THE DARKEST OF LIGHT

KINGS OF RETRIBUTION MC

SANDY ALVAREZ

CRYSTAL DANIELS

SANDY ALVAREZ
CRYSTAL DANIELS

Two Pens One Story

PROLOGUE

Bella

Staring out the living room window at the ice-covered lake and the white snow that blankets the ground, I can't help the smile taking over my face. It's Christmas time, my favorite time of year. To top it all off, my sister will be home in three days.

Alba has been away at college since August. I miss her terribly but also so proud of her. Alba was given a full ride to Montana State University in Bozeman. She's only been home once since leaving, always making up excuses as to why she can't come to visit. I can't help but wonder if she's okay, but Alba quickly squashes any doubts, telling me she's just busy with assignments.

Sofia has been thriving. She started her junior year of high school at the end of August and has made lots of friends. The guys in the club have become very protective of her. She can't even go to the movies with her friends without at least one of the prospects watching over her. I don't think she minds, though. I think it makes her feel good knowing she has a dozen big brothers looking out for her.

I've been busy decorating the house. Logan took me the other day to get a tree, only to come home with a truckload of decorations. He didn't understand the magnitude of how seriously I take Christmas. While in the checkout line he asked, "Babe, do you really need all this shit?"

I turned and gave him my best 'you're kidding, right?' look. Although, he did draw the line when he saw me hauling boxes of decorations into the clubhouse.

"Hell fuckin' no, Bella. I love you, babe, but the brothers will never let me live that shit down."

The next night Logan and I decided to go to the clubhouse and have a few drinks with the guys. I'm sitting on Logan's lap, listening to all the endless banter when the door opens. Looking over, I'm shocked when I see my sister. She wasn't due to arrive for two more days.

"Alba!" I screech. Leaping off Logan's lap, ignoring the groan that leaves his mouth when I not-so-gracefully got up.

My steps falter a bit as I run to her. I take in her red, blotchy, tear-stained face.

"Alba, what's wrong?" I question picking up my pace. Once she's within arm's reach, I grab a hold of her, pulling her in for a hug.

Her trembling body sends me on high alert. Stepping back a bit, while keeping a hold of her shoulders, I plead with her again, "Tell me what's wrong. Are you okay?"

Feeling a looming presence behind me, I glance over my shoulder and find Gabriel's tall frame standing there.

"Cariño *Sweetheart*?" he tenderly addresses her.

I watch as Alba's face goes deathly pale, and she begins to pull her heavy winter coat tighter around her body. Something is off. I can't place it. I let my eyes assess her from head to toe, looking for a sign of anything wrong, but I find nothing.

It takes me a couple more seconds to realize what's different. Letting out a small gasp, I cover my mouth.

"What the fuck?!" Gabriel growls.

1

ALBA

Seven months earlier

The party my sister held for my graduation ended several hours ago. We decided to sleep here at the clubhouse instead of going home. I've been lying in bed staring at the clock on the nightstand for the past hour. I've tried everything to get myself to relax enough to fall asleep, reading, watching television, even taking a long bath, but so far, nothing has worked.

Blowing out a frustrated breath, I get up out of bed and pad across the room, stopping in front of my bedroom door. While standing here, I contemplate whether or not I should go through with what I know is my only chance at a night of peaceful night sleep. I know exactly what I need. I need *him*. Gabriel. He's become my single source of comfort since I was kidnapped. I can still hear those men's voices inside my head telling me all the vile things they wanted to do to me. But when I'm with Gabriel, the voices disappear. And now I can't sleep without him next to me.

The nights spent at home are the worst. It's become more and more difficult to find excuses to give my sister as to why I sometimes want to spend the night here instead. Although, I'm pretty sure Bella knows. My sister is very perceptive when it comes to me, as she should be. My sister practically raised me. She has been more of a mom to me than our actual mom. Ever since I could remember, my sister has always been protecting me, shielding me from our father when we were younger and my mother's last husband, Lee. I don't remember our dad, and Bella doesn't speak of him, but I know enough to know he was not a good man. I know Bella is feeling guilty for not being able to stop what happened with Lee. What I went through was nothing compared to the horrendous experience Bella had to endure. No way should she feel bad for me. But that's the big sister in her. Always more worried about me rather than herself. I'm pretty shocked she hasn't called me out on the situation she suspects with Gabriel. My sister has no problem being in my business. Not that I mind. Bella is my best friend.

I'm a homebody and an introvert. I never made friends easily. I had one or two friends in school, but other than that, I kept to myself. I prefer it that way. It's just how I am. I know how some people look at me. Like they don't understand how I prefer to read about made-up stories instead of going out and making my own. Maybe it's lame. And perhaps I do play it safe. But for the most part, I am content with how things are. Besides my obsession with the Cuban down the hall. How I wish I had the guts to confess my feelings for him. I'm almost positive my sister knows how I feel, and as long as she's not going to bring up why I prefer the clubhouse over home, then neither will I. Most days, I would come to the clubhouse after school because Bella would be here or at work. I sometimes would feign a headache and tell her I'd rather stay.

The night the club rescued me from Los Demonios, Gabriel brought me into his room and stayed by my side for a week. He let me sleep in his bed while he slept in a chair beside me. I never understood why he felt the need to watch over me, to be my protector. He never allowed anyone to bother me unless it was Bennett or Lisa. It was like he knew I didn't want the attention. After a week, I started feeling guilty for taking over his personal space. So, with a heavy heart I decided to move back into my own room.

Gabriel did not agree with my decision. The king of broodiness responded with a simple, "No." I ended up leaving his room anyway. That night as I lay awake, unable to sleep, I regretted my decision. I soon found myself walking down the hall and sneaking into his room every night after he'd gone to sleep.

Looking back, now I realize how naïve that was of me, he could have had a woman in there for Christ's sake. No way would I have wanted to walk in on something like that, considering I had the biggest crush on the man. I would have been devastated. Gabriel was always alone, though. I would come into his room when I figured he'd be asleep and then quietly slip under the covers, always careful not to get too close. I only needed to be close enough to feel safe. The first time I snuck into his room, I woke up the next morning to an empty bed. I began to panic. Would he be mad I came in uninvited? What was he going to say to me? An hour later after working up the nerve to go downstairs for breakfast, I ran into Gabriel in the kitchen. He was standing at the counter with his back to me, fixing himself a cup of coffee.

"Morning, Cariño *Sweetheart,*" he greeted me without even turning around to look and see if it was me who was standing behind him. How did he know it was me?

"Good morning, Gabriel," I returned softly, my heart pounding.

Gabriel walked out of the kitchen, with his cup in hand, no other words spoken. I continued with this same routine night after night. Gabriel was always up and out of the bed before I woke, and he never made mention of my co-sleep dependency.

So here I stand, staring at the door. It's been a couple of weeks since I've stayed at the clubhouse, and already I'm back to my old habits. I am walking down the all too familiar hall, stopping outside the door of the man who consumes my every thought. I stand motionless. I am battling my thoughts about whether or not this is a good idea. I need to stop the dependency I have on this man. It's not healthy. I'll be leaving for college soon, then what? Shaking my head, I go to turn and head back to my room when his deep voice stops me, sending chills down my spine.

"You can come in, Cariño *Sweetheart*," Gabriel calls out.

How the hell did he know I was here?

"I can see your shadow under the door."

Well, that answers my silent question.

Taking a deep breath, I slowly open his door. The room is dark. The only light is from the small lamp on the table in the corner of the room. A shirtless Gabriel is sitting on the bed with his back against the headboard. In his hands are a sketch pad and pencil. He's every bit as beautiful as the first time I saw him. At six-foot-four, a full beard and broad shoulder, Gabriel is a beast. Almost every inch of his body from the waist up is covered in tattoos. I often wondered how far down the ink goes. His black hair is cropped short on the sides, leaving it a few inches longer on top. Deep brown eyes that most people would find off-putting, but for me, they hold kindness. His face might say fuck off, but his eyes tell the truth. You only need to take a closer look.

Standing in his room with my back against the door, we engage in an intense stare-off. I feel his dark eyes appraising me from head to toe. Feeling a tad self-conscious, I begin tugging at my oversized nightshirt. I'm completely covered with my shirt stopping a couple of inches above my knees, but maybe I should have put on some sweatpants anyway.

Nodding his head toward the spot in the bed next to him, Gabriel gives me the signal I was hoping for. Not wasting any time,

I make my way over to his bed, lift the blanket and crawl in. When my head hits the pillow, I close my eyes, relishing the smell of Gabriel's scent, and my body instantly relaxes. The last thing I remember before falling asleep is the smooth rumble of his voice, "Sleep, Cariño *Sweetheart*."

I wake sometime in the middle of the night feeling warm, too warm. It takes me a moment to realize the source of the heat. I'm lying on my side with Gabriel pressed up against my back. He has one arm under my neck and the other wrapped around my middle. Sometime in the night, my shirt must have ridden up around my waist because I feel his arm on my bare skin. My heart rate begins to pick up. This is new. Never has he touched me while we lay in bed together—both always keeping a respectable distance.

Though I've always fantasized about this exact moment, I never expected it to happen. He's so close I can feel the hard length of his cock pressed against me. He must be dreaming. No way is Gabriel hard for me. Loving the feel of him, I wiggle a bit, pushing my back into him. Tightening his grip around my waist, I feel his breath on my neck when he rumbles out my name, "Alba."

A small gasp escapes my mouth. He's not dreaming. And it's me who's turning him on. With a great deal of courage, I make the decision right then to go after something I've wanted for months. Reaching my arm around my head, I thread my trembling fingers through Gabriel's hair, while pushing my butt further back into his erection. I'm so nervous, not of losing my virginity but of him rejecting me. I've never wanted anything more than to give myself to this man.

"You sure?" he rasps, and I tilt my head back slightly.

"Yes," I whisper with a shaky voice.

As soon as the word leaves my mouth, Gabriel's hand that was around my waist slowly begins to make its way down. I feel his large hand slip inside my panties. I spread my legs slightly to give him better access. A groan escapes my lips when his long finger begins to slide through the wet folds of my pussy. "So fuckin' wet," he breathes.

Twisting my body slightly, with my hand still in his hair, I pull Gabriel to me. I want him to kiss me. His kiss will be my first. Knowing what I seek, he brings his mouth crashing down on mine. He tastes so good, like cinnamon and whiskey. His tongue tangles with mine as he gently starts to thrust his finger inside of me—my breath hitches. His fingers are a tight fit, but soon the discomfort fades. I'm so close to the edge my legs begin to shake.

I break our kiss, "I want you inside me." And I do. My body is aching for more. I see a look of hesitation on his face. He knows I'm a virgin. He was in the room with Bennett when he was examining me after my kidnapping. I had told them that I wasn't raped. Bennett wanted to give me some medication to help me sleep, but to do that, he needed to know if I was on any other medications. I confessed the only medicine I was taking was birth control. When I saw Gabriel tense, I immediately explained the pill was for keeping my periods regular. The whole exchange was embarrassing.

Wanting him to know I'm sure, I reach behind me and grab his long thick cock in my hand and squeeze. I have no idea what I'm doing. I watch Gabriel's nose flare and his eyes close while letting out a growl. I must be doing something right. Then in one swift movement, he quickly rids himself of his boxer briefs. Next, with one hand, he gently slides my panties down my legs and tosses them to the floor behind him, before taking the hem of my nightshirt, tugging it off over my head. Grabbing hold of my thigh, Gabriel brings my leg back to rest over his hip.

"Give me your mouth," he demands.

Turning my head, I give him what he asks for. A second later, I feel the head of his cock at my entrance. Slowly he pushes in, inch by inch until he's met with resistance. Fisting my hand in his soft dark hair, I brace myself for what's to come. While holding me in his tight embrace, Gabriel thrusts the rest of the way. His mouth swallows my cry. His tongue strokes mine softly, slowly, calming me down. Once my body relaxes, and I've become used to the foreign sensation of being so full, Gabriel begins to move. Pain turns to pleasure. I start rocking my hips back, meeting his thrusts. When he reaches up, pinching my nipple, I gasp, and I can't stop the noises coming from my mouth.

"I'm close," I pant when I feel my orgasm start to build. As soon as the words leave my mouth, he pulls out of me. When I begin to protest, he quickly turns me on my back, settling himself between my legs while sitting upon his knees.

"I want to look at your face when you come," Gabriel proclaims. In this position, I get a good look at this man's beautiful body for the first time. The tattoos I've wondered so much about, do stop at his waist. I'm also getting my first look at his cock, and it's perfect. I'm brought out of my trance when he reaches those big hands of his under my ass, pulling me until my lower half is lying on top of his thighs, and I wrap my legs around his waist. I watch him as he fists his cock, giving it a few strokes before he takes his shaft, running it along my slit—his actions causing my eyes to flutter. My hands fist the sheets on the bed when the sensation of his cock teasing my clit becomes too much. The look on Gabriel's face says he enjoys teasing me.

"Gabriel, please," I beg. This time it's him who gives me what I ask for. Bringing a hand on each side of my hips, he thrusts into me to the hilt. A string of Spanish leaves his mouth. I haven't a clue what he's saying. Reaching up, I grab hold of his forearms. With both hands still holding my hips, he guides himself in and out of me.

It doesn't take long before I feel my orgasm building once again. And from the tight cords in his neck, I'd say he's close himself. Leaning forward, Gabriel scoops me up into his arms, pressing his lips to mine. With me straddling his lap, we are now chest to chest. I let the motion of his hips guide our rhythm.

He breaks our kiss. "Every part of you is mine," he breathes into my ear with his arms wrapped tightly around my body, and our mouths fused once more. My orgasm crashes through me, and his mouth catches my scream. With one last thrust, he plants himself deep inside me as he growls his release. We stay in this position with him holding me, our bodies covered in sweat, and both of us trying to catch our breath. Soon my breathing slows, and my body becomes limp. I'm completely sated. Gently, Gabriel leans forward and lays me down on my back. As soon as my head hits his pillow, my eyes close, and sleep takes me. The last thing I remember is the rough feel of Gabriel's beard as he kisses my lips softly before I hear him say, "Sleep, Cariño *Sweetheart*."

THE NEXT MORNING, I wake to find Gabriel still sleeping. Sitting up in bed, I can't help but stare at him for a few minutes. Almost as if he senses my eyes on him, his pop open.

"Morning," I say shyly, slightly embarrassed I was caught ogling him.

"Mornin', babe." He grins. Scooting himself up to lean against the headboard, I take in all that is Gabriel. From his bushy beard I love so much, to his broad tattooed chest, all the way down to his cock that's on full display. Gabriel is not shy about his body. As for me, I'm clutching the sheet tightly around my exposed self.

"Babe?" Gabriel speaks loudly.

"What?" I ask.

"I asked you a question, Cariño *Sweetheart*." He chuckles.

"Oh. What was the question?"

12

"I asked what your plans were for the day."

"Well, Bella and I were supposed to start going through all my stuff at home, seeing what I wanted to take with me when I leave in a couple of weeks."

I watch as Gabriel's form stiffens. Swinging his legs over the side of the bed, he reaches down and picks his jeans up off the floor.

"That's good," he states in a robotic tone as he stands up, putting his jeans on.

"Um...I was thinking I could stay in Polson. Go to community college."

"What the hell for?" he snaps, shocking me. This is not the same man from two minutes ago.

"I just thought that we—" I begin, but he cuts me off.

"Thought what, Alba? Thought because we fucked last night, that it would be a reason for you to stay? Don't go changing your plans for me."

"Look," he says, sighing. "I had a good time last night, but it was just sex, Alba. Don't go gettin' stars in your eyes. This is not like one of your romance books you keep your nose buried in. This is real life," he says, standing there staring at me with his dark, unblinking eyes. His face showing no emotion.

I'm unable to hold back the steady stream of tears running down my face. The man in front of me is not my Gabriel, my protector. No, the man in front of me is the Gabriel that everyone else knows him to be. Had I known all I was to him was a fuck, I never would have gone through with it. That's a lie. Being with Gabriel last night was the best night of my life. It breaks my heart, knowing the feelings are one-sided.

Climbing out of bed, I drop the sheet I had clutched to my body. I feel so humiliated I'd even broached the subject of me staying. I was naïve enough to think last night meant anything.

Pulling my shirt over my head, I refuse to look at him. I open the door to his room when he calls out, "Cariño *Sweetheart*."

Without turning around, I respond in a shaky voice, "I'm not your Cariño," and walk out of his room. I ignore the sound of Gabriel's roar and the sound of shattering glass hitting the wall.

THREE WEEKS LATER, my sister and I are in my room, packing the last of my things to take to college. I never told Bella what happened that morning after I slept with Gabriel. When I came banging on her and Logan's door, asking her to take me home, she begged me to tell her. I never want to speak about what happened. And I haven't seen him since that morning. I refuse to go to the clubhouse anymore. Though I know she suspects it's something to do with a particular Cuban asshole. Bella knows I'll tell her when I'm ready.

"Alba, do you seriously need all these books? Why don't you leave them here?"

"I need my books, Bella," I huff. She doesn't understand my love of books runs deep.

Bella snickers, "Fine, you win, sis."

"Are you two finished yet? We need to get on the road," Logan asks from the doorway of my room.

"Yup, these are the last two boxes," I tell him.

Roughly four hours later, we arrive in Bozeman, where I'll be attending Montana State University studying graphic design.

My sister rode with me in my new truck while Logan followed. Bella wanted to spend as much time with me as possible. And what better way to spend four hours than listening to our favorite 80's and 90's music?

Once Logan has finished hauling my boxes up to my dorm room, my sister and I prepare to say our goodbyes, which include endless tears. Logan had to pry us apart. Okay, I'm exaggerating, but it almost came to that. Bella and I have never spent time away from one another. We've always been each other's crutch. But it's time for me to grow up. She'll be married soon, and I need to learn to stand on my own two feet.

2

GABRIEL

I haven't slept in two days. Fuckin' insomnia. It's why I'm sitting on the roof of the clubhouse at 3:00 am smokin' mota *weed*. I can't remember the last time I slept a solid six hours. Shit, that's a lie. I remember I don't want to. If I do, I'll start thinking about *her*. The roof is my spot. Everyone knows if I'm up here, leave me the fuck alone. Being up here, staring up at the star-covered sky, takes me back. Back to home. When I close my eyes, I can almost see it. The orange and purple sky transforms into darkness allowing a canopy of stars to light up the streets where my sister and I played. When night falls in Cuba, parents don't send their children to bed. No, children play in the streets as the neighbors play music and catch up on town gossip. Such an innocent time.

Now when the sun goes down and the moon takes over, there is nothing but darkness. I like the dark. It hides all my imperfections. Nighttime is when my demons come out to play. The voices have been quiet lately. The demons are never gone, only hiding in the shadows allowing me peace for a few brief moments. Now that *she's* gone, they'll be back. Reminding me of who I am and of my past.

I still remember the day my father and I left Cuba. I was ten years old. My father came into the room I shared with my sister, waking me up. It wasn't unusual for him to wake me up early and take me with him to go fishing. Only this time was different. There were no fishing poles, only a small suitcase. Arriving at a secluded part of the beach, we met up with five other men. As soon as I saw the makeshift raft, I knew what was happening. This is a Cuban's way of finding a better life. It's scary and dangerous, but being desperate will lead a person to do the unthinkable. Now my father and I were about to become those desperate people. At the time, I didn't understand why. I pleaded with him to take me home. Why were we doing this, leaving the country we love, leaving my mother and my sister?

Along with those five men, my father and I spent seven days in the Gulf with the sun on our backs. The nights were so dark you could sometimes see the glow of the creatures living beneath the sea. To say I was scared out of my fuckin' mind would be an understatement—miles on top of miles of nothing but the sea. I'll never forget the first time I stepped foot on U.S. soil. It was the start of a new life. Not a life I wanted, but one my father chose for me. While the other men were celebrating freedom, all I could think about was how much I wanted to go home. As a young boy, I didn't understand why my father would do this. Why would he take me and leave our home? What were my mother and sister going to do without my father to take care of them? My sister Leyna is four years younger than me. It was my job to always look out for her. Who was going to do that now?

It wasn't until several weeks later he told me the reason for leaving. He got himself into some trouble. He was caught skimming money from his job. My father was facing fifty years in prison. Cuban laws are much harsher than U.S. laws. He explained to me that coming to the U.S. was his only option. At least this way, he could find work and then send money home to my mother and sister.

I was so angry with him. I asked him why he had to steal. If not for him taking from his job, we wouldn't have had to leave. Once I got older, I realized my father did what he had to do to take care of his family. He didn't want to steal. He only wanted to give us a good life and keep food on the table. I knew we were poor; I just didn't realize the struggles my parents faced at the time. What kid does?

We settled in Miami with a cousin of my father's. After about a year of working two jobs, things started to change. In the beginning, we were pinching pennies just to buy bread and milk, and our lights were frequently being cut off. Then one day, we were eating endless amounts of takeout, and my father was buying a new car. Soon after that, he up and quit both jobs. Money began flowing freely. He was sending plenty of money to my mother and sister in Cuba. With the amount he was providing, they no doubt didn't want for anything.

We moved into our own house in a better neighborhood. I started a new school, a better school, and I was making friends. Overall, I adjusted well. The only part that worried me was how my father was making his money. I may have been a kid, but I wasn't stupid. Whatever my father was involved in, definitely wasn't legal. We had to leave our family and home in Cuba because of his illegal activity, only for him to come to the U.S. and do the same. I guess he didn't learn his lesson. For the most part, he kept his business away from me until I was sixteen. That's when my father's sins caught up to him—to us.

One night my father came home in an unusual mood. He seemed somber, almost defeated. When I asked him what was up, I never expected what he was about to tell me.

"I fucked up, hijo *son*," he told me. Some men were going to come for him, and they would be here soon. I told him we could run, leave town. He explained it wasn't that easy.

"You can't run from these people. They have eyes everywhere," he barely got the words out of his mouth before three men walked into our house. My father hadn't even bothered to lock the door. He knew there was no use. One of the men was wearing a suit. He was lean and tall; I'd put him at a little over six feet with black hair. This man carried himself with confidence. The other two men were in normal looking street clothes, both tall and stocky.

"Martinez," the suit regarded my father using his last name as he sat across from him at our kitchen table, "you know why I'm here." It wasn't a question but a statement.

That was the night I watched my father die. The guy in the suit, who I later learned his name was Santino, gave a signal allowing one of his men to shoot my father in the chest. I rushed over to him, catching his limp body as we both fell to the floor of our kitchen.

"Lo siento, *I'm sorry*," were the last words my father spoke to me before taking his last breath.

I'm not sure how long I sat on the floor holding my father. Minutes? Hours? All I know is that by the time I snapped out of my daze, Santino and his men were gone. The motherfucker just left. As if taking a life was all in a day's work. Like he hadn't just destroyed the life of a young man. Part of me understood why he did it. My father stole from him. You get yourself mixed up with the wrong kinds of people, only to double cross them, and you're bound to end up with a bullet in your head. But at the end of the day, I loved my father—faults and all.

Picking myself up off the floor that was covered in my father's blood, I went straight to my room to pack a bag. After packing only what I needed, I then went into my father's room and headed straight to his closet where I knew he kept a stash of money. I was sixteen and now on my own. No way was I becoming a ward of the state. I'd wait till I was out of there before calling the police. So with my bag slung over my shoulder, and roughly two thousand dollars in my pocket, I walked out of the house.

I spent three years living on the streets, bouncing around from one shitty motel to the next. Many nights were spent sleeping in the park and on the beach. I had to learn how to fight; otherwise, I wouldn't last. The first time I slept in the park, I got stabbed—all for the three lousy dollars I had in my pocket at the time. Thank fuck the asshole used a small pocketknife, so it didn't cause much damage. Not enough to go to the hospital anyway.

People had no qualms about taking what they wanted from you. If you didn't want to play victim, you had to be ruthless right along with the worst of them. Turns out I had a knack for fighting. I was quick on my feet. It also helped that I was bitter and angry at the world for the hand I was dealt. By the time I was eighteen, I was already six-foot-four and loved the rush I got from making somebody bleed. It became my addiction. That's how I found myself in the underground fight scene. It was decent money, but that wasn't my reason for doing it.

It was at one of my fights that I learned Santino's name. I remember standing outside the makeshift ring, bullshittin' with another guy. A man in the front row caught my attention, and I instantly recognized him.

"That's Santino. He's a high bidder. His guy, the one getting ready to fight, is also undefeated," he informs me.

When I cut my eyes to the man in the ring—who was currently beating the shit out of someone—it was none other than the guy who killed my father. It may have been Santino's orders, but this was the man who pulled the trigger. It was right then and there a plan was set into motion. The more fights I won, the higher in rank I climbed. The money didn't mean shit to me. I sank every dime into partying, drinking, and women.

After three months of fighting, my time had come. I was to go up against the piece of shit who took my father's life. The man had ten years and at least twenty pounds of muscle on me, whereas I had a good five inches in height on him. When the bell rang, the only thing I saw was my father's blood-soaked body lying on the kitchen floor. It was as if time had stopped, and everything was moving in slow motion. The roar of the crowd was fueling my rage. I threw punch after punch until my arms felt like lead. I soon realized how deathly quiet everything was around me. The only thing I heard was the ringing in my ears as I lifted myself off the bloody, battered, unrecognizable mess under me. All eyes were trained on me as my chest heaved, and I struggled to catch my breath.

I turned my head in the direction of Santino. My cold dead eyes met his, looking for him to show any sign of recognition. Did he know who I was? The slight lift of his chin told me he did. Why he never came after me, I'll never know. Maybe in some way, he figured an eye for an eye and all that shit. All I knew was that night would become the third most significant night of my life. Number one was when I left my home—the country I loved. Number two was the night my father was murdered. Number three was that night; the first time I killed someone. It was also my last fight, but not my last kill.

Six months after that fight I met a stranger. He came knocking on my hotel room door minutes after I robbed a gas station. After leaving the fight scene, money was scarce, and I was desperate. I never worried about cops being called after my last fight. That's not how things work on the streets, but robbing a store was different. With my gun drawn, I cracked the door open.

"No need for that, son." The stranger told me. The stranger was Jake, and he changed my life.

· · ·

SEVEN YEARS LATER, I am now the Enforcer for The Kings of Retribution. This club and these men are my life. They are my family. I still miss my little sister terribly. I send her money every month to keep her in a comfortable lifestyle. Since the passing of my mother four years ago, she has decided she wants to come to the U.S. I'm currently in the process of making that happen.

The ringing of a cell phone grabs me from my past. Cutting my eyes across the yard of the compound, I see the club's new prospect, Daniel answering his phone. The little shit is supposed to be watching the front gate, not chattin' on his fuckin' phone. Prez brought in the new guy a few weeks ago. He's been doin' okay, although something's not quite right with him. I can't put my finger on it. Call it intuition. I'll be keeping a close watch on him until he can prove his ass worthy. I watch as the prospect glances in my direction, then quickly hangs up his phone.

"Estúpido *Stupid,*" I mutter to myself. As for our other prospects, Blake, and Austin; Prez has decided to patch them in. After the way they helped handle shit when Logan's woman, Bella, was kidnapped, they more than earned their patch. The brothers will celebrate this weekend with a party.

Feeling relaxed enough to hopefully get a couple of hours sleep, I climb down from the roof and head inside. Walking through the main room of the clubhouse and down the hall, I catch Liz walking out of her room. She puts on her best, what I assume to be her seductive face. "Hey, Gabriel."

"Fuck off," I snap, not giving her a second glance. She's another one I don't trust. Myself, along with Logan, Quinn, and Reid voted against her ass staying after what went down with Cassie, but most of the older members of the club voted to keep her ass here, and as you know—majority rules. I don't want the bitch talkin' to me, and I sure as hell don't want her pussy. Liz is the only club girl we have at the moment. Some of the brothers have been bitchin' about getting some new pussy. I, for one, could care less, preferring to get mine elsewhere. Besides, after Cassie's ass betrayed us, Prez hasn't been too keen on bringing too many new people in.

Stripping off my clothes, I climb into bed, and I'm instantly hit with the sweet smell of jasmine. Fuck, definitely no sleep for me tonight.

Sitting up in my bed, I run my hand down my face and through my beard. I'll never forget the first time I saw Alba. When Prez ordered me to pick up Bella's little sister from their house, I didn't give too much thought as to what to expect. I've heard Bella describe her sister as somewhat of a shy, sweet kid who always has her nose buried in a book. When I pulled into the driveway of their house, I was not expecting the blonde beauty that stepped out the front door. "Fucking hell," I muttered to myself.

Tall, easily five-foot-seven, long, straight blonde hair brushing the top of the most luscious ass I've ever seen. I'd gotten a good eye full of her curves as she turned to lock her front door. She was about ten feet in front of me before looking up from the phone in her hands. I watched as her steps faltered before coming to a complete stop. I was met with the most beautiful blue eyes. They reminded me of the ocean at Cayo Levisa beach in Cuba. I watched as Alba raked her eyes up and down, making her assessment of me.

"Gabriel?" she questioned in a soft voice knocking me out of my stupor, and suddenly I was disgusted with myself for checking out an eighteen-year-old. She may be legal, but she's still in fuckin' high school.

I thrusted my helmet at her. "Get on, I don't have all day," I snapped. Jumping at the sound of my voice, she quickly took the helmet from my outreached hand. I immediately felt guilty for my harsh tone when I saw her hands tremble as she tried to work the strap. With a softer approach, I offered my help. "Here, let me do it for ya."

The ten-minute ride back to the clubhouse with Alba on the back of my bike and her arms wrapped around my waist felt like the longest ten minutes of my life. I knew at that moment; I was fucked.

3
___

ALBA

They told me at registration and orientation I was going to have a roommate, but so far no one has shown up. I was looking forward to not being alone on my first night in the dorm. I've spent most of my afternoon getting settled and decorating my side of the room with all the things Bella insisted on buying me. She said I need to be surrounded by comfort. Personally, I feel being here at all is uncomfortable.

Walking over to the window I peer outside, glancing around at all of the other students milling around. I take a closer look at some of the buildings and notice the library. My lips lift in a small smile, knowing that it will become a sanctuary for me while I'm here.

Sighing, I walk over and grab a bottle of water from the black mini refrigerator Logan bought and stocked for me. Inside, sitting in front of everything else, is a large bag of Peanut Butter Cups, with a small note taped to the outside.

I already know who put it there.

I grab the bag and a bottle of water and close the refrigerator. Making my way to bed, I pull the note off and sit down to read it.

Dear Alba,

I miss you already. I know it's been a long day, so I took the time to download Dirty Dancing along with the whole Fast and Furious saga, just in case you can't sleep your first night away. Enjoy your movies and snacks. I'm so proud of you.

Love, Bella

I wipe a tear from my eyes. Why am I feeling so emotional over a bag of candy? I don't care. My sister knew I would need a pick me up and I do. It's overwhelming being away from home and starting a new chapter in my life. Even if it's not something I want to be doing. For now, the distance may be precisely what I need.

I'll explore the campus tomorrow. The sun is beginning to set anyway, and it looks like I'm spending my first night alone.

I kick off my shoes, grab my computer, and settle back on my bed. I wrap my blanket around myself and pull up the movie list and click play. A good movie is what I need to distract myself. I rip open my bag of cold chocolate-peanut butter goodness and prepare to get lost in another world.

A half a bag of candy later I'm growing tired. Looking at the time on my phone, it reads 8:45 pm, so I decide to take a shower. I grab my pajamas from my dresser drawer, just in case my roommate does show up late, and head to the bathroom. It's not much to look at, but for now, it's mine and in a small way, makes me feel good. Maybe I can do this. Perhaps I am meant to be here.

With a slightly renewed outlook, I turn the shower on and climb in. I need to be more optimistic about my future. Make the most of this opportunity for now.

Then my thoughts fade to a tall, dark-eyed biker. No matter what I try to do or how far I try to push all thoughts of him away, Gabriel finds a way to creep back into my heart-the very heart he crushed.

I go to grab the shampoo from the shower caddy and drop it

when I'm startled by what sounds like the door to the bathroom clicking open.

"Hello?"

Slowly, I reach my hand through the shower curtain and grab my towel hanging from the rod and quickly wrap it around myself. Peeking out from the shower, I notice the door is closed. Getting out, I walk over to the door and turn the knob opening it. Looking around, I find no one there.

I could have sworn I heard the door open. Being alone is messing with my head right now. I walk to the bedroom door while clutching my towel and making sure it's locked, and it is. I chalk it up to first day jitters and proceed to finish drying off before getting dressed and climbing back into bed.

My phone beeps and lights up with a message from my sister. I'm surprised she waited this long to check on me. Swiping the screen, I read her text.

Bella: *I couldn't take it any longer. How was your first day on campus? Did you make any friends yet?*

I shake my head and text her back.

Me: *It was ok. I didn't explore today. Thanks for the candy. It was just what I needed.*

Bella: *Tomorrow is a new day. Love you, Sis. Goodnight*

Me: *Goodnight*

I set my alarm for 6:00 am so I can have plenty of time to find something to eat and explore the campus. Reaching over, I place my phone on my charging dock.

Before lying down, I walk over and turn the bathroom light on, leaving the door cracked open slightly. I hope my roommate doesn't get annoyed by this. I never sleep in the dark. I need a light on. Always have. My sister is the same way. We've been like this since we were little. There aren't many things I'm scared of, but the dark is one of them. I haven't been able to get over it.

Climbing back into bed, I nestle down and grab my Kindle off the nightstand, knowing the only way I'll be able to fall asleep without *him* is to read until my eyes grow heavy, closing on their own.

I AWAKEN to the constant beeping of my phone's alarm the next morning. Groaning, I unwrap myself from my warm blanket and turn it off. I'm not a morning person, but I drag myself out of bed anyway.

Digging through my clothes, I pull on a pair of black jeans and slip a loose blue tunic shirt over my head. I pair everything with some sandals and tie a low ponytail at the base of my neck. All I want is a hot cup of coffee. I'm not looking to impress anyone.

Grabbing my phone, I stick it into my back pocket and slide my bag over my shoulder before heading out the door.

I already know from the campus directory I received we have a coffee shop nearby, and they open early.

I head out the building and make my way to the opposite side of the campus. The morning air is crisp, and the smells of summer are in the air. That's one thing I love about summers in Montana —the smells. The scent of the pine trees mixed with oak and all the variety of flowers in full bloom.

I make it to A Cup of Joe Café and walk inside. It has a hipster vibe with lounge couches and chairs scattered throughout the place and low tables that sit either in front of or beside all the furniture. I notice all the outlet ports located in every section have a sign stating free Wi-Fi. I know right away that this place will become a place I frequent often.

I walk to the counter and immediately notice all of the sugary yumminess in the display case directly in front of me. Clever. They draw you in with the aromas of the coffee, then reel you in with delicious, calorie-loaded goodness on display before you place your order.

I eyeball the double chocolate chip muffin that seems to be calling out to me when the barista chimes in, breaking my trance.

"Good morning. What can I get you?" she asks me.

How anyone can sound so chipper before 8:00 am is beyond me. I'm barely coherent or can tolerate human interaction before 7:00 am, and that's with caffeine.

"A medium cinnamon dolce latte, please. Oh...and one of those double chocolate chip muffins," I tell her, pointing to the display in front of me.

As I wait for my order, I notice an older man sitting over in the far-left corner of the coffee shop reading a newspaper. It's not often you see someone who still reads a newspaper these days. Looking around, he appears to be the only one besides myself here.

After paying for what I ordered, I make my way to the opposite side of the store where a half-moon shaped couch sits. It looks quiet and cozy, far away from anyone who may enter this early in the morning.

I sit down, making myself comfortable before enjoying the first sip of my liquid courage for the day.

As I drink my coffee and eat my muffin, I gaze out the window and watch the sun completely rise. Even though I'm not a morning person, I appreciate the quiet rise of the sun. The start of a new day. A new beginning.

Digging my Kindle from my bag, I begin to read. It relaxes me, and right now, I'm a bit nervous to start my first day as a college student. Burying my nose in the story, I begin to relax.

The man in the corner catches my attention when he gets up from his lounge chair and makes his way toward the exit, but not before looking at me and smiling. I don't smile back, but continue to watch him walk past me. He's not bad looking, with light brown hair and brown eyes framed with glasses.

He doesn't spark anything inside of me. Not like a thick bearded, dark-eyed Cuban does back home. *Shit.*

There I go again. His face—his body has crept back into my thoughts. I don't get a moment's peace. My heart doesn't let me, even though I'm trying to make my head convince it otherwise.

I finish the last of my coffee and muffin before looking up at the large abstract clock on the wall that reads 8:15 am. Realizing I won't have any extra time to explore campus because I sat here much longer than I intended to, I gather my things. Throwing my trash into the garbage bin by the front door, I head out into the warm morning air.

My first class starts at 8:30 am at the art building across campus. I decided to take graphic design. I may not have wanted to be here going to college, but they do have a great graphic design program, and I got to thinking that it could lead me toward a possible career with books. Designing covers for them that is. I've been toying with the idea since my freshman year of high school. I even have dozens of covers I have designed over the past several years. I've never shown anyone my designs or also told my sister it's what I'm interested in doing. Maybe one day, though.

Entering the art building, I walk to the back until finally reaching room 106b and make my way in. The room is set up to where the desks are like sitting in bleachers, with the next row back a little higher than the first. Not wanting to be singled out or have any attention drawn to me, I take my seat in the very back of the room at the top right-hand corner.

As I'm getting into my seat, I reach into my bag and take out a notebook before digging around the bottom of the oversized tote to find the pen I want out of the 10+ I have on me at all times. I grab a handful and bring them out to make my choice for the day when I hear a masculine, husky voice beside me laugh.

"You've got quite a collection of pens there, sunshine. Mind if I borrow one of them?"

I glance up to see a tall, dark brown hair guy sitting in the desk next to me, wearing a bright smile on his face. He looks a bit ridiculous, scrunched up in the little thing before he finally stretches out his long legs.

"The name's Sam." He tells me, waiting for a reply.

"Alba," I smile at him.

"So, can I borrow one of those pens?"

"Oh, yeah, sure."

I reach my hand out, letting him have his choice.

"Thanks. So, first day, huh?" Sam asks.

"Am I that obvious?"

Laughing, he replies, "You look like a deer caught in headlights. Just a little anyway. This is my second year. I started back in Fall of last year. I'm eager to see if the new teacher replacing Mr. Johnson will be able to fill his shoes. So, where are you from Alba?"

This guy likes to talk.

"Polson, about 4 hours from here. How about you? Where are you from?"

I know he must be from the south somewhere because of his accent.

"Texas. I'm here on a football scholarship."

The happy go lucky look on his face falters the moment he tells me, but he quickly recovers.

I watch as the classroom starts to fill up with other students. Sam is sitting beside me, busy staring at his phone, as I catch some of the girls in the class, pointing at him and whispering to each other with smiles on their faces.

No one else has come in for a good three minutes when I peer up from my Kindle I had taken out of my bag and started reading a few minutes ago. I see the man from the coffee shop walk in, close the door, and place his things on the desk at the head of the classroom.

"Damn," I hear Sam whisper and glance in his direction. "I mean, the new professor is younger than what I thought he would be."

Curiosity has the better of me now as I watch the way he looks at the teacher. I don't miss the way some of the other girls ogle him too. Before I can contemplate any further, the teacher speaks.

"Hi class, my name is Professor Green, and I'll be your new Graphic Design instructor," he announces and glances over the whole class. "Okay, let's begin our morning, shall we? Take out a pen and paper, or if you wish to take notes on a tablet or laptop, please do so. Let's start by going over what this semester will hold in store for you." He continues to talk as the class takes down notes.

All in all, the class is not that bad, and before I know it, the bell is ringing, ending my first hurdle of the day. As I'm placing my things into my bag, Sam speaks.

"So, I was thinking; maybe we could become study buddies?"

I watch as a couple of girls stop a few feet back behind him and shoot daggers at me over his shoulders. *Really?*

"I don't know, Sam."

Stepping closer, he lowers his voice a bit. "Look, I'm not looking to get into your pants if that's what you're worried about. I'm looking for someone I can study with and someone who isn't distracted by all this," he sweeps his hands down his body, smirking. "And you don't seem to be the least bit interested, which is a relief."

Smiling, I agree, "Sure."

"Meet me at the library later today—say around 3:00 pm? After classes?"

"See you then."

Before he can fully turn, the two girls that were cutting me up with their glares are at his side, touching his arms and batting their glued-on eyelashes at him. He doesn't waste any time giving them a winning smile as they walk out of the classroom door.

The rest of my day goes by uneventfully. I even managed to avoid one guy in my English class who tried his best to get my attention the entire time. I had to lose him in the hallway on my way to Creative Writing. You'd think the guy would have taken the hint that I wasn't interested when I completely ignored him.

I stop by the coffee shop and grab some caffeine and a snack before heading over to the library, and I run into Sam at the counter when I walk in.

"Hey, sunshine, were you on your way to meet me?" he asks, wiggling his eyebrows at me.

"Yeah, needed some fuel first, though." I walk up to the counter to order as he finishes paying for his own cup of coffee.

"I'll wait for you."

When we're both done paying, we walk across campus to the library. It's impressive as far as libraries go. Four stories with plenty of places to find your very own corner away from everyone, along with personal cubicles scattered everywhere. As I'm searching for the perfect spot, I notice a girl with her curly, mahogany brown hair loosely piled in a bun on top of her head. She's cutting her eyes around the room, looking as if she wishes she was invisible. Pushing her glasses up her nose and tucking her feet under her, she looks back down at the book in her hands. She definitely looks like my kind of people. All she wants to do is get lost in her book, her own little world. I begin to walk in her direction, and Sam follows without saying a word.

"Excuse me. Do you mind if we sit here with you? You seem to have the best spot in the whole library."

She lifts her head and looks up at Sam and I. Taking us both in before speaking.

"I can leave," she says in a soft, quiet tone.

"No, we'd like to sit with you. If that's okay? Hi, I'm Alba, and this is Sam," I say, pointing at the six-foot-two guy beside me.

"Boyfriend?" she asks.

"No," we both say in unison.

"Umm...yeah, I guess it's okay."

Sam and I take a seat, placing our things on the table.

"You know our names, sweets. What's yours?" Sam asks in a playful but quiet way, sensing how shy she is. I'm shy too, but she seems to be much more closed up in her shell than I am.

"Sorry, my name is Leah."

"It's nice to meet you," I smile at her, and she smiles back.

The three of us ease into steady conversation talking about what classes we are taking. This is Leah's freshman year too.

"You're in my dorm building, just on the opposite side." I beam.

"I can't stand my roommate," Leah states, "All she talks about is clothes and jocks. I think she's a cheerleader. She's always bubbly and chipper, even this morning. She woke up that way. It must be exhausting. I got tired just listening to her," she jokes.

This girl is going to be a great friend. She loves books, coffee and loathes bubbly morning people. During our lengthy conversation, we learn a little more about Sam and the fact that he loves to read, though his favorite genre is paranormal romance and suspense. He likes vampire and shapeshifter stories, and his favorite author is Stephen King.

My first full day of college is complete, and I've made two new friends. We never do get around to studying. We spend the next two hours getting to know each other before Sam walks Leah and me to our dorm after we stopped and grabbed some food from the cafeteria. We part ways with plans to meet up tomorrow.

4
GABRIEL

One long fuckin' week. That's how long it's been since Alba has been gone. Four weeks since I let her walk out of my room with a broken heart and tears on her face. It took all I had in me to not go to her and kiss every one of them away. The night I spent inside Alba became another monumental moment in my life, but not the fourth. No, Alba became number one.

For months it was all I could do to keep my hands off her and fight the pull we had toward each other. The last night she spent in my bed, I couldn't hold back any longer. No way could I have her soft curves up against my body and not take what I've wanted for so long—what was mine. Consequences be damned. I'll never forget the way she looked while I took her for the first time. When Alba looks at me, she sees me—the real me. Not some tattooed monster.

Since the moment we met, Alba looked at me with wonderment and curiosity, but never fear. And that is what drew me to her the most. Most women take one look at my cut, my size, and my tattoos, and cower away. That or they are looking to slum it for one night with the bad boy. In most cases, I'd take them up

35

on the offer. Because let's be real—I'm a man and pussy is pussy. But Alba, she was never afraid of me. I'm certain she felt the same pull toward me as I to her.

When I close my eyes at night, all I see are her beautiful blue ones staring back at me with pain and devastation caused by my harsh words. I did what I had to do to get her to leave. No way was I going to let her miss out on college and not become something great because of me. And Alba would have. She would have stayed in Polson and declined her scholarship for me. I wouldn't be able to live with myself if I allowed her to do so. It makes my heart swell that someone would sacrifice so much just to be with me, to think that I'm worth that much.

Climbing out of my bed, I decide to do something I've fought not to do all week. I need to see her face. Maybe I can't have her, but I can at least watch her from a distance. After grabbing a quick shower, I get dressed, put on my cut, and make my way through the clubhouse. As I head outside, I pass Quinn in the parking lot on the way to my bike. Looking at his watch, he regards me.

"It's only 6:00 am, brother. You got an early appointment?"

"No, the shop is closed today. I've got something I need to take care of," I clip, not bothering to look at him.

"You be careful on your trip to Bozeman, man."

Catching me off guard with his statement, I snap my head in his direction.

Quinn casually leans against the wall of the clubhouse, smoking a cigarette.

"What the fuck gave you the impression I was going to Bozeman?"

Shrugging his shoulders, "I'm just surprised you lasted a week," he replies, completely ignoring my question.

"I don't know what the hell you're talkin' about, brother." I lie.

"You forget how thin these walls are, man."

Of fuckin' course. Quinn's room is right next to mine. Just how much did the fucker hear that night?

"I heard some of what you said to Alba that morning; you weren't exactly quiet. That and seeing with my own eyes, her leaving your room crying. It wasn't hard to put two and two together."

Seeing me stiffen and my eyes flair, Quinn is quick to interject.

"I get why you did it, man, really I do. Still, I can tell you now; you made the wrong fuckin' decision."

Throwing his cigarette down, Quinn walks inside, leaving me with the bitter feeling of regret because I know in my gut he's right.

Four hours later, I arrive in Bozeman and park my bike a block away from campus. No way will it not draw attention, and I don't want Alba to know I'm here. Logan knows the gist of what has happened between Alba and me. He gave me all the info he had on her. What classes she has, the dorm she's staying in, and even where the library is that she's been hanging out at. He also informed me that as far as his involvement goes, he's not risking his woman handing him his ass for helping me. Logan said Alba refuses to tell her sister what had happened, but Bella knows it's something to do with me.

It's coming up on lunchtime, so my first stop will be the library. Knowing Alba, I'm almost certain it's where I'll find her. My problem is, I don't exactly blend in well on a college campus. Like I give a fuck, though. I'm rounding the corner of one of the campus buildings when I see her. She's walking across the lawn with some short chick with glasses. Alba has her bag slung over her shoulder, and her long blond hair is pulled into a side braid hanging down the front of her shoulder. She's also wearing a blue long, sleeveless dress. I can't take my eyes off of her. She's so fuckin' gorgeous. My fingers twitch, wanting nothing more than to reach out and touch her. Seeing her smile and laugh with her friend tells me I made the right choice. This is where she needs to be—living her life, making friends. I continue to watch her until she walks into the library and out of sight. With an ache in my chest, I turn around and head back to my bike.

When I make it back to the clubhouse, I see all my brothers sittin' around having a beer. Deciding to join them, I take a seat at the bar next to Logan, and motion for Liz to bring me a drink. As I bring the bottle to my lips, our new prospect Daniel grabs my attention when I hear him talking to Blake about a fight he's participating in.

"You fight?" I ask him.

"Sure do," he tells me, puffing his chest out.

The kid is a decent height. I'd say about six-foot-one, and he's lean—maybe 180 lbs. What he lacks in muscle, I'm sure he makes up for it in speed.

"I fight at least once a week over in Missoula. The competition is decent, and the money is pretty good. The best part, though, is the pussy. Those bitches are lined up, man. Win or fuckin' lose."

"When is your next fight?" I ask.

"Three days, there's a fight every Saturday night. Why? You interested?"

"Maybe."

"Fuck man, you'd kill all those motherfuckers. And I bet you'd make some decent bank too."

I don't give two shits about the money. But I don't tell the kid that. What I need is fuckin' blood. Just the thought of fightin' again has me feeling the all too familiar rush I used to get. Making my demons want to come out and play.

"You think it's smart to go down that road again, brother?" Logan asks, bringing me out of my thoughts. He, along with Jake, are the only ones who know about my past. And how my last fight ended with me killing a man. Not that I regret it. My problem is I

38

don't always know when to stop. Sometimes that switch gets flipped, and I lose control.

"You're headed down a dark road, Gabriel. You better know what the hell you're doing. I know you got some shit goin' on in your head that needs to be worked out, but I'm telling you now, this is not the answer.

"I know what the hell I'm doing," I bite out.

"Okay, brother. Can't say I didn't warn you," Logan tells me before standing up and walking off.

I turn my attention back to Daniel, "Can you get me in on the next fight?"

"Hell yeah, man, I got you."

"Hey, prospect, you know what they say about brown-nosers, don't ya?" Quinn asks the kid. And we all know some smart-ass remark is about to follow. "You can only kiss so much ass before you choke on shit," he chuckles from the other end of the bar, causing everyone to laugh along with him.

IT'S SATURDAY NIGHT, and my body is vibrating with adrenaline for tonight's fight. Daniel informed me yesterday he got me matched with some guy named Sid. Supposedly, he's one of the best and closest to me in weight and height. I'm not concerned, though. I don't give two fucks who the fucker is or how many wins he's had. All I care about is his blood. Pounding the hell of another man is the greatest high. Am I a sick son of a bitch for feeling like I do? Probably. Do I care? Hell no. We all need an outlet, and fighting is mine. Anyone who signs up for one of these fights knows what the fuck they're getting into. So, if they get their ass handed to them, then that's on them. They get no sympathy from me.

Walking out of the clubhouse, I head to my bike and see Daniel already waiting on me. My steps falter a second when I see

Logan also on his bike, looking at me with a lifted brow while smokin' a cigarette.

"I may not agree with what your crazy ass is doing man, but no way in hell am I not gonna have your back, brother. We don't know anything about these people you're about to tangle with," Logan declares.

Grunting in response, I mount my bike, pull out of the clubhouse and onto the road with the prospect tailing behind me and my brother riding at my side.

We arrive in Missoula and follow Daniel as he directs us down a couple of winding back roads leading to the middle of nowhere. It's pitch dark. Not a fuckin' house or building in sight. We pull up to what looks like an old abandoned farmhouse. I see a few dozen parked vehicles. I glance over at Logan to see him also taking in our current surroundings. On closer inspection, the two-story building is indeed a farmhouse. The grey paint is peeling, several shutters are half hanging off the front of the house, and the roof looks like it's one heavy gust of wind from caving in. All in all, it's the perfect place to conduct such business. Not a soul around to hear the chaos and roar of chants coming from inside. It's also far enough out to stay off police radar.

Walking inside the house, I'm assaulted with the stench of cigarettes and the musky smell of sweat. I see several walls have been torn down in the old house to make a large open floor space in what was once a living room, where two men are currently pounding the hell out of each other. Men and even women take up every available empty space cheering on their choice of competitor.

The atmosphere causes my heart rate to pick up and bring back that old familiar feeling I haven't felt in a long time. This is the distraction I need. As if Logan knows exactly what I'm thinking, he turns to me.

"You're using this as a distraction to keep from going after what's yours because you believe you are doing what's best for her. Just don't take too long coming to your fuckin' senses."

I go to respond when a piercing whistle from across the room catches my attention. Turning my head, I see Daniel motioning me across the room to where he's standing next to a short, pudgy man in a cheap suit.

"Cal, this is Gabriel. The guy I was telling you about a couple of days ago," Daniel says, making introductions as I come to stand in front of them, with Logan flanking me. I give the fucker a chin lift and watch as he appraises me. His Adam's apple bobs as he swallows and takes in mine and Logan's cut.

"You're up next," he tells me. "In case Daniel hasn't already told you, we only have two rules. One—no weapons and two—the fight doesn't stop till one of you is no longer moving."

I give the man a bored look. This is not my first rodeo. He eyes me for a moment, giving me an opportunity to pussy out. Once he sees I'm not, he nods in the direction of the middle of the room where a man stands, and the crowd is circled around him.

"That's Sid. No losses as of yet. You're on in five. Good luck," he smirks and walks off.

Walking over to where my competition is, I watch as he sizes me up. Sid is about two inches shorter than I am and has about thirty pounds on me. I'm not worried in the least because once he takes his shirt off, I see the extra weight is fat, not muscle. I also note he favors his left leg a little, indicating an injury. Sid is doing a good job of hiding it. Most people wouldn't notice, but I did. Like I said, this isn't my first go around. My old fighting days and being part of the MC have taught me to size up my competition and take notice of the details.

"Fucker has a bum knee," Logan, who is standing to my right, informs me.

"Yeah, brother, I caught that too," I say, smirking at him as I

41

SANDY ALVAREZ & CRYSTAL DANIELS

remove my cut and t-shirt, handing both to Daniel, who's standing next to Logan.

"So that means you can make this shit quick. I'm ready to get home to my woman," Logan jabs back.

"I think maybe I'll have a little fun first," I say before turning and making my way into the makeshift ring. I watch Sid step forward, taking me in. He's good at masking his reaction, but I saw the twitch of his jaw and the slight hesitation in his steps when I entered the ring. Seconds later, the crowd gathers closer, encouraging their champion while eyeing me with curiosity. Bets are against me, as they should be with any newcomer. Not for long though. In a few minutes, all these motherfuckers will know who the hell I am.

Sid doesn't waste any time before he lunges toward me. He thinks he can catch me off guard. I was anticipating his move. I sidestep his swing, causing him to bow forward and lose his footing. Taking advantage, I raise my arm and bring my elbow down right between his shoulder blades. The blow has Sid stumbling to his knees. The stupid fucker obviously thought he could use his weight against me. With him down, I can easily finish this, but decide I'm not ready for the fight to be over.

I catch Logan out the corner of my eye shaking his head. He knows I'm playing with this fucker. When Sid stands back up, his face is red with anger. I smirk at him, causing him to growl and lunge at me once more. This time though, I don't move. I welcome the punch to my jaw and another to my ribs. I let the assault go on for several moments, relishing the burn in my ribs and the taste of blood in my mouth.

"Goddammit, Gabriel, quite fuckin' playing and finish this shit!" Logan hollers out at me just as my competitor lands a punch to my stomach, causing me to double over.

I raise my head and watch Sid strut around with his arms raised above his head and a smile on his face as the crowd cheers him on. Standing to my full height, I wait for the stupid fucker to turn around. When the crowd goes quiet, Sid turns, and the shocked look on his face is fuckin' priceless as I spit a mouthful of blood at his feet. This time when he lunges at me, I block his fist with my left arm and then swing my right arm, letting my fist connect with the side of his head. Then I grab a hand full of his hair, slamming his face into my raised knee, feeling the bones in his nose crunch on contact. With those two hits, his limp body crumples to the floor. Without a word, I turn away and leave him lying there.

Once I step up to Logan, Daniel hands me back my shirt and cut.

"Did you have to fuck around for so long, asshole? We could have been halfway home by now," Logan conveys with a look of irritation on his face.

"Now, what's the fun in that, Hermano *brother*?" I reply with a grin. I'm slipping my shirt and cut back on when Cal makes his way through the crowd of people, stopping in front of me.

"I can't believe you got the better of Sid," he says, handing me an envelope filled with cash. I slip it into my cut—not bothering to look at how much is in there.

"I'd like to line up another fight for next week," Cal declares.

"I'll think about it," I clip. At this point, if Sid is the best competition they have, I'm not interested.

"Really, man? You have a chance at some serious fucking cash. You'd be an idiot to walk away." Cal huffs like I've offended him. Snapping my head in his direction and stepping into his space, I watch him visibly gulp and beads of sweat drip down his forehead onto his beefy neck.

"If I were you, I'd watch my tone," I growl. "Your competition is weak. This fight was a goddamn joke and a waste of my time." Cal shrinks away and shuffles back across the room toward a man in a dark suit. I'm about to walk away when the guy Cal is talking to turns and looks directly at me when he motions in my direction.

"What the fuck?" I breathe out, not taking my eyes off this man.

"What is it, brother?" Logan asks while looking in the direction my eyes are trained.

"Do you know him?"

"Yeah, I know him," I affirm.

My blood turns cold as the man gives me a knowing look before he turns and walks away, disappearing into the crowd. It's been years since I last laid eyes on the man. Now the only question I have is—what the fuck is Santino doing in Montana?

5

ALBA

Well, I officially made it through my first week of college. Of course, Sam and Leah have had a lot to do with the fact that I haven't packed up and left already. I've talked to my sister twice this week, and both times, she's asked if I was okay, and both times, I've lied and told her I'm fine. Wanting to find out anything to do with Gabriel, I did inquire about her second consult she was supposed to have with him this week to get the final go ahead on the tattoo she's getting to cover her scars. I'm not fooling anybody, not Bella, and especially not myself, but I'm also not about to ignore the fact that he hurt me.

My roommate or lack thereof is still a no-show. In a way, it's nice not having to worry about any of my habits bothering someone. That being said, I hate being in this room alone at night, even though it's in a campus dorm full of students. I spent as long as I could hanging out at the library after class so I wouldn't have to go back and be alone.

Nights have been the worst part. I've not been sleeping well, and I almost dozed off in class this morning. Sam caught me before I face-planted onto the laptop sitting on my desk.

Thankfully, I only had one class today, and now I'm heading back to my room. Sam convinced Leah and me last night that we should all go out tonight. I plan on relaxing and maybe even get a couple of hours of sleep.

Once I enter my floor, I hear Jessica, my RA, call out to me.

"Alba, wait a second."

I met her my first day, and she is very sweet. Every morning this week, she has stopped by to say hello and kept me up-to-date on my roommate's situation. When I turn around, she is walking toward me with a vase full of white lilies and a smile on her face.

"These were sitting outside your door this morning," she says, handing them to me. "I didn't know when you would be back today and didn't want them to get knocked over just sitting there on the floor, so I kept them for you."

Who would be sending me flowers? Taking them from her, I notice the small envelope attached. Before I can inspect any further, Jessica grabs my attention again.

"Oh, the roommate you were supposed to have this semester finally called. She ended up finding off-campus housing, so it looks like you'll have the room all to yourself," she cheerfully tells me.

I suppose most people would like to have a room for themselves, but for me not so much, which made me think about the other night when Leah mentioned she is not getting along with her roommate. "Is it possible for a student to be reassigned to another room by request?" I ask her.

"Well, I suppose so. I mean, as long as the request is approved by student housing."

"Great. Thanks, Jessica."

Too curious to wait until I get to my room, I pluck the envelope from amongst the flowers and pull the small card from inside of it and read,

To my beautiful Alba.

That's it? I flip the card over, and the other side is blank.

My sister wouldn't send me flowers saying something like that, and Gabriel doesn't seem like the type of guy to send flowers. I'm baffled.

"Are they from your boyfriend? They're very pretty," Jessica asks.

"I don't have a boyfriend," I mumble.

"As pretty as you are, you don't have a boyfriend? Ooh, you have a secret admirer. That's romantic."

No, it's creepy.

I set the flowers down on a table to my left against the wall in the hallway. I don't know why, but I want nothing to do with them.

"You don't want your flowers?" Jessica calls out to me as I continue toward my room.

"I'm allergic," I lie.

"Oh. Well, okay. See you later, Alba."

Upon entering my dorm room, something feels off. Glancing around, I see everything is how it was when I left this morning. Why am I being so paranoid? This is ridiculous. I chuck my bag over onto the empty bed and sit down. Taking a deep breath and yawning, I decide to lay down for a few minutes and rest.

A soft knocking on the door wakes me. Rubbing my eyes, I sit up and look at the clock hanging on the wall. 1:00 pm? Did I sleep for four hours? Getting up, I open the door and see Leah is standing there.

"Hey, I tried texting you a few times, but you never replied," she says.

"Sorry, I fell asleep. I've been so tired lately, but I didn't mean to sleep so long. Come on in." Leah walks in and sits down on my bed.

"I figured we could get some lunch together before meeting up with Sam later."

"Sure, I'm pretty hungry. Let me freshen up really quick, and

SANDY ALVAREZ & CRYSTAL DANIELS

we can go," I tell her with a smile. I feel better. The four-hour nap helped.

Finishing in the bathroom, I grab my light blue cardigan pulling it on. We leave the room and make our way out of the dorm. Halfway toward the campus food court, Sam comes jogging up to us.

"Hey ladies," he greets, giving us the signature smile that usually makes all girls fawn all over him. "You both still game for going out?"

I look over at Leah, who looks at me. I shrug my shoulders. I do need to see more of what this town has to offer besides the confines of the campus. "I'm still game. How about you, Leah? You still want to come out with us tonight?"

Tugging at her oversized shirt, she replies, "I guess so. I mean, I don't have anything to wear, but..."

"How about we stop by your room after lunch?" I ask her. "You can grab some clothes and come back to my place to get ready with me."

Her face brightens with my invitation, and she quickly answers, "That would be great. Thanks."

"Sam, meet us outside our building at about 6 o'clock?"

Agreeing, he takes off in the opposite direction, and I turn toward Leah. "Let's go."

After grabbing some chicken club sandwiches and a couple of bags of chips, I walk with Leah to her room. I stand in the doorway and wait as she gathers some of her things into a bag when her roommate comes bouncing in with her friend in tow.

"Oh, you're here," the girl says in a snotty tone, before turning toward me. "Oh my gosh, you are so pretty. Hi, my name is Stacy. You ever thought of trying out for the cheer team? You would fit right in," she says with too much enthusiasm.

"No, it's not my thing," I tell her, scrunching up my nose.

48

"Oh. I'm the cheer captain. I thought maybe you were here to see me." She sure is self-absorbed.

"No, I'm here with my friend Leah."

"You're here with her? As in you two are friends?" She gawks with serious disbelief on her face. With her manicured finger pointed at my friend, she adds, "Why would you be friends with her, she's such a dork." The bitch and her friend giggle at the insult directed at Leah, and it's pissing me off. Especially when I see my friend shrink away. This is another reason I don't fit in here. I will never understand such immature and petty behavior.

"Yes, we're friends. We're going out with Sam McGregor tonight," I smile, giving a little attitude along with my tone. Did I have a reason to tell her our plans? No. But every girl at this school vies for Sam's attention. And I might have wanted to make her jealous. My sister did tell me, sometimes people needed to be brought down a peg or two. To be put in their place. And by the stunned look on these two girls' faces, it worked.

"Sam McGregor? The quarterback of the football team?" the other cheerleader chimes.

Completely ignoring them, I ask Leah, "You ready?"

"Yes," she says.

"Great."

Without another word, we leave. I hate superficial, stuck up people like that. I don't like it when others purposefully try to make another feel they aren't good enough. With the brief encounter I had with her roommate, I can see why Leah doesn't like her.

As we walk back to my room, I nudge her shoulder. "Hey, don't let girls like her or anyone else get to you. Her opinions don't make you who you are."

She nods her head at my statement. Leah is beautiful. Even though she does try to hide behind baggy clothes and large glasses, she's gorgeous. She doesn't see it, though. I hope I can lift her spirits with a little girl time.

Back in my room, we sit on my bed. I pull out our sandwiches, and we eat in silence until Leah speaks up. "Thank you for what you did back there. It's hard for me to stick up for myself. When I try, no one ever takes me seriously, so I usually don't say anything."

"I've only known you for a week, and I know you're a good person, Leah. Forget them if they don't see that. And you're beautiful. They're just jealous, that's all." Chewing her food, she shakes her head before taking a swallow of her water.

"I'm not beautiful."

"Are you kidding? I would die to have the curves you have. You are gorgeous. You remind me of those fifties pin-up models. Let me do your hair and makeup for tonight. What did you bring to wear?"

Setting her food down on my nightstand, she gets up and grabs her bag from the bed and pulls out two separate outfits. Both are oversized shirts and leggings like she has on now. Frowning, I look at her. "Do you have any dresses?"

"No. This is what I wear. It's what I'm comfortable in."

I'm pretty sure she could wear something I have. I get up and start digging through my clothes. "I have plenty of stuff you could borrow."

"I don't know about that. I'm much bigger than you are."

Peeking around my armoire, I look at her. "Trust me, I know I'll find something in here. I love to shop, and I made sure I brought a variety of clothes with me."

Spotting the dress I was looking for, I pull it out and let her look at it. It's a deep blue A-line cotton summer dress with a heart-shaped neckline. I haven't worn it yet. I bought it the last time I went shopping with my sister and her friend Mila, just before my nineteenth birthday. "Try this one."

"My boobs are not going to fit in that dress, let alone the rest of me," she says.

"It will work, I promise. Please try it on," I plead. I know she's uncomfortable, but I'm certain if I can get her to see for herself, she may change her mind a little. Relenting after staring at the dress and twisting her shirt in her hands, she gets up and reaches for the dress. Taking it, she walks into the bathroom, closing the door.

I'm left sitting on the edge of my bed, munching on my bag of chips for several minutes, waiting for her to come out. Finally, the doorknob turns, and she steps out, pulling at the fabric of the dress that's molded to her body.

"You look great!" I beam. She does, it looks fantastic on her. It's not as short on her as it would have been on me because I'm a few inches taller than she is, but it works.

"I've never worn anything this revealing before. I've never worn a dress before," she nervously tells me. "Are you sure my boobs won't pop out?" She starts fidgeting with the neckline, pulling on it.

"I have a white cardigan that you can wear over it if that would make you feel more comfortable. And if you really don't want to wear it, you don't have to."

Walking over to the full-length mirror on the wall, she stands and looks at herself. "I love it. I know I may seem ungrateful, but I'm not. I come from a very strict religious family, Alba. I was always told to cover up, that I shouldn't tempt others with my body. So, this is very new for me, but I really like how it looks."

Leah hasn't talked about her family, and I've not asked. I figured she'd tell me what she wants me to know, but I'm guessing by the statement she just made, I'm not going to like anything she tells me. "Will you help me find something to wear? I can be very indecisive when it comes to clothes," I ask, trying to lighten the mood and get her to have a little fun with the whole experience.

Smiling at me, she walks over to the pile of clothes I made on my bed and examines everything. "You love the color blue, don't you?" She laughs as she picks up a soft baby blue summer dress that has a pale blue lace overlay. "This one is super pretty. I say wear this one." Her eyes gleam.

"Great, I love this dress. First, we need to do our makeup and hair."

We spend the next couple of hours laughing and getting ready before its time to meet Sam outside. We both decide to wear our hair down, and I curled mine. Leah has natural curly ringlets, so all she needed was a little product for frizz control, but other than that, she has perfect hair. I'm feeling good and beautiful. My mood has a lot to do with it. I haven't felt this carefree in a while.

I'm looking forward to going out tonight.

As soon as we step outside, Sam is there waiting for us. He is wearing a pair of skin-hugging jeans, boots, and a black button-up Henley. Sam is a good-looking guy. I don't understand why he doesn't have a steady girlfriend and prefers hanging with Leah and me on most days. Turning around, a smile lights up his face.

"Damn. Look at you two. Leah, I knew you had some killer curves under those baggy-ass clothes. Damn, girl." His words cause her to blush and pull the cardigan closed.

"So, where are we going tonight?" I ask.

"I heard about this place called Crossroads. Some guys on the team said they have good food and live music. What do ya say? Wanna check it out?"

I link my arm through Leah's. "No better time to experience new things than in college, right?"

"Let's take my truck tonight. And everything is on me. I invited the two of you, so I'm paying."

As we drive to the bar, I'm taking in the scenery when I hear the rumble of a motorcycle. My heart starts racing, and I instinctively search out the source. Riding up from the passenger side of Sam's truck, I watch as the guy comes into view. I hold my breath until I realize it's not who I was thinking of. This biker is nowhere close to the size Gabriel is.

"Alba, are you okay? You look a little tense over there?" Sam asks.

Letting out a long breath, I reply, "Yeah, I'm fine. Thought I saw someone I knew was all." Determined to have a good time, I push all thoughts of Gabriel and home out of my head. I need to stop thinking about him.

Pulling into a parking spot, Sam turns the truck off. "Ready to have some fun tonight, ladies?"

"Definitely," Leah and I both answer. Her voice filled with nerves and mine filled with determination.

6

GABRIEL

I'm sitting at the clubhouse tossing back a few beers with Quinn and Reid after a long-ass day at the shop when I feel a hand slide up my arm. Turning my head, I see a chick with brown shoulder length hair, brown eyes, and fake tits hanging out of a scrap of material she calls a shirt. She's the new club pussy Liz brought around last week, and I don't have it in me to care what the fuck her damn name is. I haven't paid the bitch any mind since she walked through the clubhouse door a week ago. Not from lack of trying on her part.

"Hey, Gabriel," she purrs. "You want some company tonight?"

"Fuck off," I bark, pulling my arm free from her grasp. Feeling her hands on me causes my skin to crawl.

She huffs and storms off across the room in her too tall heels that make her wobble back over to where Liz is tentatively watching.

"You okay, brother?" Reid asks, taking a pull of his beer while sitting on the stool beside me.

"Fine," I grumble. Only I'm not fine. My mind is still reeling from seeing Santino at the fight three weeks ago. It's been seven years since I last saw him, and I can't for the life of me figure out why the fuck he would be in here. I know Santino is heavy into the fighting scene, but to show up at a meaningless fight in the middle of a small town in Montana is a far cry from what goes down in Miami. Most people don't realize how much money can be made in underground fighting. But for him to show up in nowhere, fucking Montana. Maybe it's just one hell of a coincidence. But I'd bet my left nut it's not.

On top of all that shit, I haven't been able to get a hold of my sister Leyna for the past two weeks. I call her at least every other day. She answers nearly every time. There is a sinking feeling in the pit of my stomach that something is not right. I reached out to a cousin of ours that lives several cities over. He agreed to go to Leyna's house and check on her for me. Hopefully, I hear back from him soon.

I hate that my sister is so far from me. I've been working on bringing her to the U.S., but these things take time. She insisted on staying in Cuba with our mother while she was still alive, but since her passing, we have started all the necessary steps to move her here. I miss my sister terribly. Even though we have been apart for so long, we are still as close as ever. I tell her everything. We have no secrets. Leyna knows about the club. She even knows about Alba. My sister is the only person I confide in entirely. She also told me I was an idiot for what I did, and if she were here, she'd kick my ass for the way I treated Alba. My sister has been encouraging me to go to her and to fix what I've done, but I informed her the damage had already been done.

"You plannin' on fightin' again?" Reid asks, bringing me out of my thoughts.

I shrug my shoulders. "If I get the itch, and they get some decent competition, I will."

"There are better ways to relieve stress than beating the shit out of someone," Quinn chimes in, nodding to the direction of Liz and her new minion. I choose to ignore the asshole. Quinn is doing what he does best. He's trying to goad a reaction out of me. I see the knowing smirk on his face. Instead, I turn my attention back to Reid.

"I may need you to look into something for me. I haven't heard from my sister in a couple of weeks. If I don't hear something by tomorrow, I want you to see what you can find out for me."

"Has she ever gone radio silent on you before?" he asks with a look of concern on his face. My brothers know about my sister and how close we are.

"No. She's not answering my calls," I insist. "Something about this isn't sittin' right with me. I have a cousin checking up on her; he's supposed to get back with me tomorrow. If he comes back with nothing, I want you to see what you can find."

"You got it, brother. Give me everything you have on her, and I'll see what I can do."

"Got another favor, man. I want you to get me everything you can on a Miguel Santino. This guy is big into drugs. I'm not sure the level, but my guess is he's big time, based out of Miami. He's also heavy into the fight scene."

"Is this something for the club, or is it personal?" Reid inquires.

I shake my head, "This is personal." I see the questioning look on his face, he wants to ask more, but respects my privacy enough not to.

"Alright, brother, I'll start digging tonight and get with you tomorrow."

Standing up from my stool, I nod in agreement before heading to my room to turn in for the night.

I'm GRABBING myself a cup of coffee from the kitchen the next morning after another sleepless night when I run into Reid.

"We need to talk," he says, sounding irritated as he walks past me, not bothering to stop. Following him, Reid leads me out the back door of the clubhouse to a picnic table toward the corner of the yard.

"You want to tell me why the fuck you have me digging into the biggest fucking drug lord in Miami?" he barks.

Keeping my expressions neutral, I answer him, "I told you it was personal," I remind him as I sit down on top of the table, resting my forearms on my knees.

"When you have me checking up on your sister, that's personal. It's a whole other ball game when I'm tapping into a man like Santino, Gabriel. When you mentioned drugs and fights, I imagined a low-level gang punk. If a man like Miguel Santino catches someone snooping around in his dealings, that comes back on the club."

"Thought you knew how not to get caught, brother."

"I do," Reid scoffs. "But people like Santino, have people like me making sure nobody is sticking their nose where it doesn't belong. All I'm saying is you should have fuckin' warned me as to who I was dealing with. Fucking hell, Gabriel."

"Well, now that you're done bitchin', you want to tell me what you got?" I ask, taking a swallow of my coffee.

Running his hands through his hair Reid takes a seat next to me.

"Not much to tell, man. No more than you already knew. Miguel Santino is smart. He doesn't leave a paper trail."

"Yeah, I figured as much. Thanks anyway, brother." I go to stand when he asks.

"You going to tell me what your deal is with this guy?"

Looking him straight in the eyes, I deliver to him something I've only ever told Logan.

"Miguel Santino is the man responsible for my father's death."

Turning, I walk back to the clubhouse, not bothering to wait for Reid's reaction. It's no secret that I'm a very private person. I don't divulge to anyone much about my past. Logan is the only one of the brothers that know the most. Jake only has the cliffs notes. Now Reid has a little bit more of me. I wanted him to understand the reason the information meant so much to me.

Later that afternoon, I'm at my shop, finishing a back piece for a repeat customer when the door chimes. A middle-aged man in a dark suit walks in. It's not uncommon to have suits walk in from time to time. You'd be surprised at how many of your corporate types have ink. With Blake gone to lunch, I stand up, take my gloves off, and toss them in the trash bin beside my workstation.

"Give me a minute," I tell the guy who's laid out in my chair.

"Sure, man. I need a smoke anyway," he says, getting up and walking out the door.

"What can I do for you?" I ask the suit walking in my direction.

"Gabriel Martinez?"

"Yeah, that's me," I tell him. I take a moment to size him up. The guy is about six feet tall, and his dark hair is buzzed close to his scalp. On closer inspection, he's definitely not corporate at all. Aside from his fancy suit, he looks street, right down to the scars covering his knuckles.

"I'm here on behalf of Mr. Santino. He has requested a meeting with you."

I tense at the mention of Santino.

"Not interested," I convey in a bored tone while trying to keep my anger in check.

My senses go on high alert when he reaches into the pocket of his suit jacket. In one swift movement, I slip my hand into my cut, pulling out my gun, and press the barrel to his forehead.

"You better think about your next move very carefully, pendejo *asshole.*"

Seeming unfazed, aside from the slight tick of his jaw, the man slowly removes his hand from his suit holding a card. With my gun still trained on him, I reach with my other hand and pluck it from his grasp.

"I assure you, Mr. Martinez, you want to take this meeting." Without another word, the man turns and walks out of my shop. Now I'm left wondering what the hell Santino is up to.

"Fuck," I mutter aloud. I look down at the card in my hand, which has an address written on it.

"So, are you going, man?" Reid asks me later that day at the clubhouse. After finishing with my client, I closed the shop early. I needed a fucking drink. I was still reeling from the recent invitation I received from Santino.

"Fuck, I don't know. This is the son of a bitch responsible for my father's death. I might be tempted to put a bullet in his head the moment I see him. Hell, I should have done it years ago." Blowing out a frustrated breath, I turn to Reid. "My instincts are telling me to take the meeting."

"You need to bring the club in on this, brother. Prez will be pissed if you go to this meetup alone."

"Not yet. Not going to involve the club unless I have to. I'll take the meeting, see what he wants."

"Dammit, Gabriel. Men like Santino don't request a meetup without cause. Do you think he wants to sit around and shoot the shit with you? Ask you how you have been? No. This man wants something from you, brother. He didn't stay in town and find out where you work for nothin'. My guess is he knows all about The Kings too. This whole situation reeks. And Prez is going to have your ass when he finds out what you're doing."

"I'm not involving the club," I say with finality, looking Reid in the eyes. "I'll accept whatever consequences come from not telling Jake. For now, this is my business, and I'll handle it as I see fit." My tone left no room for argument.

"Fuck," Reid mumbled, running his hand down his face. "Well,

I guess it's going to be my ass too, cause I'm coming with you. No way can I let you go alone."

"Thanks, man, I appreciate it," I say, smirking at him when he stands up from his stool, cursing under his breath.

"Yeah, yeah, asshole. I'll see you in the morning. I want to get this shit over with as soon as possible."

THE NEXT MORNING, Reid and I drive to the address listed on the card given to me. It's a local hotel a few miles from the clubhouse and not a place I pictured Santino staying. Not with the kind of money he has. But then again, Polson doesn't have much in the way of luxury hotels. Still, I was expecting our meeting to be more private. Getting off our bikes, Reid and I walk into the lobby of the hotel. Striding up to the front desk, I spot a middle-aged woman typing away on a computer.

"Can I help you?" she asks in a bored tone, not bothering to look up.

"I'm here to see Miguel Santino. Can you call his room and tell him he has a visitor?" At the sound of my voice, she startles, looking up. With her mouth gaping open, she runs her eyes over the length of me. It's not every day she has two members of The Kings strolling into her hotel. Before the stunned woman has a chance to respond, a voice calls over my shoulder.

"That won't be necessary."

Hearing the familiar voice brings back a time in my life I wish I could forget. Turning around, I stare into the eyes of Miguel Santino. My fingers itch to pull out my knife and slit his throat.

"Gentleman," Santino says, motioning to some chairs in the corner of the lobby.

I follow him over with Reid behind me. I notice three of his men throughout the lobby. I clocked them about two seconds after entering the hotel. Pretty sure that's how he knew we were here.

"I'm glad you decided to meet with me, Mr. Martinez."

"Enough of the formalities bullshit," I say, cutting him off. "Just get to the part where you tell me what the hell you want."

"Very well," Santino replies with a smile. "I want you and your club to do something for me."

"No," I snap as I stand up from my seat.

"Do you not want to hear my terms?" he presses as I go to leave.

Turning, I reply. "I don't give two fucks about your terms. My club and I aren't doing shit for you."

"That's too bad, Gabriel. I was looking forward to working with you."

I make it a few steps before he calls out.

"How's your sister?" My steps falter, and chills run down my spine.

"I don't always bank on luck, Mr. Martinez. Running into you after all these years was quite a nice surprise. When my nephew asked me to swing by and see his fight, I thought what the hell, I was in Seattle on business anyway. I never approved of his decision to get himself mixed up with biker trash, but family is family."

What the hell is he talking about?

"I see the wheels turning in your head. I believe you refer to my nephew as a prospect. Daniel told me all about your sister and has been all too forthcoming about your little club. As you know, blood is thicker than water. His loyalty lies with his *real* family."

"Fuck." I hear Reid curse under his breath. I now know why I've not heard from her. I knew something about that shit wasn't right. Standing very still, I listen to Santino speak.

"This decision was made for you when you showed up at that fight, and I spotted you across the room with my nephew. I always seek revenge, Gabriel. I know all about your club and the man you call your President. You're a pawn, Mr. Martinez. You and your club. One I plan on using."

"Leyna is a very beautiful woman. It would be a shame for something to happen to her," he says in an unpleasant tone as he stands from his seat, buttoning his suit coat. His casualness of the situation is pissing me off.

At his words, I turn and go to rush him when I feel a hand reach out and grab my bicep.

"Not here, brother," Reid warns me. And fuck if he's not right. This is exactly why Santino chose a public place.

"Hijo de puta. *Son of a bitch*," I growl, stepping right into Santino's face.

"You give me what I want, and I'll return your sister to you. It's that simple."

"I want proof she's alive," I challenge.

Pulling out his phone, Santino presses a button and places the phone to his ear.

"Put the girl on." After a moment, he hands me the phone.

"Leyna, Estás bien *You okay*?"

"Sí hermano *Yes, brother*, I'm fine. What's going on Gabriel? These men—" That's all my sister gets out before the line goes dead.

Reaching into the inside of his suit jacket Santino pulls out a cell phone.

"I'll be in touch," he says, tossing the phone at me without so much as a second glance. All I can do is watch him walk out of the hotel with his men following behind.

When Reid and I return to the clubhouse, I head straight for Daniel's room. I want the motherfucker dead. When I open his door, I see he's not here. Striding over to the closet, I yank it open and see all his shit is gone. The fucking pussy ran.

"MIERDA! *FUCK!*" I bellow.

7

ALBA

I awake with a start feeling nauseous. What the hell? I didn't even drink last night. The pub Leah, Sam, and I went to was very strict on checking IDs, not that I would have tried to drink. Suddenly my stomach lurches. I jump out of bed, running to the bathroom. I barely get the lid to the toilet lifted before I vomit, losing the entire contents of my stomach. With a groan, I pick myself up off the floor. Walking over to the sink, I look in the mirror. My skin is pale, and my eyes have dark circles. Must have been something I ate last night, making me sick. I'll see how Leah is feeling when I see her this morning for coffee. She ordered the same thing for dinner that I did.

After brushing my teeth and washing my face, I pull my hair back into a ponytail. I decide to forgo any makeup before heading to my closet to pick out something to wear. With how I'm feeling today, it's a yoga pants and t-shirt kind of day. Walking over to my desk, I grab my cell phone and keys before heading out the door. When I make it to the café, I spot Leah sitting at a table in the far corner. "Hey, have you been waiting on me long?" I ask her.

"Nope, just got here myself. And I already ordered for you."

"You're a lifesaver, Leah. I need caffeine pronto," I tell her, slumping in my chair. "I've been so tired lately. And to top it all off, I woke up this morning sick to my stomach." Speaking of that reminds me. "Didn't you order the same food as me last night? You feel okay this morning?"

"Yeah, I feel fine," she replies with concern. "You think it was something you ate, making you feel sick?"

"I don't know. Maybe. I feel better now, though. Probably just a fluke. You know stress or something," I shrug.

I change the subject. "So, my RA told me the girl who was supposed to room with me got an off-campus apartment. It looks like I'm all alone unless you try to switch dorms. Didn't you mention you're not too crazy about your roommate?"

"Ugh. Don't get me started. Stacy is awful. She acts as if everything about me offends her. My hair, my clothes."

"This is perfect," I say with excitement. "You have to see about getting transferred. Please," I beg.

"Okay, I'll talk with someone tomorrow. Won't hurt to try. Plus, I don't think I can make it a whole year with Stacy. If nothing else, I'll tell the school her choice of perfume makes my asthma act up." Leah grins.

"Wait, you have asthma? Does it get bad?"

"Sometimes, but I always have my inhaler. And I know all my limits. It's fine, Alba, I promise. Don't look at me like I'm going to have an attack on you right now."

"Sorry, it's just you're my friend. I'll always worry about you." I see Leah roll her eyes at my statement, but I don't miss the small smile she tries to hide by ducking her head.

LATER THAT DAY, I decide I need to stop by the store. Bella and Logan gave me a credit card and told me to use it for whatever I need while I'm at school.

I'm walking from my dorm to the student parking lot when I get an eerie feeling of being watched. Glancing over my shoulder, I take in my surroundings. I only see students milling around from point A to point B. Shaking the feeling off, I pick up my pace, reaching my truck. I go to reach for the door handle when I notice a piece of paper under the windshield wiper. Sweeping my head from side to side, looking around once again for someone I may recognize, but come up short. Leaning over the hood, I lift the wiper, retrieving the folded piece of paper. Opening it, I read,

Alba,

I wanted to tell you how beautiful you look today.

Okay, this is creepy. Who the hell would write me something like this? I don't even know anyone here except Leah and Sam. Something tells me this is not Sam. He's sweet, but not creepy. Suddenly, I think about the flowers I received.

Climbing into my truck, I make a mental note to ask Sam if he's messing with me. My gut is telling me no.

I'm walking down one of the isles of the grocery store in search of microwave popcorn when I run into Professor Green.

"Hello, Alba," he greets with a warm smile. I notice him holding one of those hand baskets, filled with various items.

"Hi, Professor Green. How are you?"

"Oh please, you call me Calvin when we're not in class. Professor Green makes me feel old." He smirks.

Not knowing what else to say, I fidget with my shopping basket.

"Well, it was nice to see you, Professor—I mean Calvin. I'll see you in class on Monday," I tell him, attempting to step around him. I'm the epitome of socially awkward. When he doesn't move, I look up at him. I see something pass over his face, but then it's quickly gone before smiling.

"Yeah, Alba, I'll see you on Monday," he says, stepping aside, letting me pass. *That was weird.*

Back in my dorm, I'm putting the snacks I bought at the store away, when my phone chimes with a text. Opening it, I see it's from Leah.

Leah: *I emailed student housing about putting in a dorm transfer. Fingers crossed.*

Me: *Yes! Fingers crossed!*

I send a silent prayer that Leah becomes my new roommate. Sitting down on my bed, I close my eyes, remembering the last time I slept through the night. The last time I felt completely safe.

How can one of the best memories of your life also be one of the worst? What I wouldn't give to feel Gabriel's warmth beside me. To have him wrap those strong tattooed arms around me, and to feel the scruff of his beard on my cheek when he holds me close. And no matter how much his last words gutted me, I can't bring myself to hate him or regret the last night we spent together. The way Gabriel touched me, held me, and made love to me showed me he cares. Even if his words said the opposite, it will be the memory of his touch that I'll keep with me always.

Knowing sleep is inevitable right now, I sit down at my desk and fire up my computer. Scrolling through Facebook, I see a few new releases by a couple of my favorite authors and my fingers 'accidentally' one-click. I continue to scroll down when I see an author looking for suggestions on a cover designer. Clicking on her page, I see that she's a romance writer. Chewing on my lip, I contemplate emailing her.

"Screw it," I say aloud. It won't hurt to try. Typing out an email and attaching about a dozen of my designs along with all my contact information, I then click send.

THE NEXT MORNING, I wake feeling sick, much like the day before. *What the hell is going on with me?* Probably stress. Lord knows the past several months—hell the past year—has been a nightmare. Thankfully this morning, I'm not hugging the toilet. After a few deep breaths, the wave of nausea has disappeared.

Sitting up in bed, I look up at the clock on the wall and see I have several hours before class. On Mondays, my first class isn't till after lunch. Rolling out of bed, I glance out the window and notice it's pouring rain. This makes me smile. Call me weird, but I love rainy and cloudy days. I'm just finishing in the bathroom when I remember the email I sent last night. Grabbing my laptop off the desk, I sit on my bed and pull up my email. I have a reply already. Nervously, I click to open the message.

"Holy crap!" The author wants to buy two of my designs, as is. Then she goes on asking about pricing, and do I have a website, etc. I can't freaking believe this. I spend the next couple of hours building my website and setting up a PayPal account. When I'm finished, I email the author back with what I'm charging along with my website information. I still can't believe something I created is going to be on a book.

Suddenly, I hear some scraping noises against my dorm door, and what sounds like someone giggling the doorknob. I sit there frozen, my heart pounding. Who would be trying to come into my room? Seconds later, the door flies open. Leah stands there with a couple of bags hanging from her shoulders, and she's trying to balance a box on her hip.

"You know, a little help would be nice," she chides with a smirk, knocking me from my stupor.

I smile, "Looks like you got it." That remark earns me a death glare. Walking over to her, I take the box out of her hands, setting it down on the floor. "I guess it's safe to say I have a new roommate?"

"You guess correctly," Leah says, adjusting the glasses on her face. "As soon as I checked my email this morning and saw a reply from student housing, I couldn't pack my stuff soon enough. No way was I staying around that she-beast Stacy any longer than I had too." With a huff, Leah tosses her duffle bags down on the empty bed across from mine. "You're not mad I showed up early, are you?"

"Of course not. I'm just glad you're here at all." Over the next hour, I help Leah put her things away. She doesn't have much, so she was able to bring all her things in two hauls. She wasn't kidding about wanting to get out of her old room. When I followed her into the hallway outside our door, she had all her stuff lined up against the wall. I admonished her for not calling me to help her carry all her stuff up.

With a little time to spare before class, we decide to get some lunch. I fire off a quick text to Sam to see if he wants to join us at Joe's.

"Sam said he'd meet us there," I tell Leah as we walk to my truck. When we walk into Joe's, Sam is already there. Making our way over to his table, he stands, pulling both Leah and me in for a hug. The way Sam looks and acts, you would think he's a ladies' man, but he's the exact opposite. He's sweet, caring, and respectful. In fact, I've never seen him with any girls beside Leah and me.

"How are my two favorite girls doing today?" he asks.

I'm about to answer when I notice Sam's attention has shifted elsewhere. Looking in the direction his eyes are trained, I see a guy about our age sitting at a table by the front window of the café. He has ink-black hair, and if I had to guess, he's a couple of inches over six feet tall. He's sitting across from a girl whose mouth is moving a mile a minute. But what I also notice is this guy is hardly paying her any attention. No, he keeps sneaking glances at Sam.

Suddenly, a light bulb goes off in my head. When my eyes land back on my friend, he has a slight blush on his face as he stares at me intently. Almost as if he's giving me a silent plea not to call him out. Instead, I reach across the table, taking his hand in mine and give it a light squeeze. I let my smile and my gesture do the talking for me. With a wink, I pull my hand back as Sam gives me a small smile.

Walking across campus after lunch, Sam and I part ways with Leah and head to class. When we walk into Professor Green's class, Sam has his arm slung over my shoulder. Professor Green looks up from where he stands at his podium. His lips form a thin line as he sends a scowl our way. What is with the look? Once I take my seat, I glance over at Sam with furrowed brows. He shrugs in response.

By the end of the day, I feel dead on my feet. I open the door to my dorm room and see Leah sitting on her bed with her laptop. Tossing my keys and phone onto my desk, I plop down onto my own bed. The next thing I know, I'm being woken up by someone nudging me. When I open my eyes, I see Leah standing over me.

"How long have I been asleep?" I ask, my voice sounding scratchy.

"Two hours. I figured you'd want to eat, and maybe change into your pajamas."

"I'm sorry I fell asleep on you. I don't know why I'm so tired," I say, getting up to make my way to the bathroom. "I'm going to shower. When I'm done, you feel like grabbing some tacos for dinner?"

"Yeah, tacos sound good," Leah answers while typing away again on her computer.

After my shower, I pull on some leggings and a baggy t-shirt. Foregoing the blow dryer, I decide to put my hair into a braid.

Opening the bathroom door, I see Leah is gathering her stuff and is ready to go.

"I'm starving," she announces. "My project is due by the 15th. I skipped lunch today, so I could try getting it finished by tonight. Also, can we stop at the store on the way back? I need tampons."

At that last statement, I stop in my tracks, causing her to bump into me from behind.

"Did you say the 15? As in two days from now?" I ask, suddenly feeling lightheaded, and my stomach drops.

"Yeah, why? Are you okay, Alba? You look really pale."

In slow motion, I pull my phone from my pocket, swiping the screen, and pulling up my calendar. I begin to break out in a cold sweat, and it feels like my heart is going to beat out my chest.

"No, no, no, no," I start chanting aloud while staring down at my phone.

"Alba, what's going on? You're starting to scare me."

On shaky legs, I stumble backward till I feel my bed behind me and sit. I don't want to believe it, but the pieces are starting to add up. Morning sickness, fatigue, and if that's not enough, the two months of no period is a sure sign. Fuck, how could I have missed not having my period for TWO months?

Looking over at my friend who is now sitting beside me on the bed with a look of worry on her face, I choke out, "I think I'm pregnant."

8

GABRIEL

"What the hell is going on, brother?" Logan questions while standing in the doorway of Daniel's room with Reid behind him. "I've been lookin' for your ass all morning."

"Got a fuckin' problem, I need to discuss in church," I say, cutting him off.

Logan looks at me expectantly and waits for me to divulge my information.

"Santino has Leyna. He's using her as leverage. He wants the club to do something for him. And he wants his answer...soon," I tell him. I don't have to explain who Santino is. Logan knows.

"What the fuck, Gabriel. When the hell did you talk to Santino?"

"I just found out. I had a meeting with him this morning. Reid came with me."

"Son of a bitch," Logan hisses. "You didn't think to inform any of us on what the hell you were doing?"

"I'm telling you now," I grit out.

"Fucking hell, Gabriel." Looking over his shoulder Logan

addresses Reid, "Go tell everyone we have emergency church in five." With a nod, Reid walks off doing what he's told.

I walk downstairs and enter church, taking my seat in the corner of the room, waiting for my turn to speak.

After all the men have filled in and taken their seats, Logan announces that I have the floor. The puzzled looks on everyone's faces don't surprise me. I never draw attention to myself, and I've never been given the floor before. I've never had a reason until now. I lean forward in my chair and rest my elbows on my knees, and I address my brothers.

"A man by the name of Miguel Santino has my sister Leyna. I need to get her back. His only condition is that he wants to use the club for something. I don't know what. He'll tell me what he wants us to do once we agree," I say, only giving them the short version of the situation as I look at everyone.

Prez doesn't waste any time chiming in.

"When the fuck did all this shit happen? And who the hell are we dealing with?" he barks.

Not wanting to share details about my past with all the brothers, I ignore his question and continue.

"That's not all. Our prospect Daniel is his nephew. That's how he was able to find out about my sister and details about the club." I wait for a beat and let my words sink in. A second later, everyone's booming voices fill the room. I hear the words "traitor" and "that fucker is dead." Slamming the gavel several times, bringing all the brothers to heel, Prez repeats his earlier question, looking me directly in the eyes.

"When the fuck did you find this shit out?"

"Today," I answer. "One of Santino's men came into the shop yesterday requesting a meeting. I met with him this morning."

Realizing I'm not going to divulge any more of my personal shit in front of a room full of people, Prez announces, "Church is over. Everyone who's picking up the shipment tonight, get your asses out and see Logan out at the bar. When Gabriel hears from Santino, we'll figure out a plan of action." Turning his attention back to me.

"Gabriel, you stay put," he orders as he slams the gavel on the table.

Everyone starts to leave, but not before each one passes by telling me they've got my back. I'm grateful for my brothers' support. I'm also grateful they all understand and respect the fact that I don't want to share certain parts of my past. After the door is closed, Jake sits down and leans back in his chair.

"Who is this Santino guy to you?"

Fuck, I loathe sharing. I hate talking about my past, but I'm draggin' the club into my mess, so I have to tell him.

"He killed my father; rather, he ordered one of his men to kill him." Jake stares at me for a beat with his jaw twitching, before he speaks.

"What are your thoughts on the next move we should make? You supposed to contact him, or will he contact you?" he questions.

I was expecting him to crawl all over my ass for not saying anything sooner. Hell, everything was fine until yesterday. If it weren't for the fact that my baby sister's involved, I wouldn't have said shit to anyone.

"I'm supposed to wait for a call. He gave me a burner that he'll contact me on. I have no more info other than the fact he wants the club to do some shit for him, and he has my sister. My only guess is that it's something to do with drugs. Miami is Santino's playground, so I have no clue what the fuck he's doing out west. He spotted me at a fight a few nights ago. He said he came to see his nephew. Said he knew Daniel was in with a biker club but it was just a lucky coincidence seeing me."

"You believe him?" Prez asks suspiciously. Nodding, I say, "Yeah, as fucked up as it all may seem, I believe it's only a coincidence. I don't see Santino keeping tabs on me. As for Daniel, the punk had no problem rattin' us out."

By the murderous look on Jake's face, I can tell the last part has him pissed.

Switching gears, Jake lights a cigarette then asks me the question I knew I couldn't avoid. "You fuckin' fighting again?"

"Just once."

"What the hell for? And what the hell has gotten into you lately, son?"

I stare at him, not wanting to give him my reason for fighting, why the demons have wanted to come out and play. I don't want to tell him I sent the sunshine in my life away. She was the first one to ever drown out the noise. She is quiet to my storm. Even she didn't know the effect she truly had on me.

Jake is good at reading people, and I can tell by the look he's giving me he won't press the issue. At least, not right now.

"Your fighting could cause issues for this club. You better remember that. We don't need any repercussions falling back on us due to you beating some poor fuck to death or near to it. You get me?" he warns.

I understand loud and clear and nod my head, letting him know so.

"Alright. Nothin' more can be done until he contacts you. The moment he does, you tell me. We'll sit down and figure out our next move afterward."

"What about the rat?" I ask, grinding my teeth. "No way can we let him get away with turning traitor."

With a sly grin, Prez makes a promise. "Don't worry, brother, when the time comes, that little motherfucker will be yours." Satisfied with his response, I nod. Knowing Jake, he's cooking something up.

"And as hard as it might be, we need you on this pickup today.

You did right by not going into this alone, Gabriel. We'll make sure you get your sister back."

He's right; my brothers need me today, and sitting on my ass won't make Santino call any quicker. Right now, it's a sit and wait game. A game I'm determined not to lose.

THE SHIPMENT PICK up this morning went smooth. Now we're on our way back to the clubhouse after transferring crates off the trucks at the warehouse. There's talk of getting out of the gun trade business. Word is this may be our last transaction with the Russians. Prez has decided with increased interest in club activity by the Feds, it's best we put things on the back burner. He and Logan are in talks with Volkov, our supplier, to back out for now, which shouldn't be an issue since Volkov is also our VP's dad. Fuck, it's not every day you find out your birth father is head of one of the largest Russian Mafia families.

Shit has almost come full circle for Logan, and I'm happy for him. He had a good woman come into his life who put things into perspective.

She also brought her sister with her. Eyes as blue as the Montana skies themselves and a soul as bright as the fuckin' sun, making me think a cold and empty man like myself could hold something as pure as her.

And I did—for a moment.

The problem is, I don't want to tarnish her light with my darkness—my imperfections, with the rage that lives inside of me. When Alba looks at me, I know she can see past all those things— seeing the real me, I feel it. Alba has broken past my iron-clad walls and imprinted on my godforsaken soul.

MAKING IT TO KINGS INK, I start setting up my workstation with new ink and clean, sterile equipment before unlocking the doors. My first client for the day will be showing up in about forty-five minutes. The guy is a bull rider from Cheyenne, Wyoming. He wants an upper arm piece done to commemorate his final ride. I've watched a few rodeos in my day livin' here in Montana. Those are some tough, crazy motherfuckers. Definitely badasses in their own right.

Just as I'm setting out fresh bottles of water for myself and the client, the phone given to me by Santino rings. Diggin' it out of my back pocket, I answer. "Yeah."

A chuckle sounds from the other end of the line. "Aww, come on now, no good morning?"

"Put my sister on the phone, you hijo de puta *son of a bitch*," I spit in anger at his passiveness.

His tone changes to one of authority at my attitude, and I could care less. I'm not going to kiss his ass.

"You give me your answer, and we'll see about you talking to your sister. Remember, I'm holding all the cards right now."

Clenching my fists tight, I rein in my temper before speaking to the piece of trash. "The club's in."

"Wise choice," Santino is quick to reply.

"Under one condition. I talk to her every day. And I get to lay eyes on her—today," I inform him. He may be holding the cards in this game, but I don't play by the fuckin' rules.

"Don't push my patience." Silence fills the other end of the phone before he speaks again, his voice causing my jaw to clench. "Fine. I'll text you the location. I expect to see you before nightfall."

As soon as the call is disconnected, I send out a text to Jake and Logan, letting them know what's going on. Nothing can be done until I receive information on the location. As soon as I get that, I'll send it to Reid to do his thing.

They both are quick to text back.

Logan: *We got your back.*

Prez: *Got your back, son.*

The rest of the shop crew shows up soon after I get off the phone. Blake has finally been given his own station and has a couple of solo sessions with clients of his own today. I walk over to Grayson, who started working for us a month ago. He already has ten years of experience under his belt, working at a well-known tattoo shop in New York.

"I'm gonna need you to run the place and close shop after I leave today. Think you can handle it?" I ask him.

"Yeah, man, no problem."

I hand him the keys and walk back to my workstation.

To say it was hard as fuck concentrating on the piece I'm working on is an understatement.

I'm finishing with cleanup and care instructions when the damn phone in my pocket pings with a text alert. I send the cowboy over to Aubrey, who is a new hire, to take care of the rest of his bill.

Pulling the phone from my pocket, I read the text, which gives the location of my sister, then send it straight to Reid.

Me: *Find out all you can about this location*

Reid: *got it, brother.*

Walking out the door, I mount my bike and head straight for the clubhouse. It doesn't take long for the guys to show up. Once Reid found out, so did everyone else. The text said to be at the address by 4:00 pm. That gives us enough time to try and map the location. Reid is sitting in church with Prez when I walk in, followed by Logan.

"Alright, the address is out by the country club near East Bay. Looks like a waterfront property," Reid tells us.

"Well, we have a few hours before you're due out there."

"I told Santino I wanted eyes on Leyna today."

"Did he agree?" Logan asks as he takes a drag from his cigarette.

"Yeah," I tell him.

Now it's a waiting game as Logan and I sit at the bar nursing beers while Prez sends word to a couple of other members to do a quick ride near the location Santino is staying to case the place out. I've never been a patient man—more along the lines of instant gratification. I hate sittin' on my ass like this. My sister is sittin' over there, in a house full of people she doesn't know, in a country she has never been too. If one son of a bitch has laid one finger on her, I will relish in the pain that I inflict on them. I start to grip the bottle in my hand so tight my knuckles turn white on my tan skin, and heat starts to radiate from the skin on my face with the rage boiling inside.

Slapping me on my back, Quinn saddles up on a stool beside me at the bar. "Hey, brother."

I'm through with fuckin' talkin' right now, so I lift my chin and acknowledge him.

"I have your back, brother. I'm riding with you guys. I want to see this knob gobbler for myself," he states as he takes a pull from the beer Liz handed him when he sat down.

No joke? No snarky remarks to get a rise out of me? I cut my eyes to Quinn as he continues to drink. He stares straight ahead, lost in his own thoughts. Or, he is actually giving me the space I need, which never happens. So, I don't question it. I welcome the silence and the support my brothers are quietly giving, They know I'm hangin' on by a fuckin' thread right now.

The location Santino sent is about thirty-five minutes away. The brothers Prez sent to scope the place out arrived at the club about thirty minutes ago, giving us the rundown. From what they could see, there wasn't too much activity outside, just a couple of big guys on a golf cart riding back and forth a few times in front of the property. It sounds like Santino is trying to keep himself low-key. But once we roll in, with the rumbles of our Harleys through the cookie-cutter high class neighborhood, that plan will be blown out the fuckin' water. No more words are spoken between any of us as Jake, Logan, Quinn, and I mount our bikes and head toward East Bay.

9

ALBA

"How is it you are not totally freaking out right now?" Leah asks as she stands beside me in the bathroom, and both of us are staring down at not one, not two, but three positive pregnancy tests sitting on the counter. Shrugging my shoulders, I answer, "Because freaking out is not going to change anything. And I know it's crazy, but I'm not that upset."

"Well, what are you going to do now?" Leah questions. Isn't that the million-dollar question. I turn to my friend and calmly reply.

"I'm going to take one day at a time because that's all I can do. Right now, I don't know about anything. No way am I going to have everything all figured out at this moment."

"I'll support you no matter what happens, Alba," she says, squeezing my hand with a soft smile and no judgment in her tone.

"Thanks, Leah." I'm thankful that she's not asking more questions. She never pries. I suspect it has to do with the fact that she doesn't want people asking her questions about her life. Either way, I'm relieved. Maybe once I get my head wrapped around this news, I'd be able to talk about it. It might even do me some good, to get some things off my chest, to finally talk to someone. I've got to let go of the bitterness inside me. The anger I'm carrying is not healthy for me, and it's certainly not healthy for my baby. *Baby.* At that thought, I bring my hand to my stomach and finally let my tears fall.

What I wouldn't give to have Gabriel wrap his strong arms around me and whisper in my ear that everything is going to be okay. Just like he did the night he carried me out of that house after I was kidnapped. When I close my eyes, I can feel his warm breath on my ear and feel the roughness of his beard on my cheek. Being in Gabriel's arms feels like home, and I'd give anything to go back.

I hear the soft click of the bathroom door, letting me know Leah has left, giving me the privacy I need. Resting my back against the wall, I stare at my reflection in the mirror. I can do this.

"Damn straight, I can do this," I say aloud.

THE NEXT MORNING, I wake with new determination. The first thing I do is schedule a doctor's appointment. I'm thankful Logan added me to his health insurance. I don't have to worry about money.

My designs are selling like crazy. Requests started coming in left and right ever since I sold my first two. Now I'm booked solid for the next two months. I can use my own money to pay for what I need. No way am I ready to explain any of this to Bella. I'm not ready for her to know. I don't think I could take her disappointment. All my sister has ever wanted for me was to finish high school and go to college. I couldn't tell her I never really wanted to go away to school. I like being home—with her. Every time she would bring me a new college application to fill out, she would get so excited. How could I tell my sister I didn't want to leave home and that I was content with going to community college? Bella worked so hard and sacrificed so much for me. I owe it to her to make her proud. Besides, school isn't so bad. I have Leah and Sam. The only problem is it's not where my heart is. I need to prove to Bella and myself that I can handle things on my own.

I'm going to be a mother. I'm going to work my butt off. Everything I do will be for my baby and me. Gabriel is a dream I have to let go of. My baby is all that matters now.

The ping of my phone brings me out of my thoughts. Pulling it out of my bag, I see a text from Sam asking if I want to meet him over by the campus promenade for a quick lunch. I reply yes and begin to make my way in his direction. The promenade is a short walk from my dorm. Walking across the campus lawn, I spot Sam sitting on a bench holding a takeout bag and a couple of drinks.

"How's my favorite girl?" he asks when I sit down next to him.

Returning his smile, "I'm doing okay, Sam."

"Are you sure? You look like you haven't slept in days."

God, he's so perceptive. It reminds me of Quinn. Blowing out a breath, I blurt out, "I'm pregnant." I have no idea where I found the courage to say that aloud, or why I decided to tell Sam now. My confession causes Sam to choke on the bite of food he has in his mouth.

"What?!" he wheezes out and wipes his mouth with the back of his hand. "Jesus, Alba, are you sure?"

"Yeah. The three pregnancy tests I took said yes," I sigh. "I have a doctor's appointment next week to confirm."

"What are your plans? Are you keeping it?"

Narrowing my eyes at Sam, I snap, "Of course, I'm keeping my baby."

"Hey, sweetie, I'm on your side here. It was only a question," he says, holding his hands up in surrender. "Do you mind me asking who the father is? I'm assuming he's someone from back home. I've not seen you with anyone here at school."

When I cut my eyes over to Sam, I see no judgment on his face —only concern. "Yes. There was someone back home. It was just one time."

"Was? As in you two are not together anymore?"

"We were never together," I confess, looking at the ground and willing myself not to cry. I promised myself no more tears. Feeling a finger lift my chin, Sam forces me to look at him.

"Come here," he urges me with his arm held out. Accepting, I throw myself into his waiting arms and ignore the stares we are getting. I don't care. They can all think what they want. After a few minutes, Sam kisses me on top of my head. "So, whose ass do I need to go kick in Polson?" Sam jokes, lightening the mood, and I snort. Bless his heart. He has no idea what he'd be up against.

"Ah, no offense, but you wouldn't stand a chance against Gabriel."

"Alba, the guy's name is Gabriel. How tough can he be?" At Sam's question, I throw my head back and laugh. After I get my laugh under control, I look over to my friend, and he has a scowl on his face. "I'm not liking your lack of confidence in my attempt to defend your honor," he says in mock irritation.

"Sam, Gabriel Martinez is six-foot-four and has about fifty pounds of muscle on you." I watch his eyes go big before he asks, "Christ, Alba, where did you find a guy like that?"

Deciding I can trust Sam with the truth, I tell him.

"Gabriel is a part of a motorcycle club called The Kings of Retribution," I confess.

"Are you shittin' me?" I shake my head no.

"My sister and I met them over a year ago. Bella is engaged to the club's Vice President. His name is Logan."

"This Gabriel, what's his role in the club?"

"Gabriel is the club's Enforcer," I tell him.

"Jesus fucking Christ, Alba. That's like some Sons of Anarchy shit. That man would straight up murder me, wouldn't he?" I roll my eyes.

"Relax, he's hours away. Plus, he could care less about me. I promise. You have nothing to worry about."

"Do you plan on telling him?"

"I will eventually. But right now, I'm still trying to wrap my head around it all. And like I said, Gabriel could care less. Whether I tell him today, tomorrow, or months from now, it won't change a thing."

"You sure about that, sweetie?"

Gabriel's words 'just sex' come to mind, causing my stomach to twist into knots.

"Yeah, I'm sure."

After a beat, Sam chimes in again, breaking another intense moment.

"So, want someone to go to the doctor with you?"

"No. I'll be okay on my own. Besides, we don't want to fuel the rumor mill. Someone is bound to see us. I don't want people to get the wrong idea about you."

"I don't give a fuck what people will assume, Alba. You're my friend. Whatever you need, I'm there."

I lean my head on his shoulder. "Thanks, Sam. You truly are an amazing friend."

Putting his arm around me, he gives my shoulders a light squeeze. "You're not so bad yourself, little momma." His nickname makes me smile.

I head back to my dorm after my lunch with Sam. I'm standing at the door to my room, fishing my keys from my bag. Sliding my key into the lock, I realize it's already unlocked. *Leah must be back.* Walking in, I drop my bag on the floor by the door and toss my keys on my desk. I don't see her. Maybe she's in the bathroom. Walking over, I knock on the door. "Leah, you in there?" Nothing.

Turning the knob, I open the bathroom door finding it empty. Turning back around, I glance over to her side of the room, and I don't see her bookbag, so I know she's not been back since she left for class. I suddenly get an uneasy feeling in the pit of my stomach. I was the last to leave the room. I am positive I locked the door. Running my sweaty palms down my pant legs, I begin to scan the room. Nothing seems out of place except for one thing. The top drawer to my dresser is half-open.

Walking over to my dresser, I pull the drawer the rest of the way open and find it a mess. All my bras and panties have been rummaged through. I know this because I am a neat freak. I keep my things folded and organized by color. Don't judge. That's just the way I am. Being unorganized stresses me out.

I feel like I'm going to be sick, and it's not morning sickness that has me feeling this way. No, what has the bile rising in my throat is the fact that someone was in my room, and the sicko was in my underwear drawer. The hairs on my arm stand, and I know in the pit of my stomach something is off. The flowers, the note left on my truck, and now this. Okay, Alba, deep breaths. Maybe I'm overthinking this. There could be reasonable explanations for all these things. Only I know there's not. The only people I know at school are Leah and Sam. Neither of them would do this.

My phone ringing causes me to jump. "Shit," I rasp, clutching my hand to my chest. Picking my cell up off my desk, I smile when I see Bella calling. "Hello."

"Hey, what are you up too?"

"Nothing at the moment, what's up?" I ask Bella.

"I wanted to see if you can come home this weekend."

"Um... I don't—" Cutting me off Bella adds.

"Please, Alba. All the guys are going to be gone on club business this weekend. Plus, I miss you. Come on, Alba, don't make me beg."

After thinking for a moment, I agree that maybe I should get away for a couple of days. Considering I'm a little freaked out right now, home sounds like a good idea. And Bella did say the guys would be gone. I won't have to worry about running into Gabriel.

"Fine, I'll come home. I can leave after my class tomorrow. I should be there around 5:00 pm."

"Yes!" Bella exclaims. "See you tomorrow, sis."

Chuckling, I reply, "I'll see you tomorrow."

10

GABRIEL

My blood is pumping so hard I feel the throb of my heartbeat coursing through the veins in my neck. I should have known my past would come back to haunt me in real life and not just in my dreams. I was young and blinded by revenge at the time. I didn't give two fucks about the repercussions. I never expected it to be used against my club and me seven years later. This shit right here is just the type of reason I needed—no—had to push Alba away. My past and my lifestyle have already put my sister in harm's way, and I can't put Alba in the same path of destruction.

The sooner we can find out what the hell Santino wants from our club—the sooner I can be done with him. And by done, I mean I'm going to put a bullet in him. Unless he's dead, he will always be a threat.

As soon as we pull onto Oak Street, which is about four blocks from Santino's, two Black sedans fall in behind us following the rest of the way to the meet up point, until we come up on the long driveway that leads to a large brick home located a few houses down from where we passed the country club's main entrance. No gates. No trees. A wide-open landscape with the East Bay as its backdrop. Looks can be deceiving. Someone of his caliber will have other security measures in place.

Just as we get about halfway down the driveway, the cars following slow to a stop. Not pausing, we continue to ride until we pull around into a circular driveway. One by one, we kill our bikes. Quinn lifts his chin, gesturing to the rooftop where four men walk into view, holding rifles and peering down at us over the edge. The front door to the home opens, and two motherfuckers wearing matching black suits and slicked-back hair step out. Dismounting our bikes, we walk toward the goons.

"Leave your weapons here," the one to my right says.

"Not gonna happen," Prez challenges, which causes the other guy to step forward. Jake, who isn't the least bit fazed by the guy, stands with his arms crossed in a stare-off.

"Let them in, I don't think they would be stupid enough to try anything," Santino's voice calls out from just inside the door before appearing in the doorway. He still looks the same as he did seven years ago, except for the peppered gray mixed in his dark hair.

We walk into the house, Prez leading the way behind Santino. Looking around, I see no signs of Daniel. Fucking pussy is probably too much of a coward to show his face.

"Come in, sit down," Santino says, spreading his arms in a grand gesture as we enter what appears to be a large office that's decked out in rich mahogany wood shelves and cabinets that are filled with books from floor to ceiling.

Alba would love this room. Shit. Focus.

The four of us continue to stand as he walks toward a round glass table and picks up a bottle of scotch, casually pouring himself a drink into a shot glass. "Can I offer you men a drink?"

"Cut through all this bullshit. What do you want with MY club?" Prez barks.

A flash of anger crosses over Santino's face as soon as the harsh words are spoken, but only for a second before regaining his composer.

"Mr. Martinez owes me a debt. Several years ago, he killed one of my men—"

"He killed—you had him kill my father." I step forward with my fists clenched and nose flaring from the angry breaths leaving my body. Quinn grabs me by the shoulder to keep me from moving any further.

"Rein that shit in, man. Think about your sister right now," he says to me in a hushed tone. Stepping back, I keep my eyes trained on Santino's face. The face I'm gonna beat to a bloody pulp the first chance I get.

"I always see the bigger picture, Gabriel," he tells me as he walks over to the desk in the room, reaching into a humidor box sitting on top and pulling out a cigar. Sitting down in the large black leather chair behind the desk, he clips the tip and lights it, taking a toke—the smoke billows around his head as he releases his breath.

"Where's Leyna?" I question through gritted teeth.

Santino leans back in his desk chair, "In due time..."

Having had about enough of this shit, I walk forward toward his desk. From the corner of my eye, I see the suit that stepped up in Prez's personal space earlier is now moving toward me. My hand shoots out on instinct, connecting with his thick meaty neck. "You wanna die, motherfucker?" I growl.

"Stand down men," both Prez and Santino's voices boom. The prick still in my grasp, puts his hands up. I can't find it in me to release my hold.

"Let him go, Gabriel," Jake says from behind me.

Dropping my hand, the asshole backs away and stands beside his boss.

"I'm aware of your current operations and that you hold some

SANDY ALVAREZ & CRYSTAL DANIELS

clout with the local law enforcement around here. So, I need you and your club to escort my men and their load across the state line. It's currently being loaded and will be on its way soon. Possibly in about four weeks."

I watch as Prez and Logan exchange looks. They don't look happy that someone has been nosin' around in club business. Logan crosses his arms and speaks.

"What kind of merchandise are we dealing with here?"

"That's none of your concern. I only need you on escort detail to make sure they get where they need to go. As soon as this is done, I'll hand over the girl," he informs us all.

"You gave your word Gabriel could see his sister today. I expect you to hold up your end of the deal before I agree to do a damn thing that involves my club," Prez states.

"I did." Reaching over Santino picks up the phone sitting on his desk to his right and speaking into the receiver, he tells the person on the other end, "Bring the girl downstairs to my office." He places the phone back on its dock.

A few minutes later, I watch as an exact carbon copy of my mother walks through the door. Raven dark hair that frames a heart-shaped face, with almond-shaped eyes the lightest shade of green. She's not much taller than our mother was either, maybe five feet four inches.

"Hermano *brother*," Leyna cries, tears springing from her eyes as she runs to me and wraps her arms around my waist. My hard exterior cracks a little with her embrace. I lift her chin with my finger.

"Have they touched you or hurt you in any way?"

"No, they have been good to me. Did you come to take me home with you?"

"No, hermana *sister*, not today but soon. I have to handle some business for Santino first. Until then, you have to stay here," I tell her and watch as her shoulders slump in disappointment.

90

I look to Prez, Logan, and Quinn; then, Prez turns to Santino.

"My men will make sure the shipment gets where it needs to go. You make sure NOTHING happens to this girl and that she is allowed to stay in contact with myself or her brother every day."

The fucker that escorted Leyna into the office goes to grab her by the arm but stops short the moment I lift my eyes to his. I dare him with my stare to lay one finger on her. Cutting his eyes to his boss, he waits for his instructions. Looking down at my sister, "I promise I'll be back to get you soon."

Santino nods his head, and I watch his man lead Leyna out of the room.

"You have my word; she will have access to call you anytime she wishes. Now, if you'll excuse me, I have other business to attend to. I'll be in touch soon with a date and time for our little arrangement," he says, dismissing us as he adjusts the watch on his wrist looking at the time.

Walking out of his office, I turn around and look at him straight in the eyes, "If you or any of your men touch my sister. I will kill you." His lips turn up in a deviant smile, making my blood boil even more. It takes both Quinn and Logan to lead me out of the house. My gut is churning at the thought of having to leave Leyna in the hands of this asshole.

"Let's head back to the club. I have some calls to make," Prez announces.

Throwing my leg over my bike, I decide I need to be alone for a little while. "I'm going for a ride. See ya first thing in the morning."

Turning the engine over, I peel down the driveway. It was not my intention—at first—to go there. The urge to quiet the voices in my head lead me in the only direction I might find a little peace amongst all the chaos.

It's late by the time I make it to Bozeman. I pull into the parking lot of a small hotel and park my bike and pay for a one-night stay. It's not the cleanest of places, but it is not the worst either. Walking into the room, I slip off my cut, placing it on the back of the chair.

Sitting back on the bed, I rest my head against the wooden headboard and pull a small blunt from my pocket, lighting it. Needing to take the edge off, I take three hits back-to-back, each time holding the smoke in my lungs as long as possible. I'm not chasing sleep—I'm attempting to calm the storm.

I'VE BEEN SITTING on my bike for an hour and a half.

Watching. Waiting.

Until I notice her walking out of the building. Fuckin' breathtaking.

Seeing her walking toward some guy has my ass up off my bike in less than a second. I watch the goddamn thing play out several yards away in front of me. The way he wraps his arms around her. The way she throws her head back laughing.

Just as I take a step, I feel a hand firmly grip my upper arm, and I come around swinging and watch as Quinn skillfully dodges the would-be blow to his jaw.

"What the fuck? What the hell are you doin' here? You following me, brother?" I growl.

"Yeah, I followed you. I had a feeling you might do something stupid. And I was right because here you are. You're the one that sent her away. You told her—"

"I know what the fuck I told her," I interrupt him.

"Then you know you broke her heart, man. I saw and heard the tears and heartbreak in that girl's voice that morning, and I watched as she skillfully avoided ever having to be around you every day after that," he tells me.

Diggin' the knife deeper into the wound I created in my own fuckin' chest, Quinn keeps talkin'.

"I get it. I know why you did what you did. You marchin' over there, kicking that boy's ass and saying 'Me Tarzan, you Jane' is not going to get her back. You want a girl like her back—you need to earn it, brother. You need to show her you love her."

Shit, he's right. If I did that, it would push her away more. Alba doesn't deserve to have me like this. She deserves better. The question is, can I be better for her? Can I prove to her I'm worthy of a second chance?

I peer over at her. I want her to laugh like that with me. I want to be the reason she is happy. The reason she smiles every day. I want her to be mine.

"Come on, brother, let's go home," Quinn says as he lights up a cigarette and starts to walk across the street in the opposite direction, where I see his bike parked. *That explains why I didn't hear his ass before.*

Getting back on my bike, I allow myself to glance back one last time before following Quinn back home.

Alba is my home.

11

ALBA

I debated for a minute whether or not to bring Sam or Leah with me on my weekend trip home. In the end, I chose to go alone. Frankly, I needed the time to myself, and the drive is allowing me to have just that. At least the guys are away on club business. Hiding things from my sister is my other concern. She always knows when something's not right with me. The good thing is, if she senses it, she won't push the issue. Bella has always been good at letting me have my space and waits for me to share with her when I'm ready.

The problem is, when will I be ready? A swollen, pregnant belly is not something I will be able to hide forever. Nevertheless, this is something I'm determined to do on my own. The last thing I need is a broody Cuban finding out I'm having his baby. Not yet, anyway. I need a little more time.

Feeling my stomach rumble, I stop at the next available gas station. I've got another hour before I reach home and I feel like I haven't eaten in days. Walking into the store, I head for the candy aisle and grab some Peanut Butter Cups before grabbing a large

94

bottle of water from the cooler at the back of the store. I head to the front to pay for my things when I get the feeling that I'm being watched. I scan my surroundings and find nothing and no one except for the older cashier up front. I guess I'm paranoid from yesterday. Shrugging my shoulders, I step up to the counter and place my items down.

I pay for my things and head back outside to my truck when it starts to rain. Climbing in, I get myself situated by taking the time to unwrap some candies and place them in a small plastic cup that's sitting in my cup holder, so I can munch without having to try and unravel wrappers as I drive.

Ten minutes later I'm back on the road with the radio turned up as Adele's *Hiding My Heart* blares through the speaker in the cab of my pickup truck as I cruise down the road with the wipers flicking away the drops of rain from the windshield, and I wipe an escaping tear from my eye.

Polson city limits. Another twenty-five minutes and I'll be home. On my way through downtown-main street, I pass the tattoo shop and notice the bikes sitting outside and recognize one of them as Gabriel's. *What the hell?*

Bella said that the guys were gone out of town. Maybe they haven't left yet. That's it. I know Bella wouldn't lie to me. She knows I'm avoiding Gabriel even though I haven't said so or told her why. She made it a point that I knew they would be gone.

Calm down. No one will find out anything.

I don't even make it all the way up the driveway of Logan and Bella's home when she comes bursting out the front door barefoot. A smile lights up my face. I'm genuinely happy to see my sister. My truck door is opened as soon as I park and turn the truck off. Bella is climbing in for a hug before I can even get my seatbelt off.

"Oh my god! I have missed you so much!" she sing-songs.

"I missed you too," I say as she releases me. I unbuckle, reach into the back seat, and grab my overnight bag before climbing out. Once we make it inside and Bella closes the door, Sofia comes walking down the stairs.

"Alba! It's good to see you. When did you get here? I didn't hear you come in. I was on the phone with my counselor."

"Everything okay?" I ask as I place my bag on the floor and my purse and keys on the small table by the stairs.

"Oh, yeah, everything is good. She wanted to know if I wanted to volunteer this weekend at the community outreach center. I'm going to stay over at my friend's house tonight and ride with her since she's volunteering too," Sofia says, stopping in front of me and hugging me. "I just wanted to come down and say hi before Jessica comes to pick me up." The honking of a horn has Sofia rushing back up the stairs. "That's my ride. I'm going to grab my bag, then get out of here and let you guys catch up."

Walking into the kitchen, I sit down on a stool at the large island counter as my sister grabs us both something to drink from the refrigerator.

"I thought the guys were going to be out of town this weekend. I saw their bikes in town on the way here," I question her.

Sitting a soda in front of me, Bella stands on the opposite side of the kitchen with a look on her face telling me she sees right through me.

"I'm sorry, that's what Logan told me the other day. Then plans changed, I guess. All I know is that they won't be leaving after all."

"Why didn't you call and tell me?" *Shit.* That came out kind of bitchy. It's not her fault.

Before I can apologize, she narrows her eyes and then tells me, "I didn't call you back and tell you because you might have decided not to come home this weekend. I know you have your reasons for avoiding a certain biker, and hopefully, someday you'll share that with me, but I wanted to see my sister."

I frown and slouch in my seat. All I have to do for the next twenty-four hours is stay away from the clubhouse.

"I'm sorry. I'm just really tired. And I'm happy to be here too." I need to change the subject. "I'm starving. What's for dinner?"

Smiling, she takes the hint, going along with the change of subject. On cue, my stomach growls, loudly. Besides the blueberry muffin breakfast, I ate this morning, and the candy on the ride here, I haven't had much more to eat today. I need to make it a point to eat better.

"Logan is working late. We can order in tonight. How does pizza sound?" my sister asks me. Pizza sounds amazing right now.

"I want extra cheese on mine," I respond as I stand and walk over, placing my glass into the sink.

"Why don't you get settled in your room while I call the order. We can watch a movie when you come back down, maybe talk about how those classes are going. I want to hear all about your new friends too," she speaks, wearing a smile.

I walk to the stairs, pick up my bags along the way and proceed to make my way up to my room right next to Sofia's. As soon as I step inside, my phone pings with a new message. Setting my things down on the bed, I pull my phone from my purse, swiping the screen.

Sam: You make it?

Me: Yeah, got here forty minutes ago.

Sam: Call or text if you need me. See you when you get back.

Me: Thanks. I will. See ya later.

Glancing at the time on my phone, it's 6:30 pm. I should have plenty of time to take a quick shower, so I grab my black shorts and oversized Montana State University shirt from my bag and head out into the hall and make my way to the bathroom. Once inside, I reach in, turning the water on, and letting it warm.

Thankful for all the extra space I have compared to the dorm's small bathroom back on campus, I strip out of my clothes then take my hair down, letting it fall around my shoulders. Before stepping into the shower, I glance in the vanity mirror and place my hand on my flat stomach and imagine myself a few months from now.

Will I show right away? Will I have a boy or a girl? How much will he or she look like their daddy? I hope they have his beautiful tanned skin and his thick dark hair. All I know right now is that I will love this baby fiercely, and I will always put my child first. I'll deal with Gabriel later. My focus is and will stay on me and this baby. Stepping into the spray of warm water—I relax, close my eyes, and center myself.

I'm sitting on the couch with my sister eating pizza and watching Sixteen Candles laughing so hard I feel like I'm going to pee myself, while Bella tells me about sending a sexy text and a picture of herself in some kind of sexy costume to Quinn by mistake.

"Oh my god! I would be mortified!"

"I am never sexting again," she says, burying her face in her hands. I snatch her phone from the coffee table where it was sitting and pull up her texts.

"Alba, no, give me back my phone. Don't look at it," she begs.

I'm thumbing through each photo until I find it.

"Damn. From what I've heard, this kind of stuff is right up his alley too."

"I know. I didn't realize it until it was too late, and Quinn had already gotten an eyeful before Logan walked up to him in the garage and destroyed his phone," she continues to explain.

Laughter bubbles up, making its way out of my mouth again. I haven't laughed this hard in a long time. It feels really good.

"I'm glad you're finding humor in my humiliation," she says, chunking a cheese ball at my head.

"I really have missed being home. I've missed this," I tell her.

LOGAN WALKS into the kitchen through the garage door. Looking at the time, it's already 9:30 pm. Bella has a girls' day planned tomorrow with shopping, mani-pedi, and lunch. Logan walks into the living room, and judging by the heated stare he has directed toward Bella...it's safe to say I'm officially the third wheel.

"Hey, Logan," I greet him with a small wave of my hand and a smile as I get up off the couch. "I think I'm going to turn in for the night guys. It's been a long day, and the drive kind of done me in," I tell both of them.

Bella breaks her eyes away from Logan long enough to say, "You don't have to rush off."

"No, I really am tired. I'll see you guys in the morning. Goodnight," I leave the living room and make my way upstairs, giving them their privacy.

AFTER EMPTYING the contents of my stomach into the toilet after breakfast, I clean myself up and make my way back downstairs, where my sister is waiting on me. I plaster on a fake smile because I really feel like shit. Not sleeping well and the morning sickness depletes what energy I do have. I'm determined to make the most of it though. Knowing we don't have to go anywhere near the clubhouse today already has me feeling more at ease. The last thing I need is to run into Gabriel while I'm still dealing with the news that I'm carrying his baby.

"You feeling okay, sis? You look tired," Bella questions me with a look of concern.

"Yeah, I'm fine. I didn't sleep well last night."

"Well, hopefully some retail therapy will help you feel better. The fall and winter apparel are on sale at all our favorite boutiques this weekend, and I for one, plan to find myself some new boots. I've been saving my money for a particular pair."

I might as well buy some new leggings and sweaters. They should help hide the pregnancy for awhile.

"I'm ready whenever you are," I smile.

Bella locks up, then we head out to her car, climb in and drive toward town. Before we know it, half the day is gone, and the back seat of her car is full of shopping bags. So far, today has turned out to be a good day. As we are driving down the road, I start craving chocolate cake and mint chocolate chip ice cream.

"Swing by the grocery store. Let's bake a cake tonight. A chocolate cake." I grin at my sister. I know she'll be game. Our mom would let us bake a cake together on our birthdays when we were younger, then sit down in front of the TV, each with a fork and eat straight from the cake pan and watch movies all night.

"Don't forget the ice cream," she says as she turns into the grocery store's parking lot.

I sling my purse over my shoulder and get out of the car. Walking in, I grab a handbasket and make my way to the baking aisle and grab a box of cake mix of the shelf along with a tub of chocolate icing. Knowing that Bella has the milk, oil, and eggs at home, I head straight to the ice cream aisle but get distracted by the book on the shelf. I pick it up and start to read the blurb on the back when I hear the deep timbre of *his* voice rasps from behind me, feeling it vibrate through every fiber of my being.

"Cariño *Sweetheart*?"

Gabriel.

That word spoken from his lips causes my skin to break out in goosebumps, and my heart rate increases. Taking in a slow deep breath, I collect myself and turn around. My blue eyes lock with his rich, dark brown ones and for one second, I forget about my broken heart.

"Gabriel," I speak in a soft tone.

His eyes soften, and he steps closer. He smells so good. My eyes fall to his lips. I remember the taste of his kiss like it was only yesterday. His lips part slightly as if to say something, my phone rings, bringing me back to reality. Blinking, I pull my phone from my back pocket and I see it's Sam calling me. *Perfect timing.*

Swiping the screen, I lift it to my ear and stare into Gabriel's eyes as I speak, "Hey, Sam." I say with a fake smile and watch Gabriel's face morph into one of anger before he storms away with his fists clenched at his sides.

He's the one who made the choice that there would be no us. He made that clear a little more than two months ago. What right does he have to be angry?

"You have no idea how glad I am you called just now," I confess.

"Why is that?" Sam replies, concern laced with his words.

"I just had a brief run-in with Gabriel."

"What did he do?"

"Nothing. It's what *I* almost did. Sam, that man is my biggest weakness. I need to get back to Bozeman."

"Tomorrow isn't that far away. It's a small town. It was bound to happen," he tells me. "Anyway, I wanted to check in on you. You still have that appointment this week? I want to make sure I can be there with you—for you."

"Yeah, it's this coming Friday."

I walk to the front of the store, scanning the vast area for any signs of a broody six-foot-four Cuban. Glancing down at the basket in my hand, I realize I forgot the ice cream and head back there and quickly grab it. After paying for my things, I walk out of the store and climb into the car. The whole ride home is quiet except for the music playing on the radio. Did Bella see him walk inside? Did she see him walk out? She seems to be deep in thought. My sister and I have a deep bond. I've got the feeling she is really struggling with the fact I'm not sharing something with her. I reach over, grabbing her hand. She inhales deeply before releasing her breath and squeezes mine in response. All this is set aside as we spend the rest of the evening sitting in front of the TV, eating cake out of the pan and ice cream straight out of the carton.

ON FRIDAY, I'm sitting in the waiting room at the women's clinic waiting to see Dr. Linda Turner for my first prenatal checkup with Sam sitting beside me, but wishing it was Gabriel instead. Not that I'm not grateful to have Sam by my side—I am. I just can't stop thinking about the run-in I had with Gabriel at the store this past weekend.

"Miss Jameson," the nurse calls from the open door that leads to the exam rooms in the back. I get up from my chair and nervously follow her into a room with Sam right behind me. After being given a plastic cup and making a trip to the restroom, she instructs me to undress from the waist down and gives me a sheet to cover myself with. Once the nurse leaves Sam turns around, giving me privacy until I'm seated on the exam bed.

"They have to do a pelvic exam. You can step out for that part," I instruct him.

It doesn't take long, maybe fifteen minutes before Dr. Turner is walking through the door. She's an older lady with kind blue eyes and short graying hair.

"Miss Jameson, how are you today?" She greets me with a warm smile that helps to ease my nerves a bit.

"I'm doing okay."

"Oh, I'm so sorry, I didn't see you sitting there, young man," she says when she closes the door and notices Sam sitting in the chair just behind it in the corner.

"Well, it's confirmed. You're pregnant. And from the calculations you gave us, you are right at eight weeks, giving you a due date of April 7. We are going to do a quick exam on you. Would you like your beau to stay for that?"

"Oh, no, we're not together. He's my friend. He's going to step out for this part," I explain.

Sam stands and leaves the room. The exam doesn't take long, but before she lets him back in, her kind words make this whole experience less stressful.

"It's good that you brought support today. Pregnancy can be overwhelming. I see my share of young mothers-to-be come in here, and I can tell you're going to do just fine dear," she says, patting me on my leg before she walks toward the door. I'm slipping my shoes back on when Sam walks back into the room.

"Okay, we're done here for today." The doctor says, handing me a prescription for prenatal vitamins. "I'll see you back here in four weeks. That's when we'll get our first look at the baby," she smiles.

"Do you have any questions for me?"

Honestly, right now, I can't think of one. I've been reading up on everything I could get my hands on as soon as I found out I was pregnant. I shake my head, no.

"Okay, they'll have a folder full of other information you may need at the front desk along with your appointment date and time. If you think of anything or have any questions, you can call, and I will be happy to talk to you."

"Thank you, Dr. Turner."

We exit the room, I pay for the visit and collect the folder full of pamphlets along with my next appointment, then we leave the clinic. On the short drive back to campus, I start thinking about my living arrangements. Not the fact that I share the small dorm apartment with Leah, but that I'm giving serious thought to finding off-campus living. My own place away from the hustle and bustle of campus life. Someplace quieter.

"I think I want to look at apartments off campus tomorrow," I say my thoughts aloud.

"That would be a great idea. What do you think about having an extra roommate? I'm assuming Leah would go with you if you find something, but if we all go in together, we can find a larger apartment, maybe even a condo in a decent neighborhood."

That's not a bad idea.

12

GABRIEL

I should have turned my bike around and taken what's mine. And Alba is mine. Seeing her in another man's arms caused rage to bubble up in me. Had it not been for Quinn, I would have ripped the fucker to shreds. For once, I was grateful to my brother for sticking his nose where it doesn't belong. But that's Quinn. And thank fuck. I have no doubt I'd be in jail and charged with murder right about now. Back at the clubhouse, I get off my bike and go inside with Quinn hot on my heels.

"Gabriel, you need to calm the fuck down, brother," he yaks from behind me. Several sets of eyes cut toward us. I ignored them and him as I continue to my room. "What did you expect, man? You pushed her away. Hell, you practically kicked the girl out of your bed, brother. It was only a matter of time before someone else claimed her. Alba's fucking sexy as hell."

Quinn barely gets those last words out before I have him pinned up against the wall with my forearm pressed against his throat.

"If you know what's best for you, I suggest you shut the fuck up about my woman," I snap. "And nobody is claiming her but me. As soon as I get my sister back, I'm going after what's mine," I growl.

When I see a stupid fucking grin come across my brother's face, I know what the hell he's just done. Asshole.

Letting him go, I turn and walk into my room without another word. I could hear Quinn's chuckle and parting words through my door.

"About time you pulled your head out of your ass."

That shit show happened a week ago. I'm not going to even get started on what happened when Alba came home that weekend. To say I was fuckin' shocked to see her at the store would have been an understatement. And the look on Alba's face told me she was just as shocked to see me. When she answered her phone call from another guy right in front of me, it took everything I had in me to walk away. I later found out from Logan that Bella told her sister all us guys were supposed to be gone. It fuckin' gutted me to think the only way Alba would agree to come home was because she thought I wouldn't be here. Blake knocking on my office door catches my attention.

"Hey, boss. Prez called a minute ago. Says he's calling church in an hour. I went ahead and rescheduled your last appointment."

"Alright, man. You go on ahead. I'll lock up." Forty-five minutes later, I'm walking into church, and everyone except Jake has already made it. Lighting a cigarette, I take my seat and ignore the murmuring voices around me. When Prez walks in, he takes his seat and slams the gavel.

"Reid came to me two days ago with some information he found on Santino. Miguel Santino is one of the FBI's most wanted men; has been for the better part of a decade. Recent investigations into him have been of importing and selling women and young girls," Jake informs.

"Son of a fucking bitch," Quinn hisses.

"I highly suspect that the shipment Santino wants us to take care of is not drugs, but women," Prez adds. "We have a choice here, men. We stick with our current plan, or we get the Feds involved. As you all know, ever since Logan's woman was hurt and almost killed, we voted on taking the club legit. You also know that we've not been able to shake the heat on our backs ever since either. Most recently, the question of whether or not Gabriel has any relation to Sofia."

"What exactly is it you're trying to say, Prez?" I grit out.

Not taking his eyes off of me, he answers.

"I want to hand Santino's shipment over to the FBI on a silver fuckin' platter. And in exchange, we agree to clean up our act and take the club legit."

"At the risk of my sister's goddamn life?" I challenge.

"No, son. To save Leyna's life. If Santino is selling women, your sister is as good as gone. Can you tell me that you really trust him to turn her over to you after he's gotten what he's wanted?" Jake questions. With a slight nod of my head, I give Jake my answer. With all the brothers in agreement, Prez pulls the landline phone sitting on the table toward him. Punching in a number and placing the call on speaker, the phone rings three times before someone answers.

"Agent Taylor."

"This is Jake Delane. You have a deal."

The line is silent for a moment before Taylor speaks again.

"Call me when you have a meetup scheduled." Then the line goes dead.

"Alright, now with that shit out of the way, I'm going to tell you all what's really going to happen." Cutting his eyes to me, "Gabriel, you remember that promise I made you?" I sit up straighter in my seat.

"Yeah."

"Make it quick, and no fuck-ups. I want your ass in and out before Taylor shows. And take Reid with you."

Hell, fuckin' yeah. I can already feel my fingers twitch at the thought of getting my hands on both those sons of bitches.

Quinn cuts in, "I thought you said you were handing the fucker over to the Feds?"

Lighting a cigarette, Jake continues, "No. I said I was handing his shipment over. I never said anything about Santino himself. Gabriel and Reid will handle Santino and his nephew while the Feds take care of the shipment and bring his sister to him."

Gritting my teeth, I nod. I'll be so close to my sister but have to leave her there for Taylor to take care of. If we take her with us, then the Feds would know we were there. I can only pray this shit doesn't blow up in our faces and causes my sister her life. Knowing Leyna, this is what she would have wanted. If she found out we had the chance at saving hundreds or even thousands of women's lives and didn't, she wouldn't be able to live with herself. That and she would have my ass.

THREE WEEKS LATER, I'm at work when I finally receive the call we've been waiting on. Walking out of my office to the front of the shop, I see Blake chattin' up a customer.

"I'll be back in an hour," I tell him, walking out of the shop's door and across the street to the garage. Striding through the bay opening I spot Quinn. I give a chin lift as I pass, heading toward Jake's office. Walking past the break room, I run into Bella.

"Hey, big guy. Are you here for some lunch?"

"Here to see Prez," I gruff.

"Oh, okay. I'll just fix you something to take with you when you leave. Stop by and see me, okay?"

Giving her a slight nod, I continue to Jake's office.

"Got a minute, Prez?" I ask, knocking on his door. Jake looks up from some papers on his desk.

"Yeah. What do you need?"

Stepping in front of him, I place a piece of paper on his desk.

On it is the date, time, and meeting place Santino has given me. It's one week from today.

"He only gave me the meetup spot to pick up the shipment, but no destination. He said he'd give us that info when we arrive. Not that it's going to matter since we won't be going."

Looking at Jake, I continue to keep my face expressionless and my feelings in check. I feel completely helpless in this situation. I'm the worst at waiting around for shit to happen. I'm on edge and hangin' on by a fucking thread. When Jake continues to study me, but not say a word, I decide I'm through. I turn to leave when he calls out.

"Come sit down, son."

It's not a question, and no matter how irritated and pissed at the world I am right now, I respect this man and will do as I'm told. Taking a seat, I lean back in the chair and wait for Jake to speak.

"I want you to know, son, no matter what, your sister is top priority. I have no doubt she will be coming home safe. Did you honestly think the club wouldn't have your back? I might be cuttin' a deal, brother, but don't play me for a fool."

"I can't just wait around and sit on my ass, Prez," I argue.

"You can, and you will, Gabriel. I can't risk you losing your shit. I know waitin' sucks, but it's what's smart. Your time is coming. I made you a promise. All you have to do is wait a bit longer." Fuck, I know he's right. Nodding my head, I stand, and Jake stands with me.

"Don't ever doubt my loyalty to you again, Gabriel. I saw it written all over your face as soon as I said I wanted to involve the Feds. You were thinkin' the club didn't care about Leyna."

Blowing out a breath, I nod.

"Alright, go on and let Bella feed you, and I'll make the call," Jake says, walking back around his desk and sitting down.

One week later

Reid and I are making our way through the heavily wooded area behind the house Santino is staying in. We're about 100 feet from the edge of the property line when Reid signals for me to stop. Pulling out his cell, I watch as he taps on his screen. Seconds later, the outside security lights on Santino's house cut off. With the clouds sheltering the moon, it's so fucking dark, I can hardly see my hand in front of my face. Lifting his chin, he motions for us to continue. My adrenaline speeds up the closer we get to the house.

Rounding the side of the house, we notice one guard at the front entrance. Before I can turn my head to warn Reid, the man suddenly slumps to the ground. Looking back at my brother, I see him sling his rifle over his shoulder. My brother is always on point. After assessing there are no other threats; we walk right up to the front door. Turning the knob, we walk into the unlocked house. Obviously, the son of a bitch feels confident in his security, or lack thereof. Estúpido *stupid.*

The house is quiet. The only sound I hear is the sudden creak of the stairs to my left. It only takes seconds before I hear the light ping of Reid's rifle behind me, shooting another one of Santino's men square in his chest. Pulling my gun from my cut, I signal to Reid that I'm headed upstairs, while I watch him continue toward the other end of the house. We have an understanding that if he comes upon Daniel first—he can act, but Santino is mine.

With my gun raised, I climb the last step and make my way down the hallway. The first door I pass is open, and the room is empty. The second door has me stop in my tracks. I notice it has a deadbolt on it, and my gut is telling me my sister is in that room. But as much as it pains me, I continue past. At the end of the hall is one last door. Standing outside, I take a moment and listen for any noise. Met with silence, I twist the knob opening the door.

A wicked smile takes over my face when I see Santino asleep in his bed. How I wish I had time to play, but Prez said we had to make this shit quick. Striding over to the edge of the bed, I look down at the man who took my father away from me. Tucking my gun back into my cut, I unsheathe my blade. Leaning over his sleeping form, I fist a handful of the hair on the top of his head. By the time Santino's eyes snap open, my blade is already against his throat. I can tell by the look in his eyes, he knows this is his end. Without hesitation, I deliver my parting words. The words I speak to every man I look in the eyes of as they take their last breath.

"Decirle al diablo que dije hola, *Tell the devil I said hello.*"

Then I run the blade of my knife from one ear to the next, not once taking my eyes off of his. Not until I know there is no life left inside of him. Releasing the hold I have on Santino's hair, I swipe my knife on his bedsheets, wiping away his blood when I hear a shuffling noise behind me. Turning, I see Daniel in his uncle's doorway with a gun aimed at me.

"Well, if it isn't the rat himself," I say with venom dripping from my voice. "You fucked up, kid."

"Oh yeah? What the hell are you gonna do about it, asshole? It looks to me like I'm the one with a gun."

Grinning, I reply. "You're not the only one with a gun pendejo *stupid.*" As soon as my words register, Daniel whips his head around only to be met with the end of Reid's rifle.

"Thanks, brother," I say to Reid as I step over Daniel's body.

"Anytime."

I'm pacing the yard of the clubhouse and chain-smoking my fourth pack of cigarettes. We have not heard a damn thing about my sister. My brothers all stay silent—Quinn included, which is not like him. For once, he decides to keep his trap shut. Just then, Jake's phone rings.

"Yeah?" He pauses a moment listening to who's on the other line. "Thank fuck," Prez breaths out. Hanging up, he cuts his eyes to me and gives a relieved smile.

"Reid has eyes on Leyna. She's okay. Taylor has her."

And just like that, all the tension leaves the air. I'm grateful my brother stayed behind to make sure things with my sister went smoothly.

A couple of hours later, the sound of tires crunching on the gravel alert us to Agent Taylor's SUV pulling up to the clubhouse and parking. Taylor exits the driver's seat. He's around six-foot-two with short brown hair buzzed close on the sides. He has his dress shirt rolled up to his elbows, exposing a full sleeve on his right arm. Like I said before, you'd be surprised at how many suits have tats. Besides that, everything about him screams Fed. Right down to the menacing look on his face. He definitely finds my club unfavorable. I return his look, letting him know the feeling is mutual.

Without missing a step, he rounds his truck opening the passenger door. I see him take Leyna's hand and whisper something into her ear, and she nods her head in return. When my sister's eyes turn away from Taylor and land on me, she breaks away from him and runs into my waiting arms.

"Hermano *Brother!*" she cries, burying her face into my neck.

"Shh, hermana *sister*. You're okay," I tell her quietly. Setting Leyna back on her feet, she clutches the front of my shirt using it to wipe her face, just like she would do when we were kids. "I see not much has changed. Still wiping your snot on me." I chuckle.

"Shut up, Gabe." She laughs through a watery smile.

"Let's get you inside, okay?" She gives me a nod, and I then turn my attention to the agent, who is still standing by his truck and has yet to take his eyes off my sister. "You can go now," I grind out, and my sister gasps beside me.

"Gabriel Martinez!"

Ignoring my sister, I turn my full attention to the agent.

"It's okay, sweetheart," he assures Leyna but looking directly at me. "I need to get going, got a fuck ton of shit to clean up, and about a month's worth of paperwork waiting on me. Just remember my offer stands." He slides back into his truck and drives off.

I turn to my sister, "Let's get you inside and settled. And after, we are going to discuss what that fucker meant by his offer still stands."

Leyna rolls her eyes, "Forever the big brother," she says through a watery smile.

IT'S 5:00 AM, and my sister was finally able to go to sleep. I walk out of my room and softly shut the door, careful not to wake her. After grabbing a cup of coffee, I'm walking out of the kitchen when I notice Reid limping through the main room and out the front door. I follow him out and watch as he sits down at one of the picnic tables and starts massaging his leg above the knee. When he notices me striding his way, he stops.

Sitting down next to him, I drink my coffee silently for a moment before I ask, "How'd you hurt it?"

"I'm fine," Reid bites out.

"Didn't ask if you were fine, brother. I asked you how you hurt your leg."

"Climbing down off Santino's roof," he confesses. "It'll be fine in a day or two, brother, leave it alone."

"I want to tell you I appreciate what you did for my sister. I owe you one, man."

He shakes his head, "No, you don't, Gabriel. And you're welcome."

Standing, Reid slaps me on my back, "I'm going to head in and try to get a couple of hours sleep."

Finishing my coffee, I stare out over the mountains as the sun begins to rise. I finally have mi hermana *my sister*, and there is only one thing missing—Alba.

13

ALBA

"That's the rest of it," Sam announces, closing the door to the three-bedroom condominium we signed the rental agreement for last Friday. Four weeks ago, we started looking for something off campus, and finally, after looking at several places, Leah happened upon this one located near a small walking park in a quiet neighborhood.

I have my three-month check-up today, and Leah is going with me this time. Sam is going to hang back here and get things situated. After doing some Craigslist and yard sale shopping, we found some bedroom furniture for everyone, along with a couch and two chairs for the living room. I used what money I've been making from book cover designs to take care of my share of the deposit and first month's rent and got myself a bed and dresser for my room—everything else I needed for my personal space I had already. I haven't even told my sister about the move and don't plan to just yet. At the end of the day, I need to do what I feel is right for me.

Sliding the glass door open that leads to the small back patio, I step outside. The weather is getting pretty cold now. We are at the tail end of October, and all the trees have changed their colors to variant hues of warm purple, orange, yellow, and red. The small backyard we have isn't fenced in, and it has a clear view of the park.

I wrap my jacket around me a little tighter as a gust of wind blows, picking the fallen leaves up off the ground. Today I get to see the baby. My first sonogram. It's crazy what four weeks will do. I went from not showing, to a baby bump overnight. My morning sickness is almost non-existent. I've managed to keep my bump hidden at school, wearing leggings and sweaters, trying to prevent the rumors from starting.

I hear the door slide open behind me.

"Hey, you ready?" Leah asks, poking her head outside.

"Yeah, I'm ready."

I'm lying on my back on the exam table when Dr. Turner squeezes some cold gel onto my belly. The moment the Doppler touches my skin, an image of my baby fills the screen, and I gasp.

"Look at that. I didn't even have to work for it. Baby is definitely ready for the spotlight today," she says as she clicks on various parts of the image and types away on her keyboard.

"In case you're wondering, I'm taking the baby's measurements. Making sure he or she is on track with growth. And so far, everything looks good."

Looking at the screen, I can see the nose and a little hand. With the flip of a switch, the heartbeat fills the room, and all I can think is Gabriel is missing this. Maybe I should have told him already and given him a choice to be here or not. Honestly, when it comes to Gabriel, I have no clue what the right decisions are.

"Baby's heartbeat is strong. We should be able to tell the sex in a few more weeks if you'd like to know," she smiles.

"Yeah, I'd like to know," I tell her.

Leah, who hasn't let go of my hand the entire time, has a look of wonder and amazement on her face as she stares at the monitor.

"Baby is very active right now," Dr. Turner observes.

I feel flutters all the time. The first time I felt something, I was lying in bed on my back while reading a book. It was a little flip flop. I don't know any other way to describe it. I don't think there is anything better than feeling your baby move for the very first time. The doctor wipes the gel from my stomach and helps me to sit up. Before leaving the room, she hands me my sonogram pictures.

"I'll see you November 26. Two days before Thanksgiving. Hopefully, the baby is as cooperative as he or she was today, and we can get a look at the gender. You're doing great, Alba. Everything looks as it should. I'll see you again soon," Dr. Turner informs me.

Relief washes over me. I've been so worried. With all the reading I've been doing on pregnancy and what to expect; I've also read all the things that can go wrong, and it has made me a bit paranoid. Knowing everything looks good has put my mind at ease.

"Leah, what are your plans for Thanksgiving? Are you going home? Sam told me the other day he's going home for a couple of days."

"My mom and dad are out of the country right now with the church. I'll be staying here," she answers in a detached way. I get the feeling she's relieved about not going home. From what little she has told me, which isn't a lot, her family life isn't all that great.

"My sister keeps asking if I'm going to come home. I'm not sure I want to go back home yet. If I do decide to go, will you come with me? I won't leave you here by yourself," I tell her.

She gives me a half smile, "Of course I would go with you."

THE NEXT DAY I'm on my way to my truck after leaving the counselor's office when I literally bump into Professor Green, and his hand reaches out catching me by the arm before I fall.

"Alba, I'm sorry. That was my fault. I didn't see you." He smiles, bringing himself a little too close.

I take a small step back putting some space between us, "That's okay. I wanted to speak with you tomorrow, but since you're already here, the counselor, Mrs. Reynolds, said I needed to make sure all my assignments are caught up before I start online courses. I was going to ask if you could email her and let her know." With his hand still on my arm, I gently pull out of his grip.

"Online course?" he questions. His lips form a thin line as if he's angry at what I said.

"I'm sorry. If this isn't a good time, I can come by your office tomorrow—" Interrupting me, he quickly loses the angry expression he had and replaces it with a more neutral one.

"No, I'll email her tonight, but usually, there needs to be a reason a student would change from a classroom setting to online education in the middle of a semester. What would that reason be?"

"Oh, I've talked with Mrs. Reynolds about my personal reasons already, and she said that switching over shouldn't be a problem."

"First, you move off campus, and now you're dropping out?"

Okay?

"Professor Green...me living off campus or choosing to finish my semester online is none of your business," I tell him. I mean, what the hell is up with that? He's always been a pretty nice guy and a good teacher, but being pissed about things that are none of his concern.

"I take my job as a teacher seriously, Alba. I apologize for being intrusive," he responds in a hurried clipped tone.

"I need to go," I huff.

Turning, I walk to my truck, and he calls out, "I'll take care of everything."

I look over my shoulder and answer him as I climb into my truck, "Thank you."

———————

TRUE TO HIS WORD, Professor Green, along with my other teachers, were able to send all the information Mrs. Reynolds needed, and almost four weeks later, I'm enrolled in online classes. I have to say that my level of concentration is much better now that I'm working at home instead of in the classroom. The class setting wasn't for me. This now allows me to not only continue with the degree I want but to work on my book cover business as well.

That and the fact it seems in the last three and a half weeks, my stomach has decided to double in size. And this baby is active. And more so when I get a craving for chocolate ice cream, which I try really hard not to stuff my face with. I swear I could sit and eat a half gallon in one sitting.

Then, there is the whole hiding my pregnancy from Gabriel and my sister. I feel guilty about it all the time. But with Gabriel's rejection and the possibility of letting my sister down has me keeping my mouth shut. At least till I can work up the courage to tell them. I know it will have to be soon. No matter how Gabriel feels about me, I won't keep him from his child.

I had another doctor appointment yesterday and decided not to find out the gender right now. I'm not quite ready to know. I feel like I need to share that kind of news with my sister. I'll wait until I go home for Christmas and we can open the envelope together. That's when I'll have to face the music. There will be no more hiding. I even managed to avoid going home for Thanksgiving by saying that Leah and I had the flu and couldn't make it.

Did Bella buy it? By the hurt I heard in her voice I doubt it, but again, she pretended right along with me. At the end of the conversation, she told me all she wants is for me to be happy. She misses me, and she hopes I get to feeling better. So here I am, sitting at home—not sick, eating a small turkey dinner I helped Leah cook, and I'm not enjoying a bit of it. Not that it tastes bad or anything, cause it's really good. I'm missing my family. I can sit around and blame someone else for it all, but the blame is on me. I chose to go without them. I needed to prove that I can do this—do life on my own. I needed to prove it to myself more than anything.

December-Christmas Break

"Sam, I am really sorry. I never meant for any of this to affect you," I say with remorse. Word has spread that I'm knocked up, and everyone thinks Sam is the father.

"I'm not. Fuck what everyone else thinks," he says, sitting down on the couch, placing my feet in his lap and starts to massage them. Hiding my pregnancy is no longer possible. I swear I'm going to give birth to a linebacker as huge as I am. And I'm miserable. My back hurts, and I'm getting cankles.

"You quit the team Sam, all because a couple of the guys said shit about me. You knocked one of them out. What's going to happen to your scholarship now?"

"You know I never wanted to play football professionally anyway. As for my full ride, I'll find out my fate after Christmas break. In the meantime, why don't we go out for a late lunch—my treat. Use what I can off dad's credit card before he finds out what I did today."

I rub my belly. Food sounds good. Food always sounds good.

"Leah should be back in about an hour," I glance up at him, "Mexican?" I ask.

Standing up, I tell him I'm going to take a shower. Stepping in my room and closing the door, I strip out of my clothes and throw them in the hamper. Walking over to the bathroom, I stand in front of the full-length mirror next to my closet door and stare at myself wearing nothing but a pair of boy shorts. My body has changed so much. My hips are a little wider, and my breasts are a whole lot bigger. Even my face seems like it has changed somehow. I'm not the same woman I was almost six months ago. I turn and look at my profile. I'm going to be a mom. Every day I stand in front of the mirror and look at myself, and every day I'm still in awe. I love this baby more than anything in life.

We decided on Taco Tuesdays at Jose's. You get half-off tacos, and I tried to eat my weight in them. Plus, the atmosphere here is great. I lean back in my chair.

"Why did you guys let me eat so much?" I think I ate five. But they were so good.

"I'm kind of scared to say no to you," Sam says with his eyes wide, chuckling.

"Sam, she is eating for two, you know. What's your excuse?" Leah jokes, which causes all three of us to laugh.

"Why don't we stop on the way back home and get some ice cream. I want a banana split," I say when we stand and put on our coats. They both ignore the fact that I just told them I was full and now requesting dessert. Stepping outside the restaurant, I breathe in the cold evening air. Every storefront in town is decorated. The whole street is lit up with twinkling lights and dancing Santa's everywhere.

"Can we walk for a few minutes, guys? I want to see all the decorations," I ask them. Agreeing, we walk up one side of the street then back down the other before we make our way back home.

"Guys, did we forget to turn the lights off when we left?" I ask.

SANDY ALVAREZ & CRYSTAL DANIELS

"No, I was the last one out. I know I turned everything off," Sam says.

He gets out of the truck first telling us to stay put and let him check things out. I watch him open the door to our apartment and walk inside.

"Come on, Leah, let's go inside."

"He said to stay here," she says adamantly.

I'm not listening. I climb out of the truck and make my way to the front door with Leah right behind me. As soon as I walk through the door, I see Sam coming downstairs. The whole place is trashed. The couch is slashed. The TV lays on the floor, shattered to pieces—the food that was in the refrigerator, thrown everywhere.

"They must have come through the sliding door in the kitchen. I haven't looked at all the damage upstairs yet, and whoever was here is gone," Sam tells us both. All three of us walk upstairs. My room is the first bedroom we come to, and the door is open. Sam goes in first, and I bump into his back from his abrupt stop. He quickly spins around, blocking my view with his body, trying to back me out the door.

"What the hell, Sam? Let me in," I demand.

"Sweetheart, you don't need to see anything. We need to call the police."

What in the world is he talking about? I force my way past him, and I really wish I hadn't. Hanging on my wall above my bed is my sonogram picture. It's pinned to the wall with a pocketknife, and the words GET RID OF IT OR I WILL, written in blood-red paint.

My knees go weak, and bile rises into my throat. Luckily Sam catches me before I fall to the floor.

"Who would do something like this?" Leah asks. I start to shake and then cry.

"I've had someone messing with me since school started—first flowers, then the notes. Someone was even in mine and Leah's dorm. I haven't said anything thinking whoever it was would stop, and I thought they had. I haven't had a note show up for several weeks now," I sob.

Sam bends down and picks me up and sits me on my tattered bed. "Why didn't you say anything? You should have told someone, Alba."

"I know, I know. I thought maybe someone was trying to play a prank on me at first, and when I stopped receiving notes and I figured they had moved on."

Leah grabs my hand and tells me, "We need to call the police."

I look up at both of them with red eyes and a tear-streaked face, "No, take me home."

"Alba we have to—"

"I want to go home!" I interrupt Sam.

Kneeling down in front of me, he brushes my hair from my face before speaking, "Alright, but Leah is driving you. I'll stay here and call the police." He looks at Leah, "Pack her some clothes, if you leave now, you can make it by 10:00 pm at the latest."

I watch Leah gather what she can that's not shredded and shove it into a small suitcase she found in my closet.

Get rid of it, or I will.

The image of those words keeps repeating over and over again in my head. Why would someone want to hurt my baby?

"Come on, Alba, let's go. I have what I could find. Let's get you home." I hear Leah speak, but it sounds muffled like I have water in my ears. I let them lead me to the truck, and Sam buckles me in and tells Leah to call as soon as we get there. I sit in the passenger's seat, staring out the window.

I haven't stopped crying the entire time we have been driving. I think I'm almost to the point where I have no more tears left to shed. My eyes hurt. My head hurts.

We arrive in Polson, "You'll have to tell me which way to go. I've never been here before," Leah states.

I quietly give her directions until we pull onto the long dirt road leading to the clubhouse. I don't have to worry about someone letting me in because the club put up a new security gate complete with keypad and code entry. Bella told me it was installed a month ago thanks to Logan's dad, and she gave me the code in case I ever needed it, and right now, I'm thankful she did. I give Leah the code to punch in, and the eight-foot gate slowly slides open and then closes as we pull through. After parking at the end of the building, I climb out, spotting my sister's car. On autopilot, I make my way inside.

I'm barely in the door a second when I see my sister running toward me with a smile that quickly falters, "Alba, what's wrong?" she asks as she pulls me in for a hug. Looking from Bella, my eyes connect with Gabriel's, and I pull my coat tighter.

"Cariño *Sweetheart?*" Gabriel's deep voice addresses cautiously.

My sister is staring at me then gasps and covers her mouth the moment I pull on my coat again, doing nothing to hide my pregnant belly. Gabriel's eyes drift to what has Bella's attention, and I feel my heart race even faster.

"What the fuck?" he growls. "You sure didn't waste any time spreading your legs for that ballplayer, letting him knock you up," he accuses me, his tone filled with rage.

My shock mirrors my sister's, and without hesitation my palm connects with Gabriel's cheek slapping him. The sound of my hand against his flesh echoes off the clubhouse walls. And a second later, Bella connects with the other side. How can he say such a thing? Does he really believe I would be so easy? That I would quickly sleep with someone else after being with him?

Grabbing my hand, my sister leads me through the crowd of bikers and up the stairs to my room I always used when I stayed here. Closing the door, she sits me down on the bed.

"Alba, what is going on? Talk to me. I knew you were keeping something from me and I suspected it had something to do with Gabriel, but I never thought for one minute you were pregnant with his baby," she says calmly, but with hurt in her voice. The fact that she didn't ask who the father was and assumed it was Gabriel shows me just how attentive she has really been.

"I didn't find out I was pregnant until I was two months along. And after Gabriel told me in not so many words that I was nothing to him, I couldn't say anything."

She stops pacing and sits down next to me on the bed.

"It hurts my feelings that you didn't feel you could confide in me."

"It's not that I couldn't. I chose not to. I didn't want to disappoint you."

"You could never disappoint me, Alba. You have to live life for yourself and make your own choices. I'm 100% behind you, no matter what. Don't you know that?" my sister asks. "But I get the feeling something happened, and that's why you showed up here a few days earlier than expected crying. What's going on?"

Defeated, I tell Bella everything. Every detail leading up to what happened this evening. My sister can no longer hold back her emotions. Leaning over, she holds me, and I welcome it.

"I'm going to be an auntie," she sniffles.

Hearing Gabriel's voice booming through the clubhouse catches our attention. It's muffled, but I know it's his. Oh my god, I completely forgot about Leah.

"Bella, my friend Leah brought me. She's down there right now, and those men are probably scaring her to death."

Wiping her eyes on her sleeve, she walks out the door, and ten minutes later, she's walking back in with a very freaked out Leah in tow.

14

GABRIEL

It's Tuesday night, and I'm sitting in the clubhouse surrounded by my family. I sit quietly in the corner, nursing my beer while listening to the conversation flow. Leyna is lounging on the sofa, and across from her, Logan is kicked back with a beer in one hand and the other resting on Bella's hip while she sits on his lap.

The past five months have been quiet around the club, which is a big fuckin' change from this time last year. Getting out of gunrunning will do that. Logan's father has been nothing but supportive in the club's decision to go legit. The shop and the garage have been doing well. Are we feeling the pinch with the loss of cash flow from not running guns? Yes. But it also feels fuckin' good to not deal with the bullshit that comes with it. Several of the older members were not entirely on board with the club's decision. They are set in their ways as to how the club should be, but in the end, the vote was unanimous.

Then a month ago, Logan's brother, Nikolai, came to Jake with a proposition. He wanted to start a construction business. Last year, Nikolai stayed in Polson while Demetri went back to Russia. Logan had a friend hook his brother up with a construction job.

Nikolai wanted to start making his own way. He even moved into the clubhouse. He is not a King, but he is family. It turns out, he has a knack for working construction and has been saving up his money. Nikolai asked Jake if the club would be interested in going into business together, 50/50. Prez brought the proposition up in church, and it took all of five minutes for everyone to agree. The club will put up half the money, and Reid has volunteered to work side by side with Nikolai. As Road Captain, Reid stayed busy planning all our runs, but as of lately has been without much to do, so he jumped at the chance. I respect the hell out of Logan's brother. He refuses to use his father's money. He wants to pave his own way in life.

The club even offered my sister a job. We would need a receptionist for our new company. Leyna jumped at the chance. Her being able to speak both Spanish and English will come in handy since about sixty percent of the men hired so far speak the language. Leyna has even convinced some of the brothers to learn how to speak Spanish. Except for Quinn.

My sister has refused to teach him anymore once she figured out that he was using it to hit on Sofia's Spanish teacher, which explains why he had been so eager to pick her up from school most days. One day, Sofia came home from school and told Bella how Quinn was embarrassing her at school by flirting with her teacher when he came to pick her up. So, Bella went to Leyna, and they hashed out a plan to get Quinn. Let's just say the next time he picked Sofia up from school; he came back to the clubhouse with a scowl and a very noticeable handprint across the left side of his face. All three girls busted out laughing.

"Not cool, Leyna, not cool at all," Quinn declared.

Later that day, I asked my sister what she had him say to the teacher.

"Let's just say a woman does not like being told she has a fat ass," was her response. My baby sister is a little spitfire. Don't ever let her looks mislead you. You fuck up, and she'll hand you your ass. She has laid into me on more than one occasion since she's been here. Every one of those times has been about Alba. She wasn't shy at telling me how bad I fucked up. My stomach still clenches at the thought of how I treated Alba the morning after I'd made love to her.

"Our mother did not raise you that way, and she would be disappointed in you, hermano *brother*. I suggest you get your shit together and get your woman."

And that's what I plan to do. Three weeks ago, I found a house, made an offer and I close next week. When I do get my girl back, we won't be staying at the clubhouse. Alba deserves a home of her own, and that's what she's going to get. My plan was to talk to her at Thanksgiving, but she made up some bullshit excuse not to come home. If she doesn't bring her ass home this weekend, I'll be making a trip to Bozeman.

"Hey, big guy. What are you deep in thought about over there?" Bella asks from across the room, bringing me out of my thoughts.

"Nothin'," I grunt. Giving me a warm smile, she turns her attention back to Logan. Bella is sweet and doesn't take offense to my lack of words. A few minutes later, the door to the clubhouse opens, bringing in a cold draft.

"Alba!" Bella screeches, jumping up off Logan's lap and rushes to her sister. Suddenly my senses go on high alert. Alba's face is red, and tears are running down her face. I quickly stride over to her. Alba looks at me over her sister's shoulder, and her face pales.

"Cariño *Sweetheart*," I address her softly, not taking my eyes off hers. That's until I hear Bella suck in a breath next to me and covers her mouth with her hand. Snapping my head back toward my woman, I begin to let my eyes travel over her from head to toe. And what I see has my hackles rising.

"What the fuck?" I growl. "You sure didn't waste any time

spreading your legs for that ballplayer, letting him knock you up," I grind out, fuming.

I hear Bella and Alba gasp in unison before Alba reaches out and lands a powerful slap across my face. And before I can recover, Bella reaches up and takes a shot at the other cheek. Without a word, Bella grabs her sister's hand and leads her out of the room.

The clubhouse has gone quiet, and Reid is the first to speak up. "Someone want to tell me what the hell just happened?"

Quinn is the one to answer. "That was Gabriel's baby momma puttin' him in his place. I don't think you could have put yourself in a deeper hole brother, but you sure as shit just did. I'd sleep with one eye open if I were you."

"What the fuck is Quinn talkin' about?" Jake booms looking directly at me.

"Aww now, Prez, by the look on his face, I don't think Gabriel has even fully grasped what just happened, so let's give it a minute."

I glare at my brother, but what he said finally clicks—my baby momma.

"Gabriel knocked up Alba?" Reid chimes in.

"Not only did he knock her up, but he basically just accused her of being a whore," Quinn adds.

"Son of a bitch," I hiss, hanging my head. *What the fuck have I done?*

"Wait a goddamn minute. When the hell did this happen?" Jake asks. I don't answer. All I can think about is getting to my girl. Turning away from all my brothers, I head in the direction of the room we keep for Alba. I make it about halfway down the hallway when a hand reaches out, grabbing my bicep to stop me. It's Logan.

"I think you need to let Bella calm her down before you go barging in there, man."

"You need to let me go so I can see about my woman," I suggest evenly.

"No. You need to calm the fuck down. Because the last thing Alba needs is for you to upset her even more. Think about the baby, Gabriel. Let Bella get her calmed down first."

My body tenses, and my fury is building, and I'm about to tell Logan to fuck off when we are interrupted by Austin.

"Guys, there's some chick out here asking for Alba. Said she drove her here. She looks scared as hell." Yanking my arm free of Logan's clutch, I walk back out to the main room of the clubhouse to see who Austin is talking about.

Rounding the corner, I see a short girl with wild curly hair and glasses. I recognize her as the girl Alba has been spending most of her time with at school. She looks nervous as fuck—wide-eyed and clutching her coat to her chest.

"You came with Alba?" I ask as I stop in front of her.

"Y...ye...yes," she stutters, looking up at me through her glasses. "I drove her here in her truck. Something happened, and she was too upset to drive, so I insisted I'd bring her home."

I narrow my eyes at the girl, "What do you mean something happened? Did someone hurt her?" I feel my blood heat, and my body vibrate at the thought of someone hurting Alba. Prez comes up behind me and places his hand on my shoulder, silently telling me to rein it in.

"What's your name, sweetheart?" Jake asks.

"Leah," she barely squeaks out. Then she starts rummaging through her purse. Pulling out an inhaler, she gives it a few shakes before bringing it to her mouth. After a beat, she seems to get herself under control.

"Can you tell us what happened to Alba? What caused her to get so upset she needed you to drive her home?"

Swallowing nervously, Leah answers. "She didn't want you all to know, but someone has been messing with her."

"Messing with her how?" I bark. My outburst causing this chick to shrink away.

"Gabriel, calm your ass down," Jake warns then turns his attention back to the girl. "Alright, Leah. Go on and tell us the rest." Jake encourages her to continue.

"Well, I only just found out a few hours ago, but she said she received flowers, then someone was leaving notes on her truck, things like that. Then she said she thinks whoever this person is, was in our room at the dorm we were staying in a few months ago. And tonight, we went out to eat, and when we got back to our apartment, it was trashed."

Not able to stand still any longer, I begin to pace. My vision starts to blur, and my fingers twitch. I need to hurt something, someone. I need to wrap my hand around the motherfucker's throat, who dare think they can harm my woman.

"Is that it?" Logan breaks in.

She shakes her head back and forth, "No."

Just then, Bella comes up behind us and walks up to Alba's scared friend.

"You must be Leah."

Immediately, I notice that she's been crying. Her face is red, and her eyes are swollen. When she walks past, she completely ignores me as she grabs Leah's hand, "Come on, my sister is asking for you." Stopping at the end of the stairs, Bella speaks quietly to Leah while pointing in the direction of Alba's room.

Turning around, she motions to Logan. All the men are silent as we watch Bella and Logan having an intense looking conversation. It fucking pisses me off. I want to know what the hell is going on. Logan pulls Bella into his arms and gives her a kiss before she heads back up the stairs and to her sister. My brother's grim face has my stomach clenching.

"We need to call church," Logan demands. And fuck me—I know whatever he has to tell me is not going to be good.

Five minutes later, I'm sittin' in church smokin' a cigarette while waiting for my brother to speak. Once Logan takes his seat, I watch him signal to Reid and Quinn. Both get up from their chairs and stand in front of the door, blocking the exit. Snapping my head in Logan's direction, he holds my stare, refusing to waver. When he speaks, he keeps his eyes trained on me.

"We all heard what the friend just informed us of a few minutes ago. Alba started receiving some flowers in her first week of school. Later someone started leaving notes on her truck. The first time she realized some fucker had been in her room was the first weekend she came home to visit five months ago. Alba told Bella that the sick fuck had rummaged through her underwear drawer. She confessed there had been several more incidents since then, but this last one was her breaking point. When Alba and her friends arrived back home after going out to dinner, their apartment was torn apart. Alba's sonogram picture was pinned to the wall of her bedroom with a pocketknife." Pausing, Logan cuts his eyes over to Jake, then over to the door where Reid and Quinn are still standing guard. My gut is telling me it's for my benefit because I'm about to lose my shit over what's coming next. I feel it deep down in my bones. "Written on the wall above the pictures was the message—*"Get rid of it or I will."*

Abruptly standing, my chair goes crashing into the wall behind me. In a few short strides, I go toe to toe with Quinn and Reid. "Get the fuck out of my way," I demand.

Reid denies my command, causing me to see red. "Sorry, brother. I can't do that."

I clench and unclench my fists. I've never hit one of my brother's, but at this moment, I'm seriously considering it. I get further into Reid's face, "Step aside, now." The venom in my voice is evident.

Unflinching, he still refuses. "No."

I go to lunge for him, but someone must have anticipated my

move. Suddenly, I feel an arm wrap around my neck, and I'm pulled backward. Crashing into the table behind us and then falling to the floor, I am now being held down by Logan and Reid. With a roar, I free one of my arms and thrust my elbow backward, catching Reid in the nose, causing blood to spurt out. The next thing I know, Jake is on my back with his knee digging into my spine and his forearm across my neck. I continue to struggle against him and Logan.

"Gabriel, you need to get your shit under control," Prez grinds out.

"Some motherfucker is threatening to hurt my woman and my baby!" I bellow.

"Yes, but Alba is here, and she's safe. So, you better get yourself together so we can handle the situation." Jake is right. She's here, and she's okay, and I need a clear head.

Taking a few deep breaths, I allow myself to calm down. Feeling my body relax, Jake and Logan release their grips on me and allow me to stand. Running my inked hand over my face, I cut my eyes over to Reid, who has taken his t-shirt off and is holding it to his nose. Striding up to him, I apologize.

"I'm sorry, brother."

Removing his shirt from his nose, he gives me a slight smirk and slaps me on my shoulder.

"It's all good, man. I've had worse."

Picking my chair up and taking my seat at the table along with everyone else, Prez doesn't waste any time getting down to business.

"First things first," he says looking at me. "You claimin' Alba?"

Nodding, I reply, "Sí *Yes*, she's mine."

15

ALBA

I can't believe he accused me of getting knocked up by someone else. Come to think of it; he specifically said a ballplayer. Is he referring to Sam? If so, how does he even know about him at all or the fact that he is a ballplayer?

I shouldn't even have to ask myself these questions. These men around here seem to know everything about everyone.

Hearing the doorknob turn, I get up from the edge of the bed where I was sitting and meet my sister and Leah as they come walking through the door.

"I am so sorry I deserted you down there, Leah. I was so taken aback at the moment. I can't believe I forgot you were with me."

Walking into the room further, she takes in her surroundings. I grab the suitcase she packed for me from her slightly shaking hands and set it down by the closet.

"You guys really live with all those men down there?" she asks with bewilderment as she wrings her hands together nervously. "I met Gabriel. He's umm...big," she says, giving my sister and me both a look.

I walk her to the bed and sit down with her as I watch Bella quickly close the door before responding to Leah, "Yeah, they can be a bit rough around the edges at times, but you really wouldn't find a better family to be a part of."

And she's right. This makes me feel bad for bringing chaos back into the mix when it wasn't very long ago, we all had dealt with so much. I honestly thought whoever had been leaving notes stopped. I can't wrap my head around someone threatening an unborn child.

It's unfathomable to me.

"What I don't understand is how someone was able to break into your dorm room there on campus. We made sure security was top-notch when you first checked the place out. Someone in the building must have seen something," my sister questions as she walks over to the window, pulls back the curtain a little and gazes out into the night sky.

Leah gives me a sympathetic look, knowing I'm about to have a heart to heart with my sister that I've been putting off. For far too long, I've let it fester, and it's put a barrier between us.

I sit straighter, "That's because I don't live on campus anymore. I moved a little over a month ago," I tell her.

"What?" Bella says shockingly.

"Yeah. Sam, Leah, and I are renting a condominium about fifteen minutes from campus. I felt like I needed more space since finding out I was pregnant. I like it, Bella. It was a choice I had to make for myself."

"I get all that, Alba, but why? Why is it you felt like you had to hide that from me?" she asks with hurt etched on her face.

"I thought I had to. I didn't say anything because I didn't want to disappoint you. I never wanted to leave Polson. I wanted to stay here, maybe go to community college or take online classes, but you were so proud of me and so excited for my future that I wanted to make you happy. In the end, I wasn't happy, and this baby—MY baby put so much into perspective. I'm also taking online classes now instead of on campus, and I even started a small business online designing book covers for authors. It's all coming together. I needed to make myself happy and live my life for me. I know you wanted me to have the world Bella and I do. My world just happens to be in Polson."

It feels freeing to finally say what I'm feeling aloud to my sister.

Looking up, Bella's face mirrors my own with shed tears rolling down her cheeks.

"I'm so sorry I made you feel that way. It was never my intention. You should have said something sooner. I don't ever want you to feel like you need to live life for anyone but yourself, and you could never disappoint me, Alba. If going to college is not what you want, I will support you," she says with sincerity.

Bella comes to sit in front of me on the floor. I look down at her as she looks up. Continuing, she says, "I have sat around for months knowing something was wrong. Knowing for some reason you were not happy. I heard it in your voice every time we talked, and every time you made up some excuse as to why you couldn't come home to visit. I wanted you to talk to me so badly, but I wanted you to be ready and willing to open up to me on your own and tell me what you were keeping bottled up inside. I'm your sister. I'm not here to judge you. I'm here to cheer you on. I'm so very proud of everything you do, have done, and will do in the future."

We hold hands and take a moment to collect ourselves.

We look at each other as sisters that have grown together and shared so much in life, but it's also a moment that we both are finally looking at each other as two separate women who have come so far and are both coming into their own.

Finding our own paths.

The moment is interrupted with commotion coming from downstairs.

"I'm pretty sure that's all Gabriel right now," Bella lets out with a heavy sigh and gets to her feet.

"What are you talking about?" I raise my eyebrow and ask her.

Standing a little taller, she gives me a deadpan look, "Before I brought Leah up here, I pulled Logan to the side and gave him a quick rundown of what you told me. So, I'm guessing the noises we are now hearing is the reaction from your man being told that someone has threatened you and his child," she affirms.

I stand abruptly, causing myself to get a bit lightheaded, but quickly steady myself. I can only imagine his reaction. Hell, he just found out that he's going to be a father.

A light knock on the door catches all three of our attention before hearing a soft voice from the other side, "Bella, may I come in?"

I look to my sister, wondering who the voice belongs to. She gives me a reassuring look before walking to the door and opening it. A beautiful young woman with long, black hair and stunning green eyes steps in, shutting the door behind her.

"Alba, this is Gabriel's sister Leyna. Remember me telling you about her a few weeks ago? She's been staying here at the clubhouse."

Of course. How could I have completely forgotten about that conversation? Looking to her, I say, "Leyna, I wish we could have met under better circumstances."

"Me too. And from what I overheard, it seems my hermano *brother* is going to be a papi *daddy*," she gestures to my protruding belly. "I told him he was foolish to do what he did months ago. I promise you Gabe is a good man. We are familia now, so can I hug you?" she asks with her arms stretched out in a warm welcome and a smile.

Accepting, I hug her in return.

Our introduction is cut short as the bedroom door bursts open, splintering at its hinges, causing all four of us to jump back and Leah to shriek.

Looming in the doorway is Gabriel, all six feet four inches of him.

Silence fills the room like the calm before the storm.

The stillness of the moment is defining as his intense stare carefully appraises me. His movement is so swift I don't even have time to react. Falling to his knees in front of me, Gabriel places his large hands on my belly before he hoarsely whispers, "Alba."

Overcome with emotions, I quietly sob. When he stood in the doorway, I didn't know what to expect. For a split second, I found myself afraid. Not afraid of Gabriel harming me—not physically.

Fear of rejection again.

Fear of him rejecting our baby.

I look upon his face in wonderment. A sea of pride, joy, and love for his unborn child swells in the depths of his deep, brown eyes. The heat from his touch penetrates through my shirt, causing goosebumps to cover the surface of my skin.

A lifetime, that's how long it has felt since the last time he's touched me. Somehow, this moment feels so much more earth-shattering. A sense of calm settles through my soul.

His rough, raw voice breaks through the stillness as his softly spoken words to our unborn child leave his lips.

"Your mother is my sky, and you... you are my star. I didn't know just how much my heart needed you," Gabriel's eyes lift to mine, "needs both of you. You both give me strength. You give me purpose."

Hearing sobs other than my own, I turn my head, noticing my sister, Leah, and even Leyna watching intently and quietly sharing the moment with me.

I quickly return my attention back to Gabriel. His handsome

face becomes a blur as I study him. No longer able to ignore my heart, I completely lose myself to him, and my knees go weak, then I'm lifted off my feet. Nestling my face into the crook of his neck, I breathe him deep into my lungs as he carries me out the door.

16

GABRIEL

You ever have those moments in life where you say fuck it and give in to the forces of nature? When you finally stop fighting what is obviously meant to be? When you realize your destiny has been right under your nose?

I've purposely done shit, stupid shit to fuck things up with Alba because I thought I was doing the right thing. But then again us men are always fuckin' shit up, so that's nothing new. I'm pretty sure women expect nothing less, which is why they're the stronger of the species. They take on all the bullshit we dish out, then quietly dust themselves off, hold their heads high and keep on pushing. And that is exactly what my Cariño *Sweetheart* has been doing for months.

Alba is so brave, so strong. I felt all that change, though, the moment I scooped her up into my arms. Her walls came crashing down, and her fight was gone. Her bravery had run out, and her strength vanished. Did this mean I was off the hook? Hell fucking no.

My woman has fire, and I know she will be handing me my ass soon enough. I will be taking whatever she dishes out because I sure as fuck deserve it. I can take whatever Alba gives, and it still would not equal the amount of hurt I have caused her.

Walking into her room moments ago, seeing the array of emotions play out on my woman's face literally brought me to my knees. First, there was shock, then longing, but it was the look of fear that broke me. Alba's big, beautiful blue eyes were full of fear. Like she was expecting me to lash out. To be angry at the fact that she was pregnant with my baby.

She fully expected me to reject our child the same way I had rejected her. I did that to her. My brash stupidity was the reason my woman stayed away from her home, kept secrets from her sister, and was going through what should be the happiest time in her life alone.

With Alba's arms tight around my neck, and her breath fanning my face, I stride down the hall toward my room. Walking in, I kick the door shut behind me with my booted foot before sitting down on the edge of my bed with her still in my arms. She's holding on so tight as if she's afraid to let go. There's no fuckin' chance of that happening. I'll never be able to let her go again, and I'll die before I let her be taken from me.

I need to find who the hell thought they could fuck with my woman and continue breathin'. But that shit's for another time. Right now, I need to focus on Alba and get things straightened out between us. And there IS going to be an us.

"Cariño *Sweetheart*," I choke out past my own emotion as I place my finger under her chin, guiding her to look at me. When Alba raises her face away from the crook of my neck and her gorgeous tear-filled eyes meet my dark ones, I can no longer hold back, and I crash my mouth down on hers. I should be taking things slower, but all logic is thrown out the window when Alba tugs on the front of my shirt, pulling me closer. I don't know how long we go on like this. Seconds? Minutes?

All I know is we are lost in each other. For us, time has

stopped. I will never get enough of her taste, her smell, or the feel of her soft skin underneath my rough hands. I feel at peace when she is near. Alba is the light to my dark. The mother of my child that's growing inside her. She is my home.

Breaking our kiss, I pull back an inch, keeping her face between the palms of my hands. I watch as she slowly opens her lust-filled eyes and brings her hands up the back of my neck and through my hair. No words are spoken when I stand with her still in my arms. Words will come later. I know it, and she knows it. But right now, the only thing we both need is each other.

I turn, placing Alba gently on my bed. Going down to my knees in front of her, I peer into her eyes as I clutch the front of her sweater. I make no other move until Alba gives me the signal. Lifting her arms, she gives me what I ask for, and I waste no time before bringing her top up and off over her head, where it's tossed to the floor beside me. Dropping her arms, she wraps them around her swollen belly like she's trying to hide from me. No way in hell am I having any of that. Grabbing her arms, I pull them away from where my son or daughter is growing.

"No. Don't hide your body from me. Ever," I demand, and Alba let's out a shuddered breath.

"My body has changed."

Placing my finger to her mouth, I refused to let her finish her sentence. No way will I allow my woman to be ashamed of the changes to her body.

"You are beautiful, Cariño *Sweetheart*. You have our baby growing inside of you. You and your body are providing for him, making him strong. I welcome any changes that come."

Hearing the sincerity in my voice, Alba's body relaxes into my touch as I reach behind her and unclasp her bra. Slowly, I drag the straps down over her shoulders, letting it fall and exposing her breasts. My touch causes her to shiver, and her pink nipples beg for attention. Grabbing both of her hips, I pull her closer to the edge of the bed before leaning forward and covering her breast with my mouth, and I feel her nipple harden against my tongue.

Arching her back and fisting my hair, Alba groans, "Oh god, Gabriel."

Releasing her breast, I gently push her backward, encouraging her to lie down as I kiss my way down her stomach until I'm met with blue lace panties soaked with her arousal. Not being able to resist, I tug them aside and swipe my tongue through her wet pussy, making Alba gasp and buck further into my mouth. I always regretted not tasting my woman's sweet pussy the first time we made love. Now that I know what she tastes like, I'm fuckin' addicted. I will never get enough.

Withering, Alba fists the sheets, "Please, Gabriel, I need more." At her plea, I growl and drive my tongue inside her pussy, making her scream vibrate off the walls of the room as her orgasm rips through her.

Not being anywhere near done with her, I stand, kick off my boots, and strip off my clothes. Kneeling on the bed, I wrap my arm around Alba's sated body and pull her up further into the middle of my bed before reaching up and pulling her panties off. Dipping my face, I kiss her. Our tongues tangle together in sync as I hold myself above her, making sure to be mindful of her belly.

I lean back, "No puedo respirar sin ti. Eres mi todo. *I can't breathe without you. You are my everything*," I confess right before I thrust forward, burying myself inside her.

Fuck, she feels like heaven.

And at this moment, everything feels right. Alba has managed to take over every part of me, making me feel things I've never experienced before. I knew the first time I laid eyes on her that day, when I picked her up outside of her house, that she would forever own me. Placing kisses on her shoulder and up the side of her neck, I rest my forehead on hers and then begin to move in and out of her tight heat slowly. With our mouth's breaths away,

"Who do you belong to?" I ask, not taking my eyes off hers—Alba answers without hesitation.

"You. I belong to you, Gabriel." And the tears begin to flow once again. "You destroyed me," she confesses.

"Sí *Yes*, I did, and I will spend the rest of my life making it up to you, mi amor *my love*." At my declaration, I feel Alba's body tremble as she sobs. "I love you so much, Cariño *Sweetheart*." She doesn't say it back. I know she's not ready to give me that part of her, and that's okay. This is not about me. This is about her. So, with those last words, I take Alba's mouth with mine and start showing her how much I love her.

I keep my pace slow, and even because I want to savor every moment I'm inside of her. My cock throbs when I feel the walls of her pussy flutter around it. I'm not ready to come yet, and will myself to make this moment last. Every nerve in my body catches on fire when Alba runs her soft, delicate hands up the sides of my ribs and to my shoulders where she digs her fingers into my flesh. She gasps when I pull out slowly then roll my hips burying myself deep inside her.

"I want you to ride me," I declare, changing positions and turning to lay on my back and guiding Alba to straddle me.

"Gabriel, I'm not sure... I mean, I don't..."

"Give me your mouth, mi amor *my love*," I gently demand. Once her mouth is on mine, I grab her hips and glide her wet pussy back and forth along my shaft. With her body knowing what it craves, Alba raises her hips as I grab the base of my cock and line the tip at her entrance. She then sinks down on me all the way to the hilt.

"You feel so fuckin' good," I grit out and wait a few moments, letting her adjust to the new position. Looking up at Alba, I take in all her beauty. I love the look of her round with my baby. As soon as she has this one, I won't be wasting any time before putting another one in there.

I never gave much thought to having kids—to having a family. But now a family with Alba is all I want. Reaching up, I trail my hands up and over the swell of her belly and then up to her full breasts. Bracing the palms of her hands on my chest, she begins to move. It doesn't take long for her to find her rhythm. With her back arched and her head thrown back, I know she is close when her pussy begins to squeeze the hell out of me.

Taking my eyes off her face, I look down to where we're connected. I love seeing myself disappear inside of her. The sight has my cock throbbing. Using my thumb, I begin to rub her swollen clit and feel her tight walls clamp down on my cock. I pull her forward and let my mouth swallow her orgasm. Grabbing Alba's hips, I thrust up two more times before I hold her down on top of me as we crash over the edge together.

Several moments later, after we both have recovered and I feel Alba's body go slack, I wrap my arm around her back and shift our bodies sideways, so we are lying face to face. I watch as her eyes flutter a few times before they close, and her body relaxes completely.

I begin to rub lazy circles along her hip then up her ribs until her breaths even out, and sleep takes her. After a few minutes of watching her sleep, our bodies fused together, and Alba's belly pressed against my stomach, I feel a nudge.

Seconds later, I feel it again. I suddenly realize what the feeling is—my baby. Keeping my body very still, I continue to feel as my baby decides to make himself known. And I can't help the smile that takes over my face. I'm a little amazed Alba is able to sleep through all the movement. A few minutes later, my baby settles. And even though I'm tired as fuck, I can't sleep.

I finally have my woman in my arms, and I don't want to take my eyes off of her. I've wanted this for so long. It's like I'm afraid this is all a dream. Like I'll wake up, and none of this will be real. We came really close to this moment never being a reality. Dread fills my stomach when I think about how close Alba has been to danger. So close, the son of a bitch was in her apartment. If I know Reid, he's already at work trying to figure out what the hell is going on and who the sick fuck is who dares to threaten my woman and the life of my baby.

Realizing my body is shaking from the rage building inside of me, I shut my eyes and take a few deep breaths. I need to keep my head on straight. I can't lose control. I have more than just myself to think about now. With Alba sleeping soundly, I slip out of bed, careful not to wake her. Picking my jeans up off the floor, I dig my cell out of my pocket, firing off a quick text to Reid.

Me: I want the motherfucker who's after my girl found

Reid: *Already on it brother.*

I knew my brother would be on top of shit.

Hearing a rustling behind me, I look over my shoulder and see Alba sitting up in bed with the sheet wrapped around her and her eyes scanning the floor, probably looking for her clothes. If she thinks she's about to make a quick retreat, she's got another thing coming.

"You're not going anywhere." Alba whips her head in my direction. Yep. It's time. I knew this moment was coming.

"You can't tell me what to do, Gabriel," she says, glaring at me. There's the fire I love so much.

"Sí *Yes*, I can, and I will. We have shit to work through, Alba. And we're going to do it now."

She glares, "Look, if this is about the baby, I was going to tell you. I wasn't going to keep him or her from you. I wouldn't let my personal feeling toward you affect the relationship our child deserves to have with his father. I know we'll have to figure out how to co-parent and the shared custody stuff. I just wasn't ready to deal with all that yet—"

I cut her off, "There will be no shared custody bullshit. We will raise our child together. You as my wife, and me as your husband."

"I don't know if you realize this or not, Gabriel, but this is not the 1950's. We don't have to get married just because I'm knocked up," Alba remarks dryly, "and what happened with us earlier doesn't change anything. My pregnancy hormones kinda took over my body and clouded my judgment. It was just sex, nothing more. I mean those are the words you used to describe us, right?"

Standing up from the bed with determination to put me in my place, Alba cocks her head putting a finger on her chin. "Come to think of it, those were not the only words you used to describe me. Just a few hours ago, you also called me a whore. Someone who spread her legs for 'some ballplayer'. Isn't that right, Gabriel? For all you know, this baby is not even yours," Alba finishes, her chest heaving.

"Are you finished? Because now it's my turn."

When she goes to open that sassy mouth of hers, I cut her off, shaking my head, "Number one," I say, pointing at my bed, "what we just shared together in my bed was NOT just sex, and you damn well know it. The first time I took you, it sure as hell was not just sex. That first night you gave yourself to me was the best night of my whole goddamn life. And knowing we created a life that night makes it that much more special. The lies I spewed, were just that, lies. I didn't want you to give up your scholarship and not go to college for me. So, I hurt you. I pushed you away so you wouldn't waste your opportunity on me. Number two, you are not a whore. If you ever call yourself that again, I'll tan your ass," I growl. "I should not have said what I did. Realizing you were pregnant and knowing that you have been hanging around another fuckin' man while you've been away. It fucked with my head. I jumped to my own conclusions. One thing you're going to have to get used to, baby, is that I'm a man, and men are always fuckin' up. That's why we need good women to help us rein that shit in." At my last statement, I don't miss the small smile Alba tries to hide by looking down. "Lastly, number three, I'm well aware of what century it is Cariño *Sweetheart*. We will marry because you belong to me. The baby in your belly belongs to me. Not today, and not even tomorrow, but one day soon, we will be making that shit legal."

Just as she's about to open her mouth to protest once again, I stalk toward her. With my bedsheet still wrapped around her body, Alba takes three steps backward until her back hits the wall, and I'm standing over her. Leaning down, I bring my face a mere inch from hers. Her breaths come out in pants. There is no denying the effect I have on her.

"Not only do you belong to me, but I'm in love with you. You, mi amor *my love*, are the light to my dark. You are my home."

17

ALBA

I *can't breathe.*

With my back against the wall, my eyes closed and my hands still clutching the sheet that's wrapped around my body. I feel like all the air has left my body. Gabriel is in love with me. Sure, I heard him say he loved me moments ago when he was inside me, but I figured that was just a knee jerk confession—something a lot of men probably say while they have sex-brain.

Let's be real. People can say all kinds of crazy things in the heat of the moment. But right now, Gabriel is level-headed, and his facial expressions tell me he is completely honest.

I'm trying so hard to be strong. To put up a fight. He does not deserve such easy forgiveness. I want him to suffer as much as I have. I know it's wrong to think like that, but I do. Only my will is crumbling as we speak.

Why? I was doing so well. And now, poof. All it took was for him to say those five, beautiful, gut-wrenching words.

I'm in love with you.

I can feel his breath in my face. He's so close. Only I can't bring myself to open my eyes, because once I do, the last shred of fight will be gone. One look in Gabriel's dark eyes, and I'll surrender.

"Baby, open your eyes," Gabriel coaxes.

Giving in, I open them. And I have never seen his face look so soft and tender as it does at this moment. He's looking at me so intently and watching and waiting. There is a raging battle going on between my head and my heart. It's my heart that wins.

"I'm in love with you too." I'm barely able to croak out before he responds.

"Yeah, you are," he says before his mouth comes crashing down on mine.

Releasing my grip on the sheet, I bring my hands up to his head and fist his hair, tugging him closer to me. My body instinctively seeking the heat of his. Grabbing my ass, Gabriel lifts me, and I wrap my legs around his waist as he turns and lowers me to the bed behind us.

"Hands and knees, now," he demands.

Complying, I turn over, getting on my hands and knees. When I do, the first thing I notice is my reflection. Right in front of us on the opposite side of the bed is a mirror. When my eyes meet Gabriel's, I'm hypnotized. I have a feeling this was his intention, and not once do we break the connection.

Standing behind me, I watch as he begins to stroke himself. My insides clench at the thought of having him inside me again. Seconds later he runs the head of his cock over my clit. Back and forth, teasing me. I'm so wet, and Gabriel growls in approval. With one hand on my hip he uses the other to grab the base of his shaft to line himself at my opening. Once the head of his cock is inside me, he stops, causing me to whimper. Just as I'm about to open my mouth to beg, Gabriel grabs both my hips and thrusts forward, burying himself completely, knocking the wind out of me.

"Oh, god," I mutter, throwing my head back.

"Eyes," Gabriel barks.

Meeting his stare once again, he starts to move. Only this time, it's not slow and sweet.

No, this time is hard and fast.

A claiming.

He looks so wild and feral. Gabriel is a beast. *My beast.* Without missing a beat, he brings one arm under me, snaking it between my breast and wraps his hand around my throat possessively but tenderly and urges me to sit up, leaving me no choice but to reach behind him and grab hold of the back of his head. Keeping his hand on my throat, he uses his other hand to cup my pussy, and his middle finger pressed on my clit while he continues to drive into me. With nothing but the sounds of flesh meeting flesh and our heavy breathing, Gabriel whispers into my ear before nipping my sweaty neck.

"Come, Cariño *Sweetheart.*"

And I do. I come so hard, flashes of light dance behind my eyelids. My nails dig into Gabriel's scalp, and I wouldn't be surprised if I drew blood. I don't even have it in me to care about everyone possibly hearing us because of how loud I just screamed. Gabriel continues to pump through my release for several more seconds before he finds his own.

"Fuck!" he roars as he stills behind me and fills me with his warm release.

Continuing to hold me in this position, I lay my head back against his shoulder, trying to catch my breath as he peppers my shoulder with soft, lazy kisses. My skin prickles and I hum at the feel of his soft lips and rough beard. And at this moment, I know I'm exactly where I should be. *I am home.*

I'M SICK OF SHOPPING.

Yes, I said it.

I can't believe I'm saying such filth, but I am. After Gabriel and I worked through his epic screw up two months ago, he informed me that he bought us a house. He confessed he bought it before I even came home. He said he knew he was going to do whatever was necessary to get me back, and once I was his, he wanted us to have a home we could share together.

His confession had rendered me speechless. Gabriel bought a house for us. Not out of obligation because we were having a baby. He didn't even know about our baby yet. But he bought the house out of love. He wanted to give me what he thought I deserved. He wanted to build a home and a life with me. So, when he brought me here to show me our new home for the first time, I was ecstatic.

He drove us in my truck about fifteen minutes from the clubhouse to the place we'd call home. I could not believe my eyes as he parked the truck in front of a two-story Victorian-style home. It was white with blue shutters and a blue front door. I smiled. My man gets me. There was also a large wrap around porch that extended around the entire house—and sitting on the front of the porch next to the front door? You guessed it, two blue rocking chairs. I couldn't tell much in the way of landscaping since the ground was covered in snow.

Coming up behind me and wrapping his strong arms around my belly, Gabriel's deep voice caresses my ear. "When I saw this place, I knew it was yours. Welcome home mi amor *my love.*"

Gabriel led me inside and began showing me around. When he informed me all the decorating and furnishing was going to be left up to me because he said, "I don't know anything about that shit." I could hardly contain my excitement.

So, here I am two weeks later, and I am finally finished. All the guys from the club pitched in with painting and moving in all the furniture. God forbid Gabriel catch me lifting a finger. Like being pregnant makes you an invalid. That being said, I never want to go to another furniture store or look at paint samples ever again.

Gabriel spared no expense either. He handed over his credit card and told me to get whatever I wanted. I tried to tell him I could help pay for some of the things, but he shot that idea down quickly, saying he was proud of me for starting my own business and making my own money, but I was his woman, and he was going to take care of me. He suggested I use my money and start saving for the baby. I agreed. It was a great idea.

We also had a few bumps in the road when it came to us finally moving in together. I was very apprehensive about taking such a big step. Even though Gabriel laid his feelings on the line and was clear about his intentions, I just didn't have it in me to put myself out there right away. So as much as I wanted to move into our new home and start building our life together, I held back.

I took my sister up on her offer to stay with her and Logan. Gabriel was not happy, but he understood. He knew his actions in the past are what was having me play things safe. I think a part of me just wanted him to sweat a little. Only he didn't suffer for long. Gabriel lasted only a week.

On the seventh day of staying with my sister, he showed up at her house. When Bella answered the door, Gabriel swept passed her, only stopping a fraction of a second from informing me that enough was enough. It was time for me to come home. He then stomped up the stairs and returned a few minutes later with my suitcases in hand. I sat stunned on the sofa while my sister was still standing by the front door trying to hide a smile. Logan was leaning against the living room wall nursing a beer. His raised eyebrow and bored look lead me to believe he saw this coming. I guess in a way I did too. And to tell you the truth, I was miserable the entire week.

As far as school goes, I don't miss it. I do miss my friends though. Leah had to leave the day after she drove me here. She was going home for the holidays. I could tell she wasn't looking forward to it. I invited her to stay in Polson, but she said her parents were expecting her.

I talk to Sam on the phone every day. He told me the manager of the apartment complex offered him another apartment to stay in since the one we were living in was being repainted. Sam said he didn't want to continue living in ours anyway after what had happened. I made him promise to come to visit one weekend. Gabriel happened to walk in the room at the tail end of that conversation and about lost his head. I calmly explained to him that Sam was just a friend, and he was going to stay as my friend. He was just going to have to accept that. I didn't mention the fact that I'm pretty sure Sam is gay and he has nothing to worry about, but it's not my place to oust him, especially when he hasn't even come out to me.

Walking into the kitchen, I open the refrigerator and spy the fruit salad my sister made and brought it to me yesterday. Setting it on the counter, I eye the fruit for a moment, knowing what I really want is ice cream. Giving in to the temptation I place the fruit salad back in the refrigerator and grab the mint chocolate chip out of the freezer. With my ice cream and spoon in hand, I pass by the kitchen window and spot Austin sitting on the front porch.

Gabriel has designated Austin as my bodyguard. The guys still haven't found the person who was harassing me. Having Austin around so much feels a little like déjà vu. He was a constant in mine and Bella's lives not too long ago. And here he is again, playing guard and chauffeur. I'm not allowed to go anywhere without him or one of the other guys with me.

Gabriel stayed home with me the first week I was back. He hates leaving me, but work calls. He has clients that he couldn't put off for too long. Plus, I kind of needed the break. I love the man, but he treats me as if I'm made of glass. The first couple of days he was fawning over me were great, but a girl can only take so much. I've also noticed the Gabriel I get is opposite to the Gabriel everyone else gets. With me he's this sweet, loving, gentle giant. With everyone else he's broody, asshole Gabriel.

It's like Jekyll and Hyde.

All the guys are completely unfazed by his gruff attitude. Before when my sister first started seeing Logan and we were staying at the clubhouse so much, I never really paid much attention as to how Gabriel was with everyone. I was always so caught up in how sweet he was with me. That and I spent more time alone in my room instead of socializing. I'm an introvert. I'm most comfortable being alone or around the people I'm closest to.

In the past couple of weeks, Gabriel has opened up to me about his past. I was shocked at how forthcoming he's been. He's told me about growing up in Cuba and being forced by his father to leave his country and his family. My heart broke for him when he told me about his father's death. To be left parentless and homeless at the age of sixteen. I can't begin to imagine the things he had to go through on a daily basis in order to survive. He held me that night as I cried for him and the awful events he's endured. I cried for the young boy who had lost so much, then blamed the pregnancy hormones for my emotional meltdown.

Gabriel's sister Leyna has been a daily visitor as well. We have grown close in such a short time. I feel like I've known her my whole life. I tried convincing her to move in with her brother and me instead of staying at the clubhouse, but she refused. She said that Gabriel and I needed this time for ourselves. That due to Gabe's stupidity we missed out on so much, and now was our time. Leyna was the one who told me about Santino. She didn't know her brother had not divulged that bit of information yet. Later that same day after Gabriel got home from work, I confronted him. I asked him why he hadn't told me. His response was that he didn't want to upset me. After my breakdown about his childhood, he figured I'd heard enough. He said he was going to tell me eventually, just not now. He also said my getting upset was not good for the baby.

Grabbing a blanket and wrapping it around my body I step out onto the porch. Reid, who's replacing Austin for the rest of the day, is sitting on the steps with his back against the rail smoking a cigarette. When he notices me, he quickly drops it to the ground snubbing it out with his boot. Even though we are outside, and the smoke is nowhere near me, Gabriel forbids anyone to light up within fifty feet of me.

I roll my eyes, "You didn't have to do that. Gabriel's not here to bust your balls."

"Nah, it's all good. Gonna respect my brother whether he's here or not."

I nod in response. I get it.

"So, what's on the agenda for today?" he asks.

"Well, I was thinking about taking Gabriel some lunch. Then maybe swinging by the garage to see my sister."

"Alright. You want me to drive?"

"No. I think I feel like driving myself today. Just give me thirty minutes. I need to send out a couple of emails and whip up some lunch, then I'll be ready," I tell him standing up from my chair.

"You got it, sweetheart. I'm going to shoot Gabriel a text letting him know we'll be there soon."

Back inside, I toss my forgotten ice cream back into the freezer, then make my way up the stairs to the bedroom to change. Pulling off my pajama pants, I swap them for a pair of fleece leggings. They are warm and fit over my expanding belly. Bella bought me several pairs for Christmas.

Gabriel and I celebrated our first Christmas and New Year's in our new house. It was empty. All we had was a king-size mattress on the floor in front of the fireplace and a Christmas tree. Christmas Eve dinner was pizza. It was perfect. The next day everyone went to the clubhouse for dinner. I fell back in sync with

Bella and Lisa, helping them cook. This Christmas was the best I've ever had.

And for our first Valentine's, I wasn't expecting anything, because, well, this is Gabriel we're talking about. I definitely didn't see him as a hearts and flowers type of man, and I was right, he's not. Instead, he got me an abundant supply of Peanut Butter Cups and books. Books signed by some of my favorite authors. He confessed he had some help from Bella. It was the best gift I had ever received. My man sure knows how to woo me.

After slipping on my boots and pulling on my coat, I head back downstairs and find Reid standing by the front door with his hands in his pockets, waiting on me.

"You ready? I have your truck warmed up for ya."

Stopping at the end of the stairs, I eye him with a grin. I know it was Gabriel that told him to do that.

"Yeah, I'm ready." With my purse slung over my shoulder, I follow him out the door to my truck.

"I'll be right behind you," he hollers over his shoulder on the way to his own car.

I keep my speed a little under the limit because I've only been driving for a year and a half, and the snow and ice still makes me nervous. I'm five miles from Kings Ink when I start descending a steep hill. I go to apply my brakes and realize they are not working.

"What the hell!" I pump the brakes again only to have them press all the way to the floorboard. Panic takes hold of me, and I feel my heart in my throat. "Oh god! What do I do!" I scream out to no one. Before I know it, my speed has reached fifty MPH. My hands are shaking so bad; I can hardly steer.

Looking in my rear-view mirror I don't see Reid behind me. Glancing to my left, I see his truck right beside me, with his window down. I can tell he's screaming at me by the movement of his lips, but I can't hear anything past the beating of my own heart.

With tears clouding my vision all I can think is that this is it. I'm going to crash. I'm going to die. My baby is going to die.

My thoughts are flooding my brain as my truck hits a patch of ice. I can no longer control the wheel. I feel my seat belt lock tight as my truck jerks violently to the right before it flips on its side, and I begin to roll. All I hear is the sound of screeching tires and crunching metal mixed with my screams right before my head collides with the window.

The last thing I remember is the truck coming to a stop upside down, Reid bellowing my name and then darkness.

18

GABRIEL

I've only been at work for four hours, and I can't wait to get back home to my woman. Since finding out some piece of shit threatened her and my baby, I've found it hard to leave her side. I know the club is doing what they can to find something or someone, but for weeks we have found nothing; all leads have been dead ends. Even getting our hands on the fuckin' police report has been a slow process. We know guys on the force around here, so when we needed things in the past it was fairly easy. Not so much with Bozeman PD.

I'm in my truck on my way to Reid's place. He hopped in his truck a few days ago and went back to Bozeman to see if he could dig up any new leads. He texted first thing this morning, telling me he would be back home this afternoon and wanted to go over what he's been able to find out. Reid lives downtown in an old two-story firehouse that he has turned into a large studio apartment. I slow and pull my truck down the alleyway, parking right behind his blue and white 1972 Chevy pickup that used to belong to his brother Noah. Before climbing out of my truck my phone pings with a text. Grabbing it from the console, I swipe the screen to read a message from Austin.

Austin: *I'm here, brother.*

Me: *Good.*

I should have plenty of time to talk with Reid and make it back to the shop before my second client of the day comes in. I make my way up a flight of wrought iron stairs leading to the second story door. Before I can press the buzzer, Reid's voice comes through the speaker. "Come on in, brother."

Walking in, I take in his home. Having been here several times since he bought the place, I'm still amazed by it. The architecture inside and out reminds me of my childhood in Cuba. You don't get to see this kind of workmanship anymore, and he has restored everything, making sure to keep as much of it original as possible while adding all the comforts of modern living.

I find him sitting at his large, stainless kitchen table.

"What did you find in Bozeman?" I ask him.

Sitting his coffee mug down, he slides a manila folder across the table to where I'm now standing.

"Finally got my hands on the damn police report from the Bozeman PD. It says they didn't find much. Whoever it was knew how to cover their tracks. No prints were found on anything except for a partial on one of the knives stuck in the wall. And unfortunately, at the time, the condo wasn't equipped with any kind of security system."

Grabbing the folder, I proceed to open it. The police report was filed by Sam McGregor. Forced entry through the patio door located in the kitchen. One statement from an elderly lady down the street. I flip to her statement on the next page, detailing that she saw a small silver car earlier that day that she hadn't seen before. I thumb through a couple more pages until I come across photos taken of the sonogram pictures that were stabbed to the wall and the malicious words that were used to threaten my family. My jaw twitches with tension. An intense rage starts to churn in my gut causing me to crinkle the papers in my hands.

"While I was there, I met her friend Sam. He seems like a good guy. Took care of Alba and her friend Leah since becoming friends."

Sam.

Alba reassured me that there was never anything between them, only friendship, but I don't know him, so I don't like him. I cut my eyes at Reid, letting him know I have no interest in hearing about the fuckwad.

"Got it. Anyway, we set up motion tracking cameras all around the property to go along with the security cameras I installed awhile back, which we still haven't had a hit on yet. I also talked to the old lady on the police report. After listening to her go on and on about her two cats, she finally gets around to telling me she has seen that car three times since then. This guy is going to slip up. We'll catch the son of a bitch, Gabriel," Reid assures.

Sitting around waiting for something to happen is bullshit. An uneasy feeling washes over me. I throw the folder down on the table, "So we still have nothin'," I huff out in frustration as I run my hand through my hair.

"This guy is obsessed with her, man. He'll turn up again."

I hope so. Glancing at the clock on Reid's wall I tell him, "I got to get to the shop. Let me know when you relieve Austin later. Sorry I had to call on you to sit with Alba. Prez needs Austin for something."

"Not a problem, man. I'll let ya know when I get there."

Lifting my chin at him, I turn and leave.

———————

USUALLY, tatting someone relaxes me. I get tuned into the artwork and the buzzing of the gun. Lately however with all the added stress due to all this stalker business it has had the opposite effect. My mind is elsewhere, on my woman and our child, practically every minute of the day.

My phone pings just as I'm finishing a tribal headpiece this guy wanted on his back. Pulling it from the inside pocket of my cut I swipe the screen,

Reid: I'm here. Alba wants to bring you lunch.

Me: Ok. Warm the truck up for her.

Once I'm through typing out my response, I clean the guy up and send him on his way. I don't have another appointment for another hour, which will give me plenty of time to eat when Alba gets here.

Fifteen minutes later, after I've cleaned my station, I walk to the back and into the break room to make sure we have some bottled water before Alba gets here. My mind is still cluttered with the little bit of information Reid was able to obtain when my phone rings.

I retrieve my phone from my pocket, answering the call, "Yeah," I bark into the phone, feeling a little on edge.

"Gabriel, get..." the call starts to break up with static before Reid's frantic voice comes back in, and the blaring sounds of sirens make it almost impossible to hear what he is trying to tell me, "Alba was in an accident, about two blocks from the shop, man. The ambulance is on its way," I hear Reid say from the other end of the phone.

I was running through the shop and out the door before he could finish his sentence.

"You tell her I'm comin'."

I rush and jump into my truck. My grip on the steering wheel tightens as I weave in and out of traffic. Thoughts of losing her and my child begin racing through my mind. I just got her back. I can't lose her now. Not like this.

Up ahead, I see flashing lights, and it doesn't take long for traffic to come to a complete standstill.

Fuck this.

Pulling onto the shoulder, I drive toward the chaos and blaring sirens. As soon as I get close enough, I spot her battered truck upside down on the side of the cold, wet road in a ditch.

My stomach twists into a thousand knots.

Throwing my truck into park, I burst out the door, my feet feeling like lead as I wade through the crowd of first responders.

Towards my woman.

That's when I get a closer look at the mangled mess that was Alba's truck, and my steps falter. About twenty yards ahead, I spot her, strapped to a gurney, wearing a neck brace, and by her side is Reid. Marching past the officers and firefighters I get to her side just as she's lifted into the back of the ambulance.

"Who's riding with her?" the Paramedic asks, turning to see both myself and Reid standing there.

"She's my woman," I answer.

"Climb in," he says, nodding his head.

Stepping in I sit and grab Alba's hand. The sirens roar, and we take off down the road. I take a deep breath and access her from head to toe. All the blood matted in her beautiful blonde hair has turned it crimson, along with several small lacerations that cover her left arm and a splint that has been placed on her wrist.

"She has been unconscious since we arrived on the scene. She took a pretty good blow to the head along with a broken wrist. You can still talk to her. A familiar voice may help rouse her," he informs me as he starts checking her vitals.

I choke back my own worries for both her and my child and place my other hand on top of her belly.

"Cariño *Sweetheart*," I lean down and whisper in her ear.

The ride is short. As soon as the ambulance comes to a stop,

SANDY ALVAREZ & CRYSTAL DANIELS

the backdoors fly open, and they hoist her and the gurney out, and we are rolling through the emergency room doors.

"Sir, I need you to wait out here," a young female nurse says, stopping me mid-stride as I follow my woman.

"Get the fuck out of my way," I growl, giving her a hardened stare.

"Let them do their job," the young nurse says with a quiet yet firm voice.

Fuck.

I stand there, staring at the doors they took her through. I don't know how long I'm watching for someone to walk back out, but I'm pulled from the fog when Reid shows up. I know it's not his fault, but I need some answers.

"What the hell happened?" I question. I'm losing my shit right now. I know I need to control my temper and rein in my frustration in the process.

With devastation written on his face, I watch Reid run his hand through his hair, "One minute everything was fine, she was cruising down the road at a slow pace, then a second later she's speeding up. I know Alba doesn't drive over the speed limit, ever. Once I realized something was wrong, I pulled up alongside her. The look on her face...she was so fuckin' scared, man. Then she hit a patch of ice and lost it. Fuck, I should have driven her. Gabriel, I'm sorry, brother."

As we're standing there going over the events, Bella comes running through the doors bypassing everyone. At the same time, the double doors to the back open and out walks her best friend Mila along with a doctor. I've heard Bella and Alba mention before that Mila is an OB nurse. After a quick hug between the two and some whispered words they walk toward Reid and me. Logan appears, walking in from outside and comes to stand alongside us.

Mila gives us a small smile before the doctor begins to speak, "I'm Doctor Williams. Are you all the family of Alba Jameson?"

"Yes. I'm her fiancé," I lie. "And this is her sister," I say, motioning toward Bella.

"As you know, Miss Jameson was brought in a short while ago with injuries she sustained in a car accident. She may have a concussion, so we are taking her back for a CAT Scan. She looks to have a broken wrist, as well. The on-call OB-GYN checked her out, and other than some bruising on her stomach from the seatbelt and her blood pressure being a little high, the baby looks good," the doctor informs us.

Tilting my head back, I stare at the white tiled ceiling and sigh in relief, then look back at Dr. Williams, "Thank you."

The doctor inclines his head, "I'll come back shortly after we know more." He informs and excuses himself. Mila gives me a small smile as she and Bella walk off to talk amongst themselves.

"I didn't realize she worked at the hospital," Reid wonders aloud.

Logan turns to me, "Prez and Quinn are on their way, brother." Before walking off and letting me have my space.

While pacing the fuckin' floors, I catch sight of Prez's SUV pulling into the parking lot just outside the Emergency Department.

When they enter the waiting room, their first concerns are about Alba. I look to Logan, asking him to fill them in on what the doctor told us because I'm too worked up. I feel caged. Rules or not, if someone doesn't come walking through those damn doors that are separating me from my family, I'll go searching for answers myself.

"I want Alba's truck towed to the shop. Something's not adding up with this whole picture," Prez says, causing me to pause and look at him.

"You thinkin' it may have something to do with this guy we are lookin' for?" Logan asks, folding his arms across his chest.

If this is somehow related to the piece of shit stalking my family....

My rage is so intense at this point I rear back and put my fist through the wall, needing to hit something—anything. The guys look at me, then look at the hole in the wall. No one says anything. Good thing, because I swear right now is not the time for someone to tell me to calm the fuck down.

"I'm not sure. My gut is tellin' me this shit isn't right. From what Reid recounted, it doesn't sound like a mere accident. I want to be 100% sure one way or the other though," Prez says. "Quinn, call Bennett, you guys get that truck towed to the shop today. Take my vehicle. Someone here will give me a lift home," Prez orders, chucking his keys to Quinn. Without a word, he is on his phone and out the door.

The place is quiet...too quiet.

We are the only people left waiting in the thick stillness of the waiting room for about another twenty minutes before I see the double doors that lead to the back open, and Dr. Williams rounds the corner.

Bella jumps up fast and quickly speaks, "How is she?"

At this point, us men are standing behind Bella, waiting for answers ourselves.

"Alba is doing better. As suspected, she has a moderate concussion, which is why she was unconscious for awhile, but she is starting to come around. CAT scan showed no swelling and no bleeding as of right now, which is also good. The laceration to her head was closed with a few staples. She'll be in and out of it most of the night. She also suffered a broken wrist, as well as some scrapes and bruising. And the baby is doing good; the heartbeat is very strong. They are getting her moved into a room for overnight observation. If she does okay throughout the night and another CAT scan comes out clear she can go home in twenty-four to forty-eight hours. But, she will need to rest. There will be a list of side effects to watch her for, such as confusion, slurred speech, and dizziness. Anyway, I can take someone back with me, then the rest of you can come up as soon as she is settled," he finishes saying.

Surprisingly Bella blurts out, "Gabriel is going."

I glance at her, and she smiles, "As bad as I want to be the one, she needs you more, big guy."

Her eyes water a bit with the statement, and I recognize how hard that was for her with a nod. She's a good woman—a good sister. I look at Logan for a second as he pulls her into him a little tighter. Turning on my heels, I follow Dr. Williams through the double doors.

It turns out, they already had Alba in a room on the third floor by the time we made it back there. After thanking the doctor, I walk into the hospital room where Alba is sleeping. I sit watching her for a few minutes. It's when I place my hand on her stomach; she opens her eyes and looks at me.

"Cariño *Sweetheart*," I rasp. She steals my breath every time she looks at me with those sky-blue eyes of hers. I lean over and place my lips on hers, breathing her in. Then place a kiss on her swollen belly. "My star," I say to my unborn child as Alba runs her fingers through my hair, which instantly calms me, causing my tense body to relax.

"I love you," she whispers.

Reaching up, I cradled her face in my hands and kiss her again, "Mi amor *My love*."

19

ALBA

Waking up in the emergency room and realizing not only was I alive but that my baby was okay was a huge relief. My last thoughts as I crashed were of my baby and Gabriel. No way would fate be so cruel. To finally bring us together only to rip us apart.

Shortly after I was brought into my hospital room, Gabriel was at my side. I didn't like seeing the tormented look on his face as he took in my injuries. Like now; he's sitting in a chair beside the bed, his large hand rubbing lazy circles on my belly, and his eyes are constantly bouncing back and forth between the baby's heart rate monitor and me.

I was told the OB doctor on-call was brought into the ER to do an ultrasound to check on the baby, but I was still unconscious at the time. I wish I could have seen for myself, but the constant whoosh of the heartbeat filling the room will suffice.

With Gabriel's hand rubbing my belly, my eyes begin to grow heavy. I'm trying hard to fight sleep. Afraid something may happen. Noticing my struggle, he leans over and brushes his lips across mine.

"Sleep Cariño *Sweetheart*, I've got you."

With his words of assurance, I allow my eyes to close.

I awaken some time the next morning to the feel of a hand stroking my hair. Without opening my eyes, I already know whose hand it is—Bella. Since we were children, this is something my sister has always done. It doesn't matter how old I get, my sister stroking my hair will always be a source of comfort.

Opening my eyes, I look to my right and see my sister lying in bed next to me. When my eyes meet hers, there are no words spoken. We stare at each other. Our tears are our only form of communication. We know each other so well that nothing needs to be said. Bella's tears are saying she was scared and that she loves me. Mine are saying I'm okay, and I love you too.

A moment later, Bella breaks the intense moment by pointing at my wrist. "A blue cast, Alba. What did you do, wake up from your unconscious state long enough to tell them you wanted blue?" We both giggle.

"Uh, I kinda did. I literally woke up as the doctor was wrapping it, and I believe my only words were 'blue'." My confession causes both of us to laugh harder. The sound of the door opening draws my attention, and I see Gabriel walking in with all the guys and Leyna in tow. Gabriel is the first to approach, giving me a light kiss on the lips before sitting down in the chair beside the bed. After him, each of the guys follows suit kissing me on the top of my head. Jake is the first to speak.

"How ya doin', sweetheart?"

"I'm good, ready to go home though."

"I talked to the nurse earlier. She said the doctor should be in before noon to check on you. So hopefully you can go home today," Bella informs us.

Mila comes walking in with a bright smile and a doctor trailing behind her. It was a nice surprise to find that Mila was my nurse. She happened to be working last night when I was brought into the ER. She is an OB nurse and was assisting the doctor yesterday. For that, I am thankful. Having someone you know to be the one taking care of you makes the situation a little easier to bear.

"Good morning," the doctor says, still looking down at the clipboard in her hands. Then she stops abruptly and snaps her head up with a shocked expression on her face.

"Dr. Evans?" Bella rushes out.

We're all quiet for a second before Quinn speaks up, "Well, this is some crazy ass deja-vu shit right here. How you doin', Dr. Pretty?"

"Dr. Evans, what are you doing here?" Bella questions.

Clearing her throat, she says, "I was transferred here six months ago."

Climbing out of my bed, my sister walks up to Dr. Evans and hugs her, "It's really good to see you again. I never got to thank you for all that you have done for me."

She gives my sister a warm smile, "You're welcome, Bella. And you look well."

"Would it be okay to get your number, Dr. Evans? I'd like for us to get together sometime."

"I'd like that too. And no more Dr. Evans. You can call me Emerson."

After their brief exchange, Dr. Evans turns her attention toward me, "Alba, all your tests this morning came back clear. So, we are going to let you go home today. I'd like for you to make an appointment to follow up with your OB in the next day or two."

Gabriel cuts in, "Why? Is everything okay with the baby?" he asks gruffly.

She regards Gabriel, "Your baby is doing good. The heart rate is like it should be. Alba hasn't had any contractions. I assure you all is well."

At Gabriel's questioning look, Dr. Evans continues. "How about we do another ultrasound. Let you see for yourselves."

At her suggestion, I see some of the tension leave Gabriel's body. "We'd appreciate that, thanks."

While the doctor begins to set up the ultrasound machine, everyone including my sister quietly leaves my hospital room giving us a few moments of privacy. This will be Gabriel's first time seeing our baby. With him on one side of me holding my hand, Dr. Evans sits on the edge of the bed on the opposite side and pulls the machine closer to us. Lifting my gown, she squeezes some warm jelly onto my belly. Then she takes the probe and begins gliding it around. It only takes a second before our baby's image appears on the screen.

"Here we go," Dr. Evans announces. "As you can see, the baby looks really good. And your chart says you're at thirty-six weeks."

I take my eyes off my baby, and I turn and look at Gabriel. There are no words to describe the look on his face. None other than complete wonderment.

"Have you guys found out the sex yet?"

I shake my head, no.

"Would you like to find out?"

I cut my eyes back to Gabriel, and he gives me a nod.

"Yes, we'd like to know."

Moving the probe around a bit more, Dr. Evans pauses then points to the screen. She doesn't even have to tell us what it is. It's clear as day. Our son is not shy about showing us the goods. When I turn my attention back to Gabriel, I see his face lit up with the biggest smile. The kind of smile that is reserved for special occasions. Gabriel doesn't show his smile too often, but when he does, it's beautiful.

Leaning over the bed, he rests his forehead against mine. And I faintly hear the click of the door, letting me know Dr. Evans has left. Giving us a moment.

"Did you see?" I ask.

"Sí, mi amor. *Yes, my love.* You are giving me a son."

Fifteen minutes later, Dr. Evans walks back in along with Bella and the guys trailing behind. Eagerly making her way to the side of the bed, she looks at me expectantly, "Well?"

"We're having a boy," I gush aloud.

My sister pulls me in for a hug, while the guys pat Gabriel on the back and offer their congratulations. Except for Jake, who pulls him in for a hug then murmurs something I can't hear. Jake is more than just these men's President. He serves as a father figure to them, and they love and respect him as such. I also have no doubt, he will think of himself as a grandfather to our son.

Family is not always the one you are born into, in some cases —like all of ours—it's the one we choose. And I couldn't ask for a better family. I'm not very close to my mom. We speak on occasion, and I've seen her a couple of times over the last few months. My sister has always been more of a mother figure to me than our own.

"Are you ready to go home, Alba?" Dr. Evans asks, cutting in through all the chatting voices.

"Yes! Very."

She chuckles, "These are your discharge papers, along with instructions to rest. I wrote you a prescription for some pain medicine for your wrist. It is perfectly safe for the baby. If the pain is mild, take some over the counter pain reliever for the discomfort." She goes to hand me the piece of paper only Gabriel takes it from her before I do. Rolling my eyes, I turn back to the doctor.

"Thanks for everything, Dr. Evans."

"You're welcome, Alba. And since you are officially no longer my patient, please call me Emerson."

Squeezing my arm, she turns to make her way out of the room. Just as she goes to pull open the door, Quinn pipes up.

"Excuse me, Dr. Pretty." But before he can get another word, Emerson cuts him off.

"Find your own damn coffee," as she walks out without a backward glance.

Now all of us are staring at Quinn, wondering what the hell he's done to piss Emerson off. Smirking, he looks at everyone.

"What?"

"Estúpido, *stupid*," I hear Gabriel mutter as Quinn, Jake, and Logan start to leave.

"We'll wait downstairs for ya," Jake says over his shoulder.

Never a dull moment with Quinn.

Slowly sitting up, I swing my legs over the side of the bed.

"You bring me some clothes?" I ask Bella.

"Yeah, right here," she tells me, motioning to a bag slung over her shoulder, "Want me to help you get dressed?"

"I got it," Gabriel cuts in from behind me.

"No problem, big guy. I'll wait downstairs with the guys."

I mouth a thank you at my sister as she leaves. She wants to help, but we both know Gabriel needs this. Standing in front of me, he takes hold of my hand and helps me stand.

"Let's get you dressed, Cariño *Sweetheart*."

Once Gabriel has removed my hospital gown, he takes the clothes Bella brought me out of the bag. Starting with my panties, he crouches down on one knee then motions for me to step in. Placing my hands on his shoulder, I do so. One foot at a time. Then he delicately slides them up my legs. His touch causes me to shiver.

The act of this man dressing me is so innocent, yet so intimate at the same time. Once my panties are in place, we repeat the same steps with my leggings. Next is my bra. I close my eyes and moan when Gabriel's thumbs brush over my nipples. When he reaches around me to clasp it, he runs a series of feather-light kisses along the column of my shoulder and up my neck. When he's done with my bra, he slides my sweater on, paying special attention not to hurt my wrist. Once I'm dressed,

Gabriel gives me a long lingering kiss, and I bring my hand up and run my fingers through his beard. Pulling away I ask breathlessly. "When we get home, will you help me get undressed?"

Chuckling, he swoops down, stealing one more kiss.

"Come on, baby, let's go home."

When we arrive home, Gabriel opens the front door, and I'm hit with an amazing smell. So amazing it causes my tummy to rumble.

"Did someone cook?" I ask as I begin to make my way into the kitchen. I don't make it far before I'm scooped up into Gabriel's arms.

"What are you doing?"

"Taking you to bed so you can rest," he declares while climbing the steps.

"But," I begin to protest.

"I'll bring you some food. Lisa made spaghetti."

Oh god, my mouth starts watering at the mention of my favorite food. And just then, my stomach rumbles again.

"You know I could have walked up here myself," I tell him when he sets me down beside the bed. "I feel really good. A little sore all over but no pain. I'm not even tired."

"You'll rest, just like the doctor said to do."

Picking up the blanket and pulling it back, Gabriel motions for me to get in. Deciding not to fight, I give in, and I do as he wants. This is a battle I know I'm not going to win. Besides, who wouldn't want a sexy man fawning over them, waiting on them hand and foot. This might not be so bad after all. On that thought, I smile up at Gabriel.

"My food is not going to fix itself."

Minutes later, Gabriel returns carrying a food tray with a plate of spaghetti, garlic bread, and some iced tea. What an odd sight. My man looking all domestic. He definitely looks out of place and a snort escapes my mouth. Narrowing his eyes and growling, "Only for you, Cariño *Sweetheart*."

I'm about halfway through my plate of food when Gabriel comes back into the room. I immediately can feel the change in his demeanor.

"I need to go take care of something. I'm going to have one of the guys come stay with you while I'm gone," he informs me while slipping on his cut and grabbing his keys and wallet off the dresser.

"Is everything okay?"

"Yeah, baby. Everything is fine," he assures, walking over to the bed then kissing me. I know he's lying, but I know better than to press the issue.

"Can Reid come stay with me?" At his questioning look, I continue, "He didn't come to see me in the hospital. And if I know him it's because he's feeling guilty. I want to talk to him."

Running his hands through his hair, Gabriel nods, "I'll call him."

Fifteen minutes after I hear Gabriel's truck leave, I get up out of bed and head downstairs to seek out Reid. When I walk into the kitchen, I find him sitting at the table while drinking a cup of coffee. He looks up from his cup when I approach the table. He looks like he hasn't slept in days. His honey blonde hair is disheveled, and his green eyes are dull. He also looks like he hasn't shaved in days.

"Alba, I want to tell you..."

Holding up my hand, I stop him. I know what he's about to say. Pulling out a chair, I sit down across from him.

"I don't want to hear what you were about to say. You were going to apologize for something that was not your fault. They're called accidents for a reason Reid." Clenching his jaw, he props his elbows on the table and rests his head in his hands.

A second later, he looks up, and his eyes take in the bump on my forehead and then the cast on my wrist before his tortured eyes meet mine.

"I can't get the look of your frightened face out of my head. And there was nothing I could do. Then when your truck flipped, I thought for sure that was it. I would not be able to live with myself had something happened to you on my watch Alba. You're like a sister to me. You and Bella both. I hope you know that."

He's right. All the guys in the club are like a bunch of big brothers. And they treat my sister, and I like sisters. Like I said before, I couldn't ask for a better family.

"I know, which is why I know if you could have, you would have stopped that truck yourself," I wait a beat contemplating my next statement. "I know about what happened to your brother," I say softly and his body jerks, "what you had to witness with my accident must have brought up some bad memories." Just when he's about to open his mouth, I cut him off, "Look, I know you probably don't want to talk about what happened, but I want you to know that if you ever do, then I'm here for you." I gauge Reid's reaction, hoping I've not overstepped my bounds. I watch him visibly swallow before speaking.

"Appreciate it, Alba." When he doesn't say more, I know the conversation is over. I've said my peace, and so has he. I can only pray that one day, he can see that what happened to me and what happened to his brother was not his fault.

Standing up from the table, I walk over toward the stove.

"You hungry? Lisa made spaghetti. And I'm feeling like a second lunch." I have no idea where I'm putting all this food.

"Sure," he chuckles, "I could go for something to eat."

Reid and I are just finishing our meal when Gabriel walks in the door. Striding over to me, he leans down, kissing me. He turns his attention to Reid, "I need to speak with you, brother."

Lifting his chin, Reid stands up from the table and takes his plate to the sink. Walking by me, he kisses me on the top of my head.

"Thanks for the late lunch, sweetheart."

"You're welcome," I say with a smile.

"Give me a minute with Reid, okay, baby?" Gabriel says.

I see an angry, yet worried look written all over Gabriel's face, but decide not to question him right now.

"I'm going to go take a nap. Will you come lay with me when you're done?"

"Sí, mi amor. *Yes, my love.* I'll be up in a few minutes."

Once upstairs, I change into a t-shirt and sleep shorts before climbing into bed. I must have dozed off for a few minutes because the next thing I remember is waking up to Gabriel laying behind me with his arm wrapped over my belly and his hand lying protectively over our son.

I can feel the rise and fall of his chest against my back, and I know he's asleep. With a smile on my face, I snuggle deeper into his strong embrace, and before I know it, my eyes turn heavy once again as I fall asleep in Gabriel's arms.

20

GABRIEL

I'm smiling as I pull out of the driveway of our home. We found out this morning we are having a boy. My woman is giving me a son. I still can't believe it. Seeing the image on the screen, making out his features. He is perfect. I haven't had a reason to smile in a long time. The overwhelming love I feel for my unborn child amazes me. They are my purpose in life.

Alba was released a couple of hours ago from the hospital, and even though leaving her side was hard, it was necessary because Jake called and said Alba's truck was just brought in. Logan and Quinn have already started going over everything with a fine-tooth comb, so I'm heading to the garage. If it's the cocksucker who was stalking her in Bozeman that means he was here in Polson. We need fucking answers, and fast.

Alba asked before I left if I could send Reid over in place of Austin. She knows my brother is feeling like shit about the accident. It's not his fault, but I'm guessing he is having a hard time dealing with the whole situation due to the fact he lost his brother the same way a few years ago. I called him, and he didn't hesitate.

Eager to get some answers, I pull up into the parking lot of the shop twenty minutes later and make my way inside through the front door where I'm met by Jake, who has just walked out of his office.

"Hey, brother, they just got what's left of the truck up on the lift, let's go see what they can find out," he says clapping me on the back as he passes by. When we walk into the garage, my stomach tightens into a knot looking at the wreckage again. I take a walk around the perimeter of it, really taking in the magnitude of the whole situation. How Alba wasn't hurt worse than she was is beyond me. Ducking my head, I peer underneath where Quinn and Logan are.

"Shit," Quinn remarks, which gets everyone's attention, "the fuckin' break lines were sliced."

The four of us walk over to Quinn and get a good look at the evidence before us. Sure enough, someone cut the line right behind the driver's front wheel.

"MOTHERFUCKER!" I roar, picking up a socket wrench, sending it soaring across the garage. "This guy is here in Polson, or was at some point and was able to get close enough to cut the fuckin' break lines on Alba's truck? This shit had to have happened when she was out somewhere. Either a doctor's appointment or shopping. Security is too tight at our home for this shit to happen there," I tell them.

"Who's with her now?" Prez asks me.

"Reid," I inform him.

I walk outside to get some fresh air before I explode. This asshole is in my town—around my woman and tried to fuckin' kill her and my son. He has no idea who he is dealing with. Needing to take the edge off, I light a cigarette and inhale deeply, letting the smoke burn my lungs before releasing it. I hear the door open and close behind me. Logan steps up beside me, lighting a smoke of his own.

"Prez is calling church. We need to roll out in a few minutes. Call your woman. We may be late getting home today, brother." He walks off toward his own ride, pulling his phone out, probably to contact Bella before climbing into his truck and heading in the direction of the clubhouse. Flicking my unfinished cigarette, I walk to my truck, start it up and follow him.

I'm sitting at the bar in the clubhouse nursing a beer waiting for everyone to show. Within an hour and a half, the place is packed.

"Gabriel," Doc's voice rumbles as he sits down in a stool one over from where I'm sittin'.

"Doc," I respond with a chin lift.

"How's that woman of yours today? Heard she went home a few hours ago," he inquires.

"She's good. Doc said the baby boy is good too."

"Aww shit, man, a son? Congratulations, brother!" he boasts as he raises his bottle in the air, and I lift mine in response.

Downing the remainder of my beer, I stand up and glance around the room. It looks like everyone that lives in town made it. I catch Prez walkin' from the back and making his way toward the center of the bar.

"Listen up," his gravelly voice booms over everyone else's, causing the room to go quiet, "we have a situation. I called all you brothers in today because I need all of you in the streets throughout the day tomorrow. As you know, Gabriel's woman was in an accident. She's going to be okay, but we learned this morning that someone fucked with her brake lines."

The silence in the room is broken by several 'what the fucks' and 'motherfuckers' from my brothers.

"Quiet the fuck down. We need to flush this cocksucker out, and if he is in town, we will."

When we find the bastard, he is mine.

I still can't make out who the hell could be a threat. If Santino were alive, I wouldn't put it past him to have something to do with it. But just because he is dead doesn't mean he doesn't have reach. Maybe he has family who wants to avenge him? This is definitely something I need to bring up to Prez and the other men. We can't afford to ignore any lead we can think of. If only we had something more to go on besides speculation and our own goddamn imaginations.

"Alright, men. I know it's starting to get late, and I know most of you put in a full day's work and just clocked out awhile ago. Go home. Those that can do so get out there and ask around. Find out if we have any new faces in town, and if so, where. At this point, anything you find can be a potential lead," Logan orders.

As Logan and Prez start to walk off, I stop them, "You think Santino's family could be behind any of this?"

"As I said, we leave no stone unturned, Gabriel. I'll have Reid do some digging into Santino's extended family and their locations," Prez says.

Before we get any further into our conversation, Logan's phone rings. Pulling it from his cut, he swipes the screen and lifts it to his ear, "Yeah," he clips. His eyes quickly cut to me, "You know a guy named Sam?"

"That's the guy who was living with Alba and her friend Leah in Bozeman. Why?"

"Because he's sitting out at the front gate askin' to speak with you," Logan tells me.

What the hell would he have to talk to me about? And how in the hell did he know where to find me or the clubhouse?

"Let him in," I tell Logan. Two minutes later, Sam walks through the front door and pauses to take in his surroundings before making his way in further.

"What the fuck you doin' out here uninvited, in our town, at our club?" my voice booms causing him to halt. His hands go up, "Look, man, I'm not here to stir up any shit. I'm here because I think I might have some information concerning Alba and her stalker."

"How did you know where to find me?" I ask, hardening my stare at him.

"I only know Alba's home address, but I didn't want to upset her with my suspicions, so I decided it was best that I find you first. Alba never mentioned locations or anything, so I had to be resourceful, you know, ask around a bit. Most people weren't too keen on telling me anything, but I found out enough to find my way."

Deciding we need to hear what he has to say, I pull a chair at a table to my right, "Sit," I order. He takes a seat, and Prez, Logan, and myself pull out some chairs and do the same.

Prez is the first to break through the thick tension in the air, "Son, what's so important that you went nosing' around our town? It's not smart showing up out here uninvited."

I've got to give it to him; the guy has balls showin' up to a biker compound unannounced like he did. Either that or he's stupid.

"After Alba came home, our old professor showed up at my front door asking about her. Asking why she left, and did I know how to contact her. I found it strange."

I clench my fits, trying to control the anger building inside and listen as he continues.

"Anyway, Leah was approached by him a few days later, asking her the same thing. When she recounted what he said, I went looking for him the next day. Teacher or not, he's messing with my friends and snooping, and I don't like it. I had an office worker dig up his address for me. I showed up at his doorstep that same day and couldn't get an answer. He hasn't been back either. It seems as though he just up and left. I've asked around, and no one knows why," Sam finishes.

"Damn, brother, you think this guy is the one connected with Alba's accident?" Logan questions.

"An accident. Was Alba hurt? Is she okay?" Sam frantically asks, looking to each of us for answers.

I abruptly stand from my chair, causing it to skid across the floor. I can't take this shit. Sam takes my movement as a threat and stands.

"Sit the fuck down," I growl at him. He has nothing to worry about at the moment, but he doesn't know that, so he continues to stand.

Jake takes the opportunity to calm everyone's nerves. "Sit down, son. None of us are a threat to you. Gabriel here is wound tighter than normal right now. Someone tried to hurt his woman yesterday by tampering with her brakes. She and the baby are going to be okay," Jake tells him.

Giving me a final glance, Sam sits back down.

"Look," he says, "I'm telling you something isn't adding up. And now knowing about her accident, my gut is telling me Professor Green has been the guy all along."

He isn't the only one. My gut is tellin' me the same thing. We need to find out who the hell this Professor Green is.

I motion to Prez and Logan to walk over toward the bar, leaving Sam to sit alone.

"I need to get home and talk to Reid."

"What do you want to do about pretty boy over there? You know he's probably going to want to see your Alba," Logan smirks, knowing god damn well the same thing would have already crossed my mind. I think it's time Sam and I get a few things straight. I've claimed what's mine and dipshit sitting over there needs to know it. I walk back toward the table and look down at Sam.

"You got plans to see my woman while you're here?" I ask.

"I do. I booked a hotel room in town," he answers.

"Alba's mine. Are we going to have issues with that? Because if

SANDY ALVAREZ & CRYSTAL DANIELS

your dumb ass came here thinking you could sweep in and save the day and get the girl, it ain't happening," I warn him.

"I can assure you; Alba and I are and always will be just friends. She's a beautiful and caring woman, but she's not the one for me. I promise you," he assures me.

"Make sure you keep it that way, and we won't have any problems," I warn him.

Turning away, I lift my chin to Prez and Logan and walk out the door, leaving them to finish with Sam. The sun is getting ready to set, and I want to get home to my family and bring Reid up to speed with our new-found information.

When I make it home and walk through the door, I find Alba and Reid sitting at the table. Striding toward her, I lean down, kissing her, then turn my attention to Reid, "I need to speak with you, brother." Standing up from the table, he takes his plate to the sink, telling Alba thank you. I turn back and face Alba, "Give me a minute with Reid, okay, baby?"

"I'm going to go lay down. Will you come join me when you're done?" she asks.

"Sí, mi amor. *Yes, my love.* I'll be up in a few minutes." Once Alba is upstairs, I find Reid waiting in the living room. "Sam showed up at the clubhouse."

"No, shit? That was ballsy of him. What for?"

"Suspects one of the professors at the school of being Alba's stalker. He was going around asking questions about her, then vanished and hasn't been seen since. Too much of a coincidence if you ask me," I tell him.

"You got a name for me?"

"Calvin Green."

Grabbing his keys from the coffee table, I walk with Reid toward the front door.

"I'll see what I can dig up on him. I'm assuming we need to be at the clubhouse in the morning?"

184

I nod my head.

"See ya in the mornin', brother."

I wait until I see his taillights fade at the end of the driveway before locking up the house and making sure the security alarm is set before I head upstairs. I find Alba sound asleep in our bed, so I grab myself a hot shower. After drying off, I climb in behind Alba and wrap my arm around her, laying my hand protectively over our son. Completely relaxed, a few minutes later, I fall asleep.

21

ALBA

I wake the next morning in the exact position as I was when I fell asleep the second time with Gabriel's arm around me. I can tell it's still early because the sun is just starting to peek through the bedroom window. I don't want to move. I want to stay in this protective bubble of strong inked arms forever, but my bladder has different plans. Along with a baby who is currently kicking the heck out of said bladder.

Trying very carefully to get out of bed without disturbing Gabriel is proving impossible. When you're eight months pregnant, getting up out of bed can be a task and not a graceful one either. By the time I wiggle myself into a sitting position, I look over my shoulder at Gabriel and find him wide awake. He has one brow raised, and his lips quirked.

"Not one word," I say, glaring at him.

"I wasn't going to say anything, Cariño *Sweetheart*. I very much would like to keep my balls," he teases.

Rolling my eyes, I get up and walk to the bathroom. After finishing my business, I come back out into the bedroom to find Gabriel standing in front of the dresser in all his glory. The sight of him still takes my breath away. My eyes roam over every inch of his body. From his thick arms to his broad tattooed shoulder. Then my eyes follow the light dusting of dark hair on his chest that leads down.

A growl brings me out of my trance. And when my eyes land on Gabriel's face, I see pure desire.

"Stop lookin' at me like that," he warns.

My breathing speeds up, and I lick my lips, "Why?"

"Because when you look at me like that, I want nothing more than to bend you over the edge of the bed and drive my cock into your tight pussy."

His words cause my breath to hitch and my core to tingle. "I'd be okay with that."

Growling again through clenched teeth, he shakes his head, "You just got out of the hospital, baby. You need time to heal."

"But..." I go to argue only to have him cut me off with a sharp look. "Fine," I mutter.

Once downstairs, we both head to the kitchen. I go about gathering the contents to make an omelet when Gabriel orders me to sit. I do as he asks and sit down on a stool at the bar. Propping my elbow on the counter, I rest my chin in my palm and enjoy the view of Gabriel shirtless and in a pair of grey sweats that hang low on his hips. I'm pulled from yet another dreamy state when the doorbell rings.

Glancing at the clock on the wall, I see it's 7:30 am and smile because I have a pretty good guess as to who it is. Stepping down from the stool, I go to answer the door.

"I'll get it," Gabriel says.

"It's probably just Bella. I'm surprised she held off until the sun was up to come over."

A moment later, Gabriel walks back in the kitchen with my sister trailing behind. She walks straight to me and pulls me in for a hug.

"How are you feeling today?"

"Really good. My wrist was bothering me a bit when I woke up, but it's fine now."

Gabriel turns his attention from the stove. "You didn't tell me you were in pain," he scolds.

"I'm not. I said it was bothering me a little. I took some pain reliever when I was in the bathroom, and now I'm fine."

"You should have told me."

"Why? So, you could have fed the medicine to me like a baby? I can do things for myself, you know."

My last statement causes Gabriel to glare and my sister to snicker, which earns her a glare from Gabriel as well.

"I hope you two don't mind, but I called Mila and asked if she would mind stopping by here before her shift to check up on you. If big guy," she says, pointing her thumb at Gabriel, "is anything like Logan, then he'd feel better if you were checked out."

The glare disappears on Gabriel's face, and it's replaced with one of gratitude, "Appreciate ya, Bella."

"No problem, Gabriel," she says sincerely.

My sister and I are finishing breakfast Gabriel cooked when we hear a knock at the door. I don't even attempt to answer it this time.

When Gabriel reenters the kitchen, it's with Mila. Bella and I both step down from our stools and greet her with a hug.

"Hey, Alba. How are you feeling this morning?"

"I feel okay. But these two are being worried warts. So, I'm glad you could stop by on your way to work. Maybe once they see I'm fine, they will stop hovering, and Gabriel might let me do things for myself."

"It's nice having someone to worry about you. It just means they care," Mila states somberly. God, why did I have to open my big mouth? Mila is a single mother. Ava's father passed away before she was born. Bella has told me on several occasions Mila doesn't date, and she knows she gets lonely. And here I am complaining about the people who love me showing too much attention. I swallow past the knot in my throat, "Mila, I'm sorry. I shouldn't be complaining. I know how lucky I am."

She waves her hand at me, "I'm the one who's sorry. I had no right to overstep."

"You didn't overstep. You spoke the truth. I should not speak as though I'm ungrateful." After hugging Mila, I lead her into the living room where she proceeds to check my vitals, and then she moves on to the staples on my head.

"All your vitals are normal, and your head is already starting to heal nicely. How's your wrist feeling?"

"It was a little achy this morning. I took some pain reliever, and it helped."

"Have you made a follow up with your OB yet?" Mila asks as she begins packing her blood pressure cuff back into her bag.

"Yep. I have an appointment with her tomorrow."

Mila slings her bag over her shoulder, and I walk her to the front door.

"Thanks for stopping by. We really appreciate it."

"No problem, Alba. I was happy to. And anytime you two need anything, you can call me, day or night," she says, looking to both me and Gabriel.

"I need to be going too. I'll walk out with you," Bella announces.

"Call me later, okay?" then turns toward Gabriel, "Thanks for breakfast, big guy." He gives them both a chin lift as they walk out the door.

An hour after my sister and Mila left, Gabriel informed me that he needed to go to the clubhouse and take care of a few things. When I asked who was babysitting today, he gave me the best surprise.

Now here I am standing on my front porch, shifting from foot to foot as I see a familiar truck making its way down our gravel driveway. Before the truck is even in park, I'm down the steps and throwing myself into Sam's arms. I've missed my friend so much. It's been months since I've seen him.

"Hey, little momma," he beams, scooping me up in his arms.

"Why didn't you tell me you were coming?" I scold once he releases his hold.

"I wanted to surprise you."

"Well, I'm definitely surprised. Come on, let's go inside," I urge, grabbing his hand and tugging him along behind me. Walking back up the steps to the front porch, we pass Gabriel. He leans in, kissing me, and then he and Sam exchange the usual guy acknowledgment of chin lifts before Gabriel heads in the direction of his truck.

Walking inside, I shut and lock the door before setting the alarm. Something Gabriel insists I do even when one of the guys is here with me. But now that I'm thinking about it, I'm wondering what sort of conversation Gabriel and Sam must have had yesterday. I'm shocked he has allowed Sam to be alone here with me. That he trusts Sam to watch over me without one of the guys. Knowing Gabriel, he probably threatened Sam.

No matter what was said, all that matters is, he trusts Sam enough to let him be here alone with me. Plus, one look at my friend, and you can clearly see he would have no problem protecting me. He may not be as big as Gabriel, but then again none of the other guys are.

We sit together in the living room and talk about trivial things. I notice that every time I bring up school and ask about his classes, he diverts my questions. Even when I ask about Leah, his answer to everything is fine. Sitting up straighter on the sofa, I narrow my eyes at Sam.

"Alright, what's going on? Why do I get the feeling you're keeping something from me?"

Hanging his head and pinching the bridge of his nose, Sam lays it on me.

"I dropped out of school."

I look at him with a stunned expression, "What? Why? When did this happen, and why have you not told me before now?"

"After I quit the team, my father refused to pay my tuition, so I had no choice. All this happened after Christmas. I didn't tell you because you have enough shit on your plate to worry about. I know you already blame yourself for me quitting the team. You didn't need that kind of stress, Alba." Seeing the tears well up in my eyes, Sam shakes his head at me.

"Hell no, Alba, no tears. Absolutely none of that shit that went down was your fault. So, don't go getting upset, you hear me?"

"That fight was my fault, Sam. Had you not been defending me, you would still be in school."

"Sweetheart, me kicking that guy's ass was a blessing. I was forced to face my father and come clean about some things in my life. One of them being I did not want to play football. Football was never my dream; it was my father's. I'm happier now than I have been in a very long time, Alba. I'm no longer living my life for someone else. I'm living my life for me. You taught me that."

I give him a confused look.

"What do you mean I taught you that?"

He shakes his head. "Look at you. Look at where you're at. The moment you found out you were pregnant, you said 'fuck what everyone thinks'. You faced the challenge head on. And school. School was never for you. So, what did you do? You created your own path. You decided to live your life the way you wanted. Not the way others thought you should."

By the time Sam is finished talking, I'm a sobbing mess, "I'm really glad you finally stood up for what you wanted, Sam. As long as you're happy, I'm happy for you."

Several minutes later, after my tears have dried, Sam speaks up again. "Now that that truth is out of the way, I suppose I should keep going since I'm on a roll."

"What are you talking about?"

"I'm talking about Leah."

"What about her? You said she was doing well."

"Leah is in trouble. I think she needs help. The kind I can't give her. And I'm hoping that you might be able to help. Hell, after meeting Gabriel and some of the men in the club, I'm convinced you can."

Oh god. I have a horrible feeling in the pit of my stomach. This has something to do with her family. I just know it. Leah has never come right out and told me any details about her parents. But the way she acts, and some of the things she has said, I'm certain her home life is not good.

"You know I'll do anything for her, Sam. Now tell what's going on."

"You know, I wouldn't normally say anything that would upset you, given your current state, but I feel her situation is time sensitive."

"My current state? You all need to quit acting like being pregnant means I have some sort of disability or that I'm incompetent for Christ's sake. Now tell me what the hell is going on!" I demand with a raised voice.

Taken aback a moment by my raised voice, Sam finally continues, "When I arrived back to our apartment after spending Christmas with my parents, Leah was already home. I wasn't expecting her until after New Year's, and she clearly wasn't expecting me to come home so early. Because when I got there, she was in the middle of packing. I could tell immediately something was off. From the moment I stepped into her room and started to ask questions, she did everything she could to avoid even looking at me. I walked up to her and grabbed hold of her arm to get her to stop packing and talk to me. When she finally turned toward me that's when I saw it."

"Saw what?" I ask. But I'm not sure I want to hear the answer. Leaning over with his elbows resting on his knees, he places his head in his hands. Swallowing past the knot in my throat. I repeat myself. "What did you see, Sam?"

Looking back at me, he answers, "She was beaten, Alba. Both of her eyes were black. One was nearly swollen shut. Her lip was busted. She couldn't even walk without being hunched over. Even though she wouldn't let me see, I know the rest of her body matched her face. At first, she refused to tell me anything. But no way was I going to give up. When she realized I wouldn't back down, she broke. Leah told me everything, Alba, and it's not pretty." Looking at me with hurt and anger in his eyes, Sam tells me what I already suspected. "Her father did that to her. You want to know why? Because he's been having someone from his church spy on her. Because of the dress she wore when we went out to the club together. Her father said she was presenting herself like a whore. He also found out she was living with me. A man. She had kept that a secret from her family. Leah had no idea her father had been spying on her."

Standing up from the couch, I begin to pace the living room.

"Sam, please tell me you didn't let her leave. Please tell me she didn't go back home."

"Fuck no, I didn't let her go back. She was going to. Her father demanded she pack all her stuff and return. But after what she told me, and after seeing what that motherfucker was capable of, no way was I about to let her leave. What we did was finish packing up her shit, then we packed up mine, and we moved. I found another apartment on the other side of town. Leah had to quit school. Luckily, I still had some money in my savings to get us by for a while. I was able to find a job in construction. The pay is decent enough. The problem is I can't hide her in Bozeman forever. Her father is going to find her, and she's terrified of what will happen when he does. She can't live the way she has been for the past couple of months. She's scared even to leave our apartment."

Holding up my hand, I stop him. "She can come here. Leah can stay with Gabriel and me." I watch as Sam's shoulders slump in relief. "Why didn't she come with you? Is she okay being home alone while you're gone?"

"She said she would be. I tried to get her to come with me, but she didn't want you to find out about what happened. She said if you started asking questions, she knew she wouldn't be able to lie to you. Leah made me promise not to say anything. This was one promise I had to break though. I don't think her staying in Bozeman is safe anymore. Leah still hasn't told me everything about her family. Only that they are super religious and strict, all I know is what her father did to her was not anything God would have wanted."

When Sam finishes replaying the horrible event of him and Leah, I stop my pacing and return to my spot on the couch next to him.

"How attached to Bozeman are you?" I ask.

Giving me a thoughtful look, he replies, "I don't know, I like it well enough. It's better than living at home. Why?"

"How would you feel about both you and Leah moving here to Polson?"

Sam seems to be pondering my question as I nervously bite my lip. What I wouldn't give to have two people who have come to mean so much to me move here. When I see a wide smile stretch across his face, I know what his answer is, and I throw myself at him.

Over the next several hours, we make a plan and iron out all the details of his and Leah's move. The plan is for them to make a move within the next month. That gives him time to find a place for the two of them and hopefully line up some work. I told Sam I'd ask Gabriel if maybe Reid needed some help. His and Nikolai's business is doing so well, so I'm hoping they can hook Sam up. When we hear Gabriel's truck pull up outside, Sam stands.

"Well, that's my cue."

"Are you sure you have to go now? You can stay for dinner."

"Naw, I need to get back home. I don't want Leah to stay another night alone."

I shake off my disappointment at the mention of our friend.

"Okay. Call or text me when you get home. And tell Leah I'm going to call her tomorrow."

"I will, little momma," he says, kissing the top of my head.

Walking over to the front door, Sam is sliding on his coat when Gabriel walks in.

"Cariño *Sweetheart*," he acknowledges me first with a kiss and pulls me into his side before offering his hand to Sam.

"Gabriel," Sam greets in return. Once he's in his truck and begins to drive away, I give one last wave before closing the door.

"Everything okay, babe?"

With a heavy and hopeful heart, I answer him. "It will be."

22

GABRIEL

Before leaving the house, I shoot a text off to Prez because I'm supposed to be at the clubhouse right now with the rest of the men, but I'm running late. I wasn't leaving Alba until I knew someone was with her. I don't want her left alone in the house until I find and eliminate the threat to her and my baby. Sam isn't my ideal as to who she should be left with, I would prefer one of the brothers, but my woman was too excited when she found out he was coming out for a visit for me to protest. Putting aside the fact that I still don't like him, I waited for him to get here before I left. I'm banking on Reid being able to dig up some answers to who this Calvin Green is.

Church is well over by the time I get out to the clubhouse. Being a weekday, most of the guys need to get to their day jobs. Time doesn't stop for no one, and several of my brothers have families to take care of. Hell, even my client list is starting to back up at the shop, but they aren't my top priority right now. My family is.

As I'm pulling up to the clubhouse gate, Prez is in his SUV

about to come out from the other side. When the gate opens, we roll up next to one another, stop then put down our windows.

"You get your woman squared away this morning?" Prez leans out his window and asks me.

"Sam is with her. Sorry I missed church, Prez. I couldn't leave her by herself," I tell him.

"Don't worry about it. Until this shit is resolved, she shouldn't be alone. Reid and Quinn are the only ones left back there. I'll let them fill you in on everything. I gotta run down to that new construction site on the south end of town and meet Nikolai. You need me you call, and Logan is at the shop if you can't reach me," he informs.

"Got it," I answer before he rolls up his window and proceeds down the dirt road. I drive through the gate and up to the clubhouse parking my truck. I don't have to go looking for anyone because both Quinn and Reid are sitting at the table drinking coffee in the main bar area. Both their heads lift in my direction as I approach the table, "What we got this morning?" I ask.

"To start, I can't find shit on this Calvin Green. I dug around in the school's database. Here is his headshot they had on file," he hands me the 4×6 photo. "They have him listed as a former employee who quit two weeks ago. All his credentials on the surface seem legit, but a background check pulls up nothing. I think you will have to make a run to Bozeman tomorrow," Reid says.

Fuck.

Quinn takes a swallow of his coffee then looks up at me, "Prez wants you and I to go out to Charley's and ask around. See if any newbies have been seen passing through. Austin just called before you walked in and gave Reid a list of locations he drove Alba to the other day. There's a possibility we can get into some security feeds or Department of Transportation cameras to pinpoint any activity in those areas on that day."

SANDY ALVAREZ & CRYSTAL DANIELS

We're going in circles and running off of theories at this point.

"Did Prez have you dig into Santino's family for me? Can we rule them out?"

Reid leans back in his chair and closes his laptop, "I looked into it last night. I'm pretty sure we can rule them out. He didn't leave too many people behind. No wife, no kids. This Calvin Green, I have a feeling this is where our main focus is going to be. Grace's Bakery was on the list of places the truck was parked the other day. Since we know her, why don't you stop by there sometime today and see about taking a look at her security feed."

Finally, a direction and a person of interest. Right now, I'm thankful for Sam showing up when he did, or we would still be chasing empty leads because we had absolutely none. Knowing what this guy looks like definitely helps in the attempt to catch something or someone on a camera somewhere. That is, if Reid can find anything. If anyone can do it, he can. His hacking skills have spoken for themselves over the years in helping this club in more situations than I can count.

Now my only issue is getting through the day stuck with Quinn. The fucker talks too damn much. The man can't seem to appreciate silence like I do; even when the conversations are usually one sided, he still tries. It's nothing personal, it's just not who I am, and he knows that. It doesn't stop him from trying, though.

"Call me if you find anything, brother," I tell Reid.

He lifts his chin, "Will do. I'm heading to my place. Catch up with you later."

I turn toward Quinn, "Taking my truck, your car is too fuckin' small, let's go."

"Aww, come on, man, don't talk about my baby like that. She's a classic. And she's not small. Your ass is too damn big, squatchman," he says, standing from his chair and walking past me to the front door.

We both climb into my truck and get on the road. Quinn reaches over and turns on the radio, and I reach over, turning it off.

"Come on, it's too damn quiet in here," he complains.

"Leave it alone," I order. He digs a pair of earbuds out of his pocket, placing them in his ears and takes his phone out. The rest of the thirty-five-minute ride he doesn't talk. I pull into Charley's parking lot. It's a local bar that a bunch of us visit several times a month. Charley was a friend of Reid's old man; they both served in the Marines together. He even rides with us from time to time when we do charity runs. We might do some shady shit and live by our own rules, but our club supports its community and the people in it. We give back where it counts, and our country's veterans are one of them. Those men deserve more than what they receive. I respect Charley.

Being that its noon, the place is dead except for the few usual barflies and the couple of lot-lizards we see walking around in the back parking lot designated for the truckers to park at when they need a place to stop and rest. Charley gets a lot of them coming through with their loads, and it has helped bring in more business, and it being at the edge of town near the interstate makes it a convenient location.

Steppin' into the bar, we hear the low music from the old jukebox in the far corner of the low-lit room and three old men sitting at the bar watching ESPN on the TV above the bar with no sound coming from it. Charley is behind the bar chatting with them. He looks up as soon as we get closer. "Well, hell. Quinn, Gabriel. I haven't seen you guys in here for awhile. How have you been?" he speaks with a huge smile on his face as he greets us with a firm handshake.

"Aww, Charley, you miss me?" Quinn teases.

"I make good money when you fellas come around. You draw

in the pretty ladies too. What can I do for you guys? I take it this time of day it is business," he states.

I nod my head, and he leads us to the other end of the bar.

Pulling out the picture of Calvin Green, I sit in on the bar for him to look at, "Need to know if you've seen this guy come in here recently, specifically this past week?"

He studies it for a few seconds. "Hmm, we get a lot of truckers passing through, it's hard to say. You should ask Kinsley. She was waitressing those nights. She's in the back getting ready for her shift. You guys can go on back and ask her. Sorry I couldn't help. You can also check my security feeds. You know where everything is. I'll let you do your thing. Come say your goodbyes when you're done, alright?"

"You bet, Charley, thanks," Quinn says.

Picking the picture up, I lead the way toward the back and walk into the break room where we see a young woman sitting at the table, scribbling in a notebook.

"You Kinsley?" I ask her, my voice booming and bouncing off the walls of the room, causing her to jump in her seat. Quinn takes it upon himself to take over.

"Shit, man, don't scare her. Hey, darlin', we're a couple of Charley's buddies. You waitressed this past week, correct?"

She squares her shoulders, trying to look less intimidated by us.

"Yeah, I started my first night this past Tuesday. Why?" She's a pretty little thing, but she's nothing compared to Alba. "You by chance see this guy in the bar those nights?" I show her the picture, and she takes it from my hand to get a closer look.

"Yeah, I remember him. He kept to himself. Didn't drink either. Just asked for water, and when he asked for a menu, I told him we only serve burgers and fries made to order. He acted as I offered him shit on a platter. He sat in the back-corner booth glued to his phone."

My blood starts pumping. We've got proof the fucker was in town. One step closer to pinning this asshole to all the shit going on with Alba.

"You remember when he left that night?" Quinn asks her.

She looks to him, then hands me back the photograph, "No, I'm sorry I don't have an exact time. It was busy that night, but it was too late. He stayed until last call, and that was around 2:00 am the next morning," she informs us as she starts to put her things away in a bag, then slides out of her chair.

"I've got to start my shift soon. Anything else I can help you fellas with?"

"Well, now that you mention it, you could..." I don't let Quinn finish the sentence because I know where he was going with it.

"No, we'll leave you to it," I cut in as I spin Quinn around and give him a small shove toward the door.

As we make our way to Charley's office, he speaks up. "Man, just because you have yourself a fine-lookin' woman at home doesn't mean you get to mess with my game, brother. That woman was built for sex. Did you see that ass?"

"Quit thinking with your dick right now. We got shit to take care of," I tell him while pulling up the security feed and going back to last Tuesday night.

"Killjoy," he mumbles.

I dig around in Charley's desk lookin' for a USB I can download a copy of the file to and finally find a few in the bottom drawer that hasn't been labeled with anything and plug it into the computer. I watch the feed for a few minutes with Quinn watching over my shoulder.

"Wait, back it up. Right there. That guy there looks pretty close to this Green guy," he points out.

I examine him and compare the image to the picture in my hand. The image isn't clear, and it's a side profile showing him leaving in a small black car. The old lady in Bozeman said the car she noticed was silver, but he could easily have swapped vehicles. I'll take this to Reid and have him zoom in on the guy's face and his car, clean the picture up a bit. "Alright, let's take this and get going. I still need to stop by Grace's," I tell Quinn. We walk back out to the front of the bar.

"You boys find what you were lookin' for?" Charley asks.

"Yeah, we got what we needed. Thanks, Charley," I tell him.

"Alright, stay safe," he tells us as we walk past the bar and out the door.

As soon as I get inside the truck, I send a text to Alba, checking on her.

Me: *You good?*

Cariño: *I'm good. Love you*

Me: *Te amo más* Love you more

Satisfied, I start the truck and head back toward town.

By the time we make it to the bakery, it has started to rain. Luckily, it looks like Grace doesn't have any customers. The parking spaces out front are all empty, which means we can be in and out. I step out of the truck and fuck if it isn't colder than it was when I headed out this morning. Some bikers, including a few of my brothers, are hardcore. It doesn't matter what type of weather there is. They are on their bikes. I love my ride. Ain't nothing better than feeling the breeze on your face and the open road, but I'm not about to freeze my balls off during wintertime in Montana.

My stomach rumbles from the smell of sugar cookies filling the air as we walk inside. Alba brought some of those things home the other day. The crack of sweets is what they are. I nearly ate the whole damn box by myself. I walk into the back of Quinn when he abruptly stops, almost knocking him over in the process. Over in the corner of the store back behind the register is the broad back of our Prez, who has a tiny Grace caged in with his hands on the wall—on either side of her—her back pressed against the wall.

"What do we have here? Another sweet tooth, Prez?" Quinn goads as he saunters up to the counter and leans forward on it. Seriously, the man has no filter.

"Fuck off, Quinn," Prez growls.

A blush creeps up Grace's cheeks as she ducks under Jake's arm. Composing herself, she walks to the counter, wearing a smile.

"Hey, guys. What can I get for you? Gabriel, how's Alba doing today?" she asks.

Clearing my throat, I regard both her and Jake, who has stepped back around the counter to join us.

"She's doing good. Grace, Alba was here the day before her accident, can we get a look at your security feed?"

"Sure, but the only camera I have is located inside the store. Will that help you with what you're looking for?"

Shit. Probably not, but it's worth a look anyway. "Quinn, go take a look at that feed, would ya? I need to talk with Prez a minute."

Grace looks to Jake, and he gives her a brief smile, then she turns and leads Quinn toward the back.

"We went out to Charley's and got the feed from Tuesday night with a possible image of the guy. I'm taking it to Reid for him to clean it up, so we can have a better look at it. She showed the picture to the new waitress that was working that night, and she remembers him coming in."

He runs his hand through his hair, "Alright, I'll contact Logan. Wrap this up. We'll be meeting up at Reid's in about forty minutes since he's the closest, and everyone is here in town at the moment," he informs me.

Quinn and Grace walk back out, "Nothin', brother. All it shows is Alba walking in, getting a cinnamon roll, and walking out."

I turn toward Grace, "Can you box up some sugar cookies for Alba?" After watching her place about a dozen cookies into a pink box, she hands it to me, "No charge. I hope she starts feeling better.

Tell her to call me when she's up for a visit," she says with a warm smile. I can see why Jake likes her.

Quinn was on his phone as soon as we walked out the doors letting Reid know we were heading his way and that Prez and Logan wouldn't be too far behind us. We find him downstairs in his computer room. Turning in his chair, he looks in our direction. Reaching into my front pocket, I get the USB drive and toss it to him, "I know Quinn briefed you on what we found, but can you clean it up? The picture quality is shitty," I ask him.

Grabbing a chair from the other side of the room, I sit down beside him and watch him do his thing. Within five minutes, he's scanned through the feed and starts enhancing the image, and the picture on the screen becomes clearer. On the second computer screen, he mentions the headshot he obtained from the college files last night.

Reid's doorbell chimes, and his phone goes off. He swipes the screen and taps an app. When he does an image of Logan and Prez standing outside his door fills the screen. He taps out a code unlocking his door letting them in, "Come on in. I'm downstairs in my office with Quinn and Gabriel," he informs them through the speaker outside.

After making their way downstairs and walking into the room, Logan hands Quinn a bag. "Here, Bella cooked lunch earlier, some country fried steak sandwiches and potato salad," he tells us.

"Thank fuck. I'm starving," Quinn says as he quickly plunders in the bag and unwraps one and shoves it into his mouth.

I turn my attention back toward the two screens.

"Brother, I think we have the same man here," Prez says as he looks between the two images.

"Looks like we're taking us a ride to Bozeman in the mornin', men. You still keeping this from Alba?" Logan asks, addressing me.

"I want more answers before I put this stress on her," I tell him, never taking my eyes off the two images on the screens in front of me, "Reid, can I count on you to protect my woman while I'm out of town tomorrow?"

"We protect our own, brother. You know I will."

Good. Because I'm about to do a little hunting of my own. This motherfucker is a dead man walking.

23

ALBA

I just finished heating up the premade chicken alfredo sauce Lisa made and taking the garlic bread out of the oven when Gabriel comes striding through the front door. That woman put enough food in my freezer to last a month. I'm beyond grateful because, unlike my sister, I'm not in love with cooking. I only cook because it's a must, not because I like it. Coming up behind me, Gabriel nuzzles me in the crook of my neck.

"Smells good, babe."

"It does. You have Lisa to thank for it. My sister must have told her how much I like anything pasta because she cooked every pasta dish known to man."

While Gabriel walks over to the kitchen sink to wash his hands, I go about pulling plates down from the cabinet to set the table.

"Is Austin still outside? Do I need to set a place for him?"

Drying his hands on the hand towel, "No, he went back to the clubhouse," Gabriel informs. "I told him I needed to talk to you about something."

I turn my attention toward him, "Talk to me about what? Is everything okay?"

Taking me by the hand, he leads me into the living room. When he sits down on the couch, he pulls me down onto his lap.

"I was at the garage with Quinn and Logan today. They were checking out your truck. After your accident, I had a feelin' something about it was off. Prez had it towed so we could check it out ourselves."

I take a shuddered breath, "Why do I get the feeling that I'm not going to like what you found."

With his palm on my hips, Gabriel squeezes gently, "Your brake lines were cut."

Feeling the bile rising in my throat, I slap my hand over my mouth and rush down the hallway to the bathroom. I barely get the lid to the toilet raised before I empty the contents of my stomach.

Whoever threatened me while I was in Bozeman has found me, and he's trying to make good on his promise. In fact, he almost succeeded.

"Fuck." I hear Gabriel curse behind me. Then I feel my hair being lifted away from my face and a cold washcloth placed on my neck. Helping me stand, Gabriel guides me over the sink where he pulls open the drawer taking out a spare toothbrush and toothpaste we keep here in case we have guests.

After washing my face and brushing my teeth, I meet his concerned yet venomous eyes in the mirror.

"He's found me, hasn't he? He tried to kill me. He's doing exactly what he said he would," I state in a shaky voice. I have held my shit together for months, but right now, I feel like all my bravery has run out. "I don't have any fight left, Gabriel. I'm so tired of trying to hold it together."

Scooping me up in his arms, I bury my face in the crook of his neck as he carries me out of the bathroom and up the stairs.

"You don't have to fight mi amor *my love*. That's what I'm here for." Setting me down on my side of our bed, he takes my face and encases it in his hands. Looking me in my eyes, I see fierceness and determination.

"Baby, no-fuckin'-body is going to harm you or our son." Closing my eyes, I nod. "You are the bravest person I know. Had it not been for my own fuck-ups, none of this shit would be happening."

I shake my head. "Gabriel, we're past all that. I've forgiven you. It's time you forgive yourself."

"I'll never be able to forgive myself, Alba. Knowing you were out there having to go through this pregnancy alone and feeling like I didn't care for you. I will never forgive myself for doing that to you. But never again. From now on, I will carry you, Cariño *Sweetheart*. And I will do all the fighting," he declares, brushing my tears away.

Sensing my tiredness, Gabriel reaches down and takes my shoes off. Then he pulls the blanket back, "Lay down, baby." Doing as he asks, I let out a heavy sigh once my head hits the pillow. Leaning over me, Gabriel kisses my lips, then he moves down and places a gentle kiss on my belly.

"Sleep, baby, I've got you."

I AWAKE SOMETIME LATER to Gabriel's light snoring beside me. The rumble of my tummy alerting me to the fact that I haven't eaten. Climbing out of bed, I make my way downstairs to the kitchen. I fully expected to find our forgotten dinner still on the stove, but to my surprise, the kitchen has been cleaned, and the food put away, aside from a single plate wrapped in foil sitting on the counter. I smile because I know Gabriel was thinking of me. He knew my stomach would wake me.

Once I've reheated my dinner, I carry my plate down the hall to the office. I can get some work done while I eat. Getting lost in my work always helps with taking my mind off things. As the time ticks by, I'm so lost in my current book cover project, I don't even hear when Gabriel comes in.

"What the hell is this?" he rumbles over my shoulder while staring at my computer screen.

Letting out a yelp, I jump in my chair and clutch my hand to my chest.

"Jesus Christ, Gabriel. Don't sneak up on me like that." I chastise.

"Sorry, baby. I didn't mean to scare ya."

"I know you didn't, but for a big guy, you sure are stealthy," I tease. I see the amusement on his face before turning his attention back to my computer.

"Mind telling me why there is a half-naked man on your computer, Cariño *Sweetheart*?"

"Um, I'm working. I woke up and was hungry, and I decided to try and finish one of my projects."

With a confused look, Gabriel asks, "I thought you did book shit." I roll my eyes at his colorful description of what I do.

"I design book covers, mostly romance. This is one here," I tell him, pointing at the man who he described as half-naked. He has jeans on and is shirtless. When he still doesn't say anything, I elaborate, "The book is an erotic romance. The author is going for sexy and sex sells," I finish with a shrug.

"Sex," Gabriel says gruffly, "Is this the kind of shit you read? Books with people fuckin'?" I can feel myself blush at his question.

"Umm, yeah. Some of what I read has sex."

Giving me a crooked grin, Gabriel's stare goes molten, "You like readin' porn, babe?"

"What? No! It is not porn. It's romance."

SANDY ALVAREZ & CRYSTAL DANIELS

My embarrassment seems to amuse him because he starts chuckling.

"Cariño *Sweetheart*, if there is fuckin', then in my book, that's porn."

"Whatever," I huff, "can we please change the subject?"

Leaning in closer to me, bracing one hand on the desk and one hand on the back of my chair, Gabriel's lips graze my ear, "I don't think I want to change the subject. Tell me something, baby. Does reading your books turn you on? Does your pussy get all wet when you read about those people fuckin'? Do you think about me doing those things to you, Alba?"

My skin prickles, and my body shivers at the deep rumble of his voice. His words are turning me on. So much so, I rub my legs together to try and ease the ache. Gabriel's dirty words always have this effect on me.

"I bet if I stuck my hand in your panties right now, your pussy would be soaked."

"Yes," I barely whisper once I am able to find my words. With a growl, he takes me in his arms, picking me up as if I weigh nothing. Then he carries me out of the office and up the stairs to our room.

Within seconds Gabriel rids me of my t-shirt. And before I know what's happening, I'm lying on my back on the bed, and he is rushing to pull my leggings off, taking my panties with them.

Dropping to his knees, Gabriel wraps his large hands around the undersides of my legs and pulls my body to the edge of the bed. Then without warning, his mouth is on me, and he's dragging his tongue up my center.

"Oh, God!" I shout, digging my fingers into the blanket on the bed. Gabriel is devouring me like he's starved for my taste. The feel of his hot mouth and rough beard is like heaven.

Just when I start to feel my orgasm building, he pulls away. I whimper in protest, and just as I'm about to demand he keeps going, the words die on the tip of my tongue when I see him stand and begin shedding his clothes. I'll never get over how stunning Gabriel is. His body is literally a work of art.

Kneeling on the bed, he slides an arm underneath my shoulder blades and slides me up farther up to the middle of the bed. The whole time his dark eyes never leave mine. He's holding himself up away from me, always mindful of my belly. Even with pregnancy his size makes me feel small, reminding me of a gentle giant. Some people may look at Gabriel and think of him as anything but gentle. But I know differently. I know this side of him is only for me.

Needing to touch him, I reach up and thread my fingers through his hair, then down his face until I grab a fist full of his beard, forcing his mouth down on mine. Then I press the heel of my foot to the back of his thigh to force him closer to my core.

"Gabriel, please," I moan against his mouth when I feel he's not giving me what I want.

"Slow, mi amor *my love*," he rasps. Rising up, he reaches down with one hand and guides the head of his cock to my entrance. I close my eyes and relish the feel of him as he sinks every thick inch into me. Once he is fully seated inside, he stills for a moment waiting for me to become accustomed to being so full. I love the way he fills me. Every time with Gabriel feels like the first. A few moments later, he begins to move. His strokes are long and slow. Every time he feels me getting close to the edge, he changes position. Soon my moans turn to whimpers.

When I feel like I can't take it anymore, and I'm so desperate to come, I beg once again, "Gabriel, please."

Shaking his head, he keeps with the same torturous, unrelenting pace. My hips are moving in perfect sync with Gabriel's rhythm, and I am once again on the brink of orgasm, only to have him pull out of me completely. My need to come is so strong I almost want to cry.

Gabriel doesn't waste any time lying on his back and pulling me on top of him. Straddling his hips, I sink down onto his cock. This position has him going even deeper.

"Fuck," Gabriel hisses as he runs his hands up over the swell of my belly then cups my breast. I brace my hands on his chest for balance and begin to rock against him. It doesn't take long for me to find my rhythm. And this time, when I am on the brink of orgasm, Gabriel does not stop me from seeking my release. Using both hands, he grabs my ass and begins thrusting his hips upward.

"Come now, Alba. Come with me," he demands. And my body listens. Digging my fingers into his chest, where I am almost certain I will leave marks. I come shouting Gabriel's name as he too stills, planting himself deep inside me growling his own release with my name on his lips. Holding me close, Gabriel rolls us on our sides. Once our breathing is under control, he is the first to speak.

"Was that better than your porn?"

"It's not porn," I giggle. Then add, "It was way better."

24

GABRIEL

I grab my weapon and secure it to my side before pullin' on my cut. Alba went downstairs fifteen minutes ago to let my sister in. The two of them will be here alone for awhile today until Reid can make it out. I checked the whole property earlier this morning, and everything is running the way it should, and the camera feed is working properly as well. Knowing I can tap into the live feed with the app on my phone gives me a little comfort leaving her without one of the brothers for a couple of hours.

We have a long drive ahead of us and having so many miles between me, and my woman has me on edge and nursing a mild migraine this morning. So far, Reid hasn't been able to dig up much on this Calvin Green except for the facts we already knew. I'm hoping we turn up some more information once we get to the only address we have on the guy.

To top it off, we have a snowstorm threatening to move north of us later tonight. It's about a four hour drive we have ahead of us just to get there, then the drive back, so we'll be taking Logan's ride since his truck is best suited for the rougher weather and he can throw his plow attachment in the bed of his truck.

On my way downstairs, I replay the way Alba got upset last night when she found out her brake lines were cut, and someone intentionally tried to harm her. It may not be the smartest move, but I couldn't tell her who we are trying to dig dirt up on because I fear the stress will overwhelm her at this point. She rescheduled her doctor's appointment until tomorrow, and she'll be hunkered down in the house with someone by her side all day. Maybe with the men having made their presence known in town the past few days it will have made this guy think twice about showing up in our town again.

Maybe.

I find Leyna and Alba sitting on the couch in the living room in front of the roaring fire I started in the fireplace this morning. Walking around the edge of the couch, I bend down, giving her a deep kiss. "I need to go. Logan is waiting for me down at the bike shop," I tell her.

"I'll miss you. I promise I'll be fine. Your sister and I are going to sit here and enjoy this fire. Please be safe. The weather could get worse before you get back home," she says with worry.

Alba knows I'm not telling her everything but hasn't pressed the issue. Giving me a beautiful smile, she grabs hold of my hand, "I love you."

"Yo te quiero más *I love you more*," I bend down and whisper into her ear, "I'll check on you soon."

As I'm walking out the front door and setting the alarm from my phone, I can't shake this uneasy feeling I have. Brushing it off, I climb into my truck that's been sitting out here warming for the past ten minutes and make my way down the long driveway to the main road and head toward town.

When I make it to the shop, Logan is out front sitting in his truck waiting on me. I park mine, lock it, and walk over to the passenger's side of his and open the door.

"Hey, brother. You ready for this long ass ride this morning?" he asks, lookin' really fuckin' tired himself.

"Yeah, lets hit the pavement and make some time, brother."

I climb in and shut the door. He hands me a large thermos that I know has hot coffee in it.

"Bella made it. I have my own over here, so help yourself."

Untwisting the lid, I pour some into the cup attachment. Nothing is going to relax the tension I have built up in my shoulders and neck, but it tastes good going down.

An hour later, my phone chimes with a text alert. Pulling it from my pocket, I swipe the screen. It's from Alba,

Cariño: I'm ok

She knows I'm worried about her, and I'm sure throughout the day she will send texts my way to let me know she is doing alright. Pulling up my security app, I tap into the camera feeds from outside the house. Seeing nothing I put my phone back into my pocket.

So much for the damn weather report, it looks like the storm is moving in quicker than they predicted. We've been on the road now for almost four hours, and about half an hour ago the snow started falling and it's steadily increasing.

"I think we're keeping ahead of it. It's a good thing we're only one exit away from being in Bozeman," Logan remarks.

Leaning forward, I enter this guy's address into the GPS system —752 Claremont Blvd. and it lets us know our destination is another twenty minutes from the first exit. So fuckin' close to finding answers.

The nearest neighbors look to be about two miles down the road. He lives on the outskirts of town in a rural area. After taking in the property, we both check our weapons and pull gloves over our hands, so we leave no evidence that we were ever here, before getting out of the truck. Once done casing the perimeter of the home, we make our way around back.

Yesterday, Reid showed Logan how to reset the alarm system once we gain access to the home with a universal hack code he can punch into the keypad. Pulling a small leather case from his coat pocket, Logan uses a set of tools to pick the lock, and after a couple of tries, the lock pops. We walk inside, and as I'm closing the door, he disarms the alarm. I didn't even know someone could do that shit until he got to talking about it on the ride here. Ever since, my mind's been running a mile a minute. I thought my system at home was top notch and now I'm not so sure.

Quietly Logan and I make our way through the house, doing a sweep through every room. I take the upstairs while Logan takes the main floor. I come upon the only room I find furniture in. A queen-size bed that was slept in at some point because the bedding is disheveled, and there is a chest drawer to my left. I walk to it first, pulling open the drawers only to come up empty. They had nothing but clothes inside them. I notice the only bedside table and proceed to dig through it, coming across a piece of mail with his name on it, a rent receipt. Thinking we can possibly lift a full set of prints from it, I take a plastic bag from my back pocket and place it inside and seal it shut. I find nothing else of importance, so I head back down to find Logan. As I'm rounding the stairs, I notice a small door underneath the staircase. Logan comes walking from the kitchen, "No signs of the guy. What did you find upstairs?" he asks.

"His room and a rent receipt. I stuck it into a bag, so we can check it for prints later. Where do you think that small door leads?" I ask him, pointing to the door I notice to my left.

"We have one of those. It's usually a storage space," he says, walking to the door and opening it.

Peering inside, we see nothing—at first, but upon closer inspection, I notice a handle attached to a door on the floor. "Does yours have that?" I point.

A puzzled look crosses his face, "No."

Squatting down, I grab the handle and pull. The fucker is locked. Logan digs the lock pick tools out of his back pocket and hands them to me. I haven't picked a lock in years. It takes three attempts before the locking mechanism on the inside clicks. Handing the tools back, I lift up on the handle and find stairs leading down underneath the house.

"He had this locked for a reason. Let's get down there and see what we can find."

Trying to fit my large frame through the small and narrow stairwell wasn't easy, and the thick stagnant air that engulfs us as we make our way down is suffocating. I pause, trying to let my eyes adjust to the darkness as I reach inside my jacket pocket and pull out a flashlight.

A dim light comes on overhead, and I turn my head to see Logan has found the switch on the wall next to the stairs and a stunned look on his. I spin around, ready to take some fucker out only to be met with a sea of pictures covering the wall in front of us.

All of the pictures of Alba.

The cords in my neck tighten, and my breath gets caught in my throat. I'm looking at some kind of shrine. There have to be at least fifty pictures pinned to the old wood wall. This guy has been watching her for months. Even before she left for college because one of the photos I recognize is from the day of her party when she wore that breathtaking blue summer dress. I reach out and rip it off the wall.

"Brother, focus. We need to dig through here and find anything to help us figure out who this guy is and where he could have gone."

Logan's voice is muffled. I can only half make out what he said through the rush of adrenaline that has started pumping through my veins. Desperately trying to shake it off, I start canvassing the room and come upon another door located near a shelf full of boxes by the back of the room. When I turn the knob, it opens without hesitation, and I walk inside.

What I find makes my stomach knot. Shackles are hanging from cold, damp walls. Off to the right is a twin-size bed and a toilet in the corner of the small room. It's a small fuckin' cell is what it is.

Did this guy have plans to take my woman and keep her prisoner in here? The more I take in, the more my heart rate increases. It's to the point I hear it roaring in my ears.

"Gabriel," Logan shouts from the other room, "I found something."

"Yeah, I found something too, brother," my voice catches in my throat as it echoes off the bare stone walls. I hear his footsteps as he walks up behind me, flashing his light inside, getting a look at what has me rooted in place.

"Fuckin' hell, man," he says, stunned by what's in front of him as he hands me a stack of papers mixed with photographs. "It seems this psycho has done this before. He has various pictures of women and tons of news clippings about their disappearances. And that's not all, man," he hands me one more bundle, this time containing more pictures. I know right away by the look on his face I'm not going to like what I see. I look down and shine my light on the stack of photos in my hand.

I am never going to be able to get these images out of my head. The site of these women as I sift through them one by one chained to the wall. Some of them so emaciated you can make out their backbones, and their backs are scarred with slash marks.

A sudden need to call and check on Alba hits me. I haven't gotten a text from her lately. I need to hear her voice to settle the storm brewing inside me.

Handing the pictures back to Logan, I dig my phone out and swipe the screen bringing up her number then putting the phone to my ear. Nothing happens. I look at the screen, noticing that I have no bars.

"Need to go upstairs. Can't get a signal down here," I tell Logan. I let Logan lead the way back up the narrow staircase opening and back into the foyer area of the house. Once I check my phone and make sure I have reception, I tap send calling Alba again.

"Hello," her sweet voice says.

"Hey, babe, how you and my sister doin'?"

"We're good. Your sister just fixed us the most amazing coconut pastry turnovers."

"We're about to head back. I needed to hear your sweet voice a moment. See ya soon, mi amor, *my love*." I tell her.

"I love you," her voice softly says before hanging up.

Logan strides toward me, "Get on out to the truck and start it for me," he tosses me the keys, "I'm about to trip this alarm so Bozeman's finest can find all the shit down there."

Walkin' out the door, I make my way to his truck, get in and start it up and wait. As soon as he jumps into the passenger seat, I take off.

Before we reach the exit to Polson, Logan is on his phone talking with Prez filling him in on what we found. I decide to check on Alba again and pull my phone from my coat pocket. The snowfall is heavy, so I pull off to the side of the road before swiping the screen. It rings but goes straight to voicemail, so I try again.

It rings and rings.

Come on, baby, answer the phone.

Nothin'.

"Wasn't Reid heading to your place over two hours ago?" Logan asks, "Maybe she is away from her phone or something."

"Yeah, I'll call him," I inform, as I'm pulling up Reid's number, then hit send and wait.

"Motherfucker! He ain't answering."

"Okay, listen. I'll call Prez and tell him what's going on. We'll get someone out there to check on things," Logan tries to reassure me even though worry flashes across his face when he says it.

"Fuck!" I yell. Starting the truck, I pull out onto the road. We're roughly thirty minutes from my place, and we'll probably make it before someone else does.

Five minutes later, my phone rings. Reid's number lights up the screen, and I hand my phone to Logan, so I can pay attention to the road. "Put it on speaker," I tell him.

REID

I'M in my truck driving out to Gabriel and Alba's house. He and Logan left for Bozeman a few hours ago. My ass should have been out there already, but I fell asleep sitting at the damn computer earlier.

I was up all night trying to find out who this Green fella is, and I'm nowhere closer than I was. I'm pretty sure he's done this kind of thing before. No fingerprints or paper trail anywhere. This guy knows how to hide his tracks. I'm positive Calvin Green isn't his real name, which makes finding the asshole a lot harder. Maybe Gabriel and Logan were able to find something—anything.

It's a fuckin' mess out here on the roads. When I make it out to Gabriel's place, I'll have to borrow a room or the couch for the night. There's no way I'm going to be able to make it back out in this mess if it continues coming down the way it is. It's getting heavier by the minute. Thirty minutes just to drive fifteen miles... this is fuckin' insane.

Finally, I'm able to pick up my speed once I get outside the downtown area, where it looks like most people have chosen to stay off the roads. About another five minutes and I should be pulling off the road onto their driveway.

I get why a lot of the guys live out here, and I almost bought myself something not far from them until the owner of the old firehouse put a for sale sign up. She was selling the historical building to help pay for her husband's medical expenses.

"FUCK!"

Bright red flashing lights come out of nowhere, snapping me from my thoughts, causing me to jerk my steering wheel hard to the right. To avoid hitting the stalled vehicle, I maneuver my truck off the road before skidding to a stop.

Once I regain my train of thought, I put the truck in park, leave it running and get out checking for any damage. My door doesn't even close completely before squealing tires catch my attention, and a white SUV comes barreling toward me. I try to move out of the way, but I'm not fast enough.

The force of the impact sends me flying. Instantly I'm finding it hard to breathe, and the pain radiating through my body is indescribable. A few seconds later I realize I'm on the ground because the cold from the snow-covered ground is starting to seep through my clothes.

"You still breathin'?" A male voice I don't recognize speaks from above me. I open my eyes to look at him. "Looks like you're pretty busted up there," he says as he kneels down to the ground, "She was supposed to be mine, you know. I paid those dirty fucking bikers for her, and then you guys took her."

It takes me a few seconds to process his words before it hits me.

"I think I'll leave your broken body right here. You'll be dead before anyone finds you in this storm, and I'll have what's mine before anyone knows what happened. Don't worry. I'll let Alba know you won't be making it after all," he spews.

Lying on the ground, I watch him walk off. The only thing I can see through the snow are the taillights as he pulls away.

I'm screwed.

I'm busted up good, but somehow, I need to find a way to get to my truck because my phone is sitting on the seat next to my laptop. I start trying to move my limbs and instantly realize I can't feel much from the waist down. As much as I want to take a moment to curse the situation, I need to focus all my energy on trying to drag myself toward my truck, which looks to be about twenty yards away. The pain that pulsates throughout my body as I put weight onto my right forearm and pull causes my vision to blur. And with each pull I cough up blood and gasp for more air.

I have no idea how long it takes me or how many times I was on the brink of passing out, but I find myself near the passenger's door. My body is so cold at this point; I have lost all feeling in my hands. Reaching up I fumble with the handle of the door. I'm able to pull on it enough for it to swing open. Spent, I lay there on the ground wondering if I have another ounce of strength to give when I hear my brother's voice inside my head—

You fight. Fight for her and that baby. Fight for yourself. Fight for me. Get your ass up, Reid.

His voice sounded so real it felt like he was right beside me as I took my left arm and used whatever was left in me to hoist my body into the floorboard of the truck and reach for my phone. I can't get my chest to expand enough to take in a full breath anymore, and I know I'm about to lose consciousness at any moment because adrenaline and willpower have all but gone. I pull up Gabriel's number, swipe the screen, and wait.

"Where the fuck are you?" he asked frantically as he answers the phone.

I suck in every last bit of air I possibly have left in my body, "He's here."

25

ALBA

"Okay, girl, spill it," I hedge while sitting on the sofa next to Leyna. She stopped by earlier for a visit and said she would stay with me until Reid got here. She has been glued to her phone for the better part of an hour. Every time she reads an incoming text, she gets a huge smile on her face. And there is no hiding the blush that has taken over her cheeks this very moment.

"What?" she feigns innocence and quickly slides her cell back into her pocket.

"Don't what me, I'm not blind. Now tell me who he is. And before you try denying it again, I know it has to be a guy. Only a man could put a smile like that on your face. Not to mention you're blushing."

Rolling her eyes, she confesses, "It's nothing really. It can never be anything because my brother would hate me and kill him."

I scrunch my brows, "What does Gabriel have to do with anything? He just wants you to be happy. As long as this guy is good to you, that's all that matters."

She shakes her head, "No, I know my brother wouldn't

approve. It would never work, Alba," she insists. Now she really has my attention.

"Who is it, Leyna?"

Throwing her body against the couch, she rests her head on the back and closes her eyes tightly. I see the strain in her face. Whoever this guy is, she cares for him, but for whatever reason is afraid for anyone to know. Reaching over, I grab hold of her hand and give it a little squeeze. Turning her head, Leyna looks at me. Letting out a deep groan, she drops the bomb.

"Lex."

Tilting my head to the side, I rack my brain. Lex?

At my confused expression, she continues, "Alexander Taylor. As in Agent Alexander Taylor."

Suddenly recognition dawns on me, and my mouth falls open.

"You mean the FBI Agent who rescued you?"

She nods her head in confirmation, "Sí, the one and only."

"Holy shit," I say, staring at her.

Groaning again, Leyna throws her arm over her face and lays her head on the back of the couch.

"You see why I can't tell my brother. The club and the Feds do not mix. I mean, you should have seen them the day Lex rescued me and brought me to Gabriel. If looks could kill, they both would have dropped dead on the spot." She waves her hand in dismissal, "It doesn't matter anyway. We're just friends."

I narrow my eyes at her with suspicion, "Just friends?"

When Leyna refuses to look at me, I know she's not only lying to me; she's lying to herself. It's written all over her face. It has been all day.

"Friends don't make you smile the way you have been smiling all day every time you pick up your phone."

Scooting myself closer to her, I place my hand on her shoulder, and when she looks at me with a pained expression, I know her feelings are torn.

"I don't want to overstep, but may I give you some advice?" I ask.

"Yes. I think I could use all the advice I can get."

Not sugarcoating my words, I tell it to her straight, "I say go for it with this Lex guy. Life is too short to worry about what other people think, Leyna. The most important thing I have learned over the past eight months is if you spend all your time worrying about what others think and trying to please everyone around you, then you are wasting the precious life YOU have been given. Will Gabriel be upset? Probably. And you know I love your brother more than anything, but who cares what he thinks? As long as you are happy and Lex is good to you, then Gabriel will eventually have to come to terms and accept that. Please, Leyna, never be afraid to go after what is going to make you happy. I will stand behind you when it comes to your brother." Leyna's shoulders slump forward. I hope she lets my words sink in. Everyone deserves happiness, and she is no exception. I have faith Gabriel will one day understand.

After a few moments, Leyna finally speaks, "I know you're right, Alba, but I also know it's going to be easier said than done."

"No," I say, "giving up is easier. Standing up for what you want is going to be hard, but worth it in the end."

Leyna lets out an unsure laugh and gives me a bright smile, "You're very smart in the ways of the world for someone so young."

"Trust me. I'm not that smart." I chuckle, "I just had to live and learn the hard way and suffer some consequences along the way. I don't want to see you do the same."

Leyna is about to open her mouth to respond when her phone chimes with an incoming text, causing me to smile and Leyna to roll her eyes. "He's relentless," she smirks.

"I like him already," I tell her. Staring down at the phone in her hand, Leyna blurts out, "He wants me to come to Seattle."

"Are you going to go?"

"I don't know yet," she shrugs. "We constantly text and sometimes talk on the phone for hours. I remember the first time he contacted me. It was a couple of months after the rescue. He said he had been thinking about me and wanted to see how I was doing. And then, I don't know. One phone call turned into another, and now it's just so intense. I feel like I've known Lex my entire life. He's become my best friend."

"Only a friend?" I hedge.

"Honestly, I don't know. I want there to be more, but I'm not sure about him. Lex hasn't given me any signs that he sees me as anything more."

I raise my eyebrow, "You sure about that? Because the way he makes you blush says different."

"Lex can be a flirt sometimes, but honestly, I think that's just how he is. I'm not going to read anything into it. A man like him can have any woman he wants. Don't get me wrong. I'm not saying I'm unattractive or anything. I'm not one of those kinds of women, but I do know there is no way I can hold a man like Lex's attention. I've always been the kind of girl that guys see as 'the friend'. I've been friend-zoned more times than I can count. And I'm okay with that. I'm used to it. That is why I will not get my hopes up when it comes to Alexander."

I can tell Leyna is trying to play the situation off as if it's no big deal. Her words don't match her body language or the catch in her voice. I have a sneaky suspicion her radar is way off. I have no doubt things will play out in her favor in the end. Not wanting to push the issue, I decide to change the subject, "I'm starving, how about I order some pizza? Or do you want something else?"

"No, pizza sounds great, I'm surprised they still deliver in this weather, the snow is really coming down out there." Standing up from the couch, I make my way into the kitchen, "Well, fingers crossed they will, and I'll order two since Reid should be here any minute." Glancing at my watch, I see it's getting a little late. I figured he would have been here by now.

Making my way back into the living room, I grab the remote control for the TV off the end table. "Want to watch a movie?" I ask Leyna.

"Yeah, something funny, though," she adds.

I'm scrolling through movie choices when the doorbell rings. "No way is that our pizza. I just ordered five minutes ago," I say aloud.

"Maybe it's Reid. Wasn't he supposed to be here?" Leyna asks.

"Yeah, but he has a key. Maybe he forgot it," I mumble to myself as I walk over to the front door to let him in. Punching in the code disarming the alarm, I flip the locks and open the door, "Did you forget your key?" I ask, expecting to see Reid. Only that's not who greets me.

"Hello, Alba."

I'm stunned, and it takes me a moment to respond, "Professor Green? What in the world are you doing here?" I ask, still confused by his presence. "And how did you know where I live? This is a little inappropriate, don't you think?"

I begin to feel very uneasy when he just stands there looking at me with a scowl, not answering any of my questions. Something is telling me I need to get away from him. He looks almost wild with his disheveled clothes and his unshaven face—nothing like his usual polished self.

When I go to slam the door in his face, he quickly counters my move by forcibly shoving his way into my house. This move causes the door to slam into my face and knock me to the floor.

Thankfully, I land on my butt. Feeling a sharp radiating pain in my nose and wetness seeping down my face, I bring my hand up to cup my face, and I use the sleeve of my sweater to try and control the bleeding.

"Alba, what's going on?" I hear Leyna asked as she walks in the room. "Oh my god," she gasps, running over to help me off the floor.

Once I am on my feet, we both turn our attention back to my former teacher, who has already closed the front door. I notice through my blurry vision he is holding a gun, and has it pointed straight at us.

Leyna is the first to speak, "Who the hell are you?" She takes it upon herself to step in front of me, knowing she is doing it to protect my baby and me.

Training his gun directly at Leyna, Professor Green finally opens his mouth, "Shut the fuck up bitch," he seethes. "What I want is what was supposed to have been mine. I want what I was promised." This guy is crazy. I have no idea what the hell he is talking about.

"You need to leave," I demand, finally finding my voice, "my boyfriend will be home any minute."

Barking out a menacing laugh, Professor Green delivers a gut-wrenching blow, "Your biker trash of a boyfriend is miles away, and that other one is lying on the side of the road dead. I took care of him on my way here."

I realize he's talking about Reid. That's why he never made it. The professor's confession has me doubling over. I feel like I can't breathe. Reid is out there somewhere dying or already dead because of me. Feeling rage build up inside me, I let my anger take over. Standing up to my full height, I dart around Leyna and charge. Momentarily, he is stunned when I rush him and land a solid punch to his cheek.

"Alba, no!" Leyna shouts, but it's too late. The professor quickly regains his composure and then swiftly backhands me across my face. Luckily, Leyna is there to catch me this time before I fall.

"You stupid, fucking whore!" Walking over to us, Leyna once again places herself between the Professor and me. Giving her a shove, he orders us into the kitchen. "Move! Both of you get in there and sit."

Leyna and I make our way into the kitchen with our hands clasped together. Glancing back, we both keep our weary eyes on the ticking time bomb walking behind us. I keep thinking back to what he said moments ago, something about him wanting what was supposed to be his.

"Sit!" he shouts from behind us, and we both scramble to the kitchen table, choosing to sit at the end, furthest away from the man who is currently pacing back and forth in front of us. I can hear him mumbling to himself, but I'm unable to make out his words. It's like he's in his own little world right now.

Leyna and I continue to watch him for several moments when, without warning, I feel a gush of wetness between my legs. Feeling my heart rate pick up, I look down and notice the puddle under my seat. This can't be happening right now. I give Leyna's hand a tight squeeze, gaining her attention. When she cuts her eyes to me, I moved my gaze to the floor beneath me. Not wanting to alert Professor Green, we stay silent.

Suddenly, my first contraction hits. It's not bad, but a bit more uncomfortable than one of those Braxton Hicks contractions. Closing my eyes, I take a deep breath and breathe through it. When I open my eyes, I realize the professor is quiet, and his attention is on me. The way he is staring at me and not saying a word unnerves me and causes my skin to crawl. His eyes are boring into me. It's as if he's trying to figure me out.

"What do you want?" I ask, refusing to break eye contact. I'm scared out of my mind, but I don't want him to know that. I don't want him to feel like he has that kind of power over me. Maybe if I can get him talking, it will buy us some time. I only pray Gabriel figures out something is up sooner rather than later. He calls me pretty frequently, and when I don't answer he might send someone out. Time is not on my side though. It's been about ten minutes since my water broke. I don't know how much time I have.

"I want what I was promised. Those bikers gave me their word. I paid for you. I want what's mine," he declares.

"What do you mean you paid for her?" This is coming from Leyna.

"Los Demonios. As soon as I saw your picture and they told me you were pure, I knew I had to have you. But then your filthy biker ruined everything. And you gave yourself to one of them. You gave away what was mine, you fucking whore," he seethes. At the mention of Los Demonios, everything starts clicking. My professor is the man who had bought me?

"The flowers, the notes. All that was you?" I ask, already knowing his answer.

"Yes, it was me. I got a teaching job at your school, so I could be close to you. Waiting for the right time to make you mine. That's until I learned you are having a biker's baby. You were a bad girl, Alba, giving away what was mine. But don't worry, as soon as we get rid of that little problem," he swings the gun toward my swollen belly and points, "you will be mine."

I place my arms around my belly at the mention of getting rid of the problem. He's talking about my baby. He's the one who wrote those vile words on the wall of my old apartment.

With bloodshot eyes and an evil grin, Professor Green begins striding in my direction. Standing abruptly from my chair, I back up a few feet. "What are you doing?" I ask, this time, there is no hiding the tremble in my voice. Not answering my question, he continues forward.

With his back turned away from Leyna and his full attention trained on me, I notice her taking advantage of his distraction. Leyna quickly stands up from the table and runs to the kitchen counter. She goes straight for the drawer with the knives. Professor Green is so fixated on me he doesn't notice.

I take two more steps back until my back is pressed against the wall. With my arms still clutched around my belly protectively, I am now facing the very man who wants to take my baby from me. He's so close I can smell the stench of sour coffee on his breath. Leaning closer into me, he picks up a lock of my hair, bringing it to his nose and inhales, "Mmm," he hums.

Without warning, a roar rips through his mouth, and he stumbles backward, away from me. Behind him is Leyna holding a bloody knife, and I realize she has stabbed him.

Not missing a beat, Leyna grabs my hand, and we both start to make a run for it. Just as we are about to turn the corner of the kitchen, a shot rings out, and I feel my arm being jerked.

I stumble a bit as Leyna falls to the floor and I see blood seeping from her stomach. Falling to my knees beside her, I scream out her name. Seeing blood gushing from the wound in her stomach, I place my hand over it in an attempt to stop the bleeding. It only takes seconds before I am covered in her blood.

Noticing the knife lying beside her body, I go to reach for it, but I'm violently jerked back. I let out a yelp at the pain radiating through my shoulder as Professor Green wraps his hand around my arm and proceeds to drag me across the floor back into the kitchen.

Letting me go, he goes to step over me, and when he does, I use all the strength I have and kick. This causes him to lose his balance and tumble to the floor, knocking his gun from his hands. Scrambling to my hands and knees, I shuffle toward the weapon ignoring the pain in my wrist and the tightening in my belly as another contraction hits.

Just as I grab the gun, I feel a hand wrap around my ankle. When I am tugged backward, I fall from my hands and knees and onto my belly, and the pain causes a blood-curdling scream to rip from my body. Flipping me on my back, the professor straddles my legs and begins wrestling me for the weapon.

Rearing back with a closed fist, I prepare myself for the blow. Seconds later, his fist slams down on the side of my head, and I instantly see little black spots. He uses my dazed state to wrap his hand around the gun, still in my grasp. I continue to put up a fight even as I feel myself slipping away.

The last thing I remember before darkness takes me is the sounds of another gunshot echoing in my ears.

26

GABRIEL

As soon as I hear Reid's voice croak out, 'He's here', my heart sinks to the pit of my stomach, and my foot presses the gas pedal to the floor. Time comes to a standstill. My only thought— save Alba and my sister.

"Reid, where are you?" I hear Logan ask. And for what feels like minutes, we hear dead silence on the line.

"Reid, tell us where you are," Logan barks into the phone frantically just as we catch a glimpse of a blue truck off on the side of the road.

"Shit, stop the truck," Logan yells. I slam the brakes causing the ass end of the truck to fishtail slightly before coming to a stop.

"Get your ass to Alba," Logan yells and jumps out. I don't wait. I lay on the gas again, spinning tires as they try to get traction on the snow, slick roads.

Spotting my mailbox ahead, I make a hard left barreling down the driveway only to be met with a white SUV parked sideways right in my path. I don't have enough time to slow down before slamming into the side of it.

Coming to a stop, I waste no time flinging the door of the truck open and jumping out just as a single gunshot echoes in the air. Breaking into a full-on sprint, I run toward the house.

Reaching the porch, I ram the front door with my shoulder, causing it to splinter from its hinges.

The first person I see is Leyna lying in the fetal position at the kitchen entrance, with blood pooled at her side. Rushing to her, I drop to my knees, quickly checking for a pulse. As soon as my finger grazes her neck, she flinches and opens her eyes. Quickly looking her over I find her wound. A gunshot to the abdomen. Yanking off my jacket along with my cut I rip my shirt off my body and apply pressure, causing her to flinch and groan in pain.

"Leyna, I need you to hold pressure on your stomach. I've got to find Alba. Can you do this for me?" I calmly say to her. Slowly nodding her head, she replaces my hand with hers and holds the shirt. "I promise I'll be right back," I assure her.

Getting up, I make my way fully into the kitchen. I'm not prepared to see my woman on the kitchen floor pinned under the body of a man, and blood spreading across the wood floor. Rushing over, I grab hold of the guy's shirt, yanking hard enough that the force sends him thudding against the kitchen floor.

Dropping to my knees, I hover over Alba's body, swing my arm around, and aim my gun at the guy ready to pull the trigger before taking in the fact he isn't moving. His limp, lifeless body is lying there, with the look of death in his empty eyes.

Placing my weapon on the floor beside me, I scoop Alba into my arms, "Cariño *Sweetheart*, open your eyes for me," I urge her as I desperately run my hands and eyes over her body to see if the blood covering her belongs to her or the dead man on the kitchen floor. A moan escapes her lips just as she begins to open her eyes. When her beautiful blue eyes meet mine, I lean down and kiss her forehead, "Alba, you hurt anywhere?" I ask her.

Immediately she grabs her stomach, "I don't think so, but my water broke earlier." Peering over my shoulder, she gasps, "Gabriel, your sister..."

Tires crunching gravel, then heavy feet pounding into my home have me clasping my gun from the floor beside me and aiming it toward the direction of my front door. As I'm ready to pull the trigger, Prez, along with Doc, comes rushing into view. Relief washes over me. They take in the scene for a brief moment, and after noticing I have Alba, Doc rushes to my sister's side on the floor.

"Gabriel, any of that blood Alba's?" he quickly asks as he starts to examine Leyna.

"No, but she said her water broke awhile ago," I tell him.

"Alba, honey, have you started having any contractions?" He addresses her directly, and I look to her for her answer.

"Umm, yes, but they haven't been close together," she lets him know just as her grip tightens on my arm, and she holds her breath.

"Babe, you having one now?" I brush the hair from her forehead with my hand. All she can give me at the moment is a nod as she tries to breathe through what looks to be an intense contraction.

Prez walks over to Green to confirm whether or not he's dead. Once checking for a pulse, he looks at me and shakes his head. *Good.* My only regret is that I'm not the one who pulled the trigger.

Kneeling, Prez gets eye level with me on the floor, "Listen, Logan contacted us, he said he called 911 and is waiting on an ambulance to arrive and pick up Reid. He said Reid doesn't look good, brother," his voice breaks with emotions before clearing his throat.

Alba doesn't take the news well and begins to weep.

"Stay strong, sweetheart. It'll all work out," Prez says to her then stands. Walking by Doc, he puts his hand on his shoulder before walking over to the kitchen window, most likely to compose himself.

"You're going to be alright, sweetie," I hear Doc calmly say to my sister as he pulls his phone from his coat pocket. He taps the screen then puts the phone to his ear as he lays my sister onto her back, "Need an ambulance out here at 204 Sky Rd. Two victims, one with a gunshot to the lower left abdominal area," I watch as Doc gently rolls her onto her side, her face grimacing in pain at the movement, "exit wound lower left kidney region on her backside. Another victim is a nineteen-year-old female, thirty-six weeks pregnant. No evident signs of trauma, but her water has broken, and she is experiencing contractions," he tells the dispatcher over the phone. After telling them he needed both hands to apply pressure to my sister's wound, he taps end to disconnect the call then drops his phone to the floor to give all his attention to Leyna.

Alba starts to cry harder. Pulling her tighter into my body, I try to calm her with my touch.

"She got shot trying to protect me. She stabbed him with a kitchen knife, and then he shot her," she sobs. "I'm sorry. I should have never opened the door," she starts to shake violently. Her adrenaline is wearing off, and the shock from the whole ordeal is starting to set in, "I shot a man. I killed someone, didn't I? Gabriel, I'm..." another contraction cuts her off.

"Breathe through it, Cariño *Sweetheart*," I encourage her. With all that's going on, there is no way I'm going to get her to calm down enough to concentrate. The fact that she shot the fucker to protect herself and our baby fills me with pride. She fought to stay alive. She fought for our son. My sister fought for her family. I spin around and position myself behind her. I spread my legs, settling her between them to support her back to my front.

"I need you to focus right now, baby. The ambulance is on its way, and Doc has control of Leyna. Focus on the baby right now."

Knowing that it's something Bella has done to calm her sister in the past, I soothe her by stroking her hair, which I notice helps her immediately.

Looking off to my side, "How much longer, Doc? Did they give you an ETA?"

"We should hear those sirens at any moment. Luckily the weather has let up, so it will make it easier to get here. Although getting their trucks around the wreckage in the driveway will cause them to go through the grass, so let's hope those heavy rigs don't get stuck in the wet ground out there."

Fuck, I forgot all about that SUV and Logan's truck. I'll carry them out if I have to.

Another twelve or so minutes go by, and Alba makes it through another contraction. I look over at my sister. Her eyes are closed, and her face is very pale. "Doc, how's she doing?" I ask through a lump in my throat.

"She's going to be fine," he says, but his words are to ease both my sister and Alba. The look he gives me though says she needs help, and fast. The sound of sirens finally fills the air. As all the first responders pull into the front yard, I hear footsteps approaching.

The police announce their presence upon entering my home, "Polson PD." They walk in and around the corner with guns drawn. Instantly, I recognize the two officers—Lawrence and Perkins. The club has dealt with them on many occasions. Lucky for us, we have a good rapport with these two.

They spot Prez standing off to their left by the window, "Shit, Jake?" then Perkins spots Green lying on the floor. "This guy dead?" he asks as he's holstering his weapon after making sure the room is clear of threats before the paramedics come in. I have no time to answer him. He walks over, kneels down, and presses his two fingers to the guy's neck. Alba goes into another contraction, this one taking her by surprise, and by the moan escaping her lips is much worse than the one before.

A couple of paramedics, along with two EMTs, appear with their gear in tow. Things happen extremely fast after that. My sister is prepped and loaded onto a stretcher as Doc stays by her side while they wheel her out.

Alba is loaded onto a stretcher soon after. I leave the cops with Prez to do his best and wrap shit up here. If they have questions for the rest of my family or me, they'll have to wait. Following alongside my woman, I wait for them to load her into the back of the ambulance for a second time within the span of a week before climbing in behind them.

The ambulance carrying my sister has already left. When the EMT driver goes to close the backdoor, officer Perkins stops him and pokes his head just inside the door, "Listen, I'll be needing statements sometime soon. And I thought you'd like to know I heard over the radio a while ago that one of your members was brought into the ER just before we arrived on scene," he tells me. My nod gives him my thanks before stepping back, allowing the driver to finally shut the door.

My mind is racing with a thousand thoughts right now and kicking my own ass because I wasn't here to prevent everything that has taken place. My sister and my brother are fighting for their lives right now, and it's crushing me.

Turning to look at Alba, I focus all my energy on her. As I try to help Alba through another contraction, the paramedic asks, "Is this your first pregnancy?"

"Am I that obvious?" Alba says as she catches her breath.

"You're doing good. The first one is always the hardest. I felt like I didn't have a clue what I was doing either with my first child," her glance lands on me then back to Alba, "but I didn't have someone to help me through it. You look like you have an abundance of support."

Alba looks my way and squeezes my hand a little tighter, "I'm definitely lucky, even if I'm totally terrified."

"Given the circumstances, I can understand," she says, putting her hand on Alba's arm and giving her an understanding smile, "we'll be pulling up to the hospital in five minutes."

Logan is the first one I spot as we enter through the ER doors standing over by the triage room talking with Dr. Evans, whom I notice is in regular clothes instead of scrubs.

Alba turns to the nurse who took over as soon as the paramedic wheeled us in and asked him to stop for a second and looks up at me, "Go find out about Reid and Leyna, please. I'm fine. I'll be in the room waiting. I promise to have someone come bring you up just as soon as they get me settled."

She's just as worried about the two of them, if not more than I am. I give her a brief kiss on the forehead, "I'll be there soon, mi amor *my love*."

"Gabriel, how's Alba doin'?" Logan asks as I make my way toward him and Dr. Evans.

"In labor. Heard any word about Reid or my sister?"

"I was just talkin' with Emerson. Why don't I let her fill you in?"

Craning her neck to look up at me, she gives me a weary smile, "As I was telling Logan, I talked with my colleagues tending to both your sister and Reid. Leyna suffered a gunshot wound to the lower abdomen. It was a clean shot, but since she has signs of internal bleeding, they have to take her to the OR to open her up and find the source. She lost a good bit of blood as well." I clench my fists and swallow through the knot forming in my throat as she finishes.

"She's stable, and the doctor is confident she will make it through. As for Reid, he's busted up pretty bad guys. The impact of being hit by a vehicle caused a good bit of damage to his body. He has four broken ribs, one of which punctured his right lung—causing it to collapse. Broke his right arm in two places, and may or may not have fractured his lower spine. Everything is so swollen and inflamed right now. They'll need to wait and reassess him later. If nothing more, there may be nerve damage because he can't feel much of his lower half. That's all I can tell you at this point. I'm really sorry. If you'll excuse me, I need to get ready for my shift. I promise to let you know more as soon as I can."

We watch her walk off and disappear through the double doors. They're both going to make it but at a price. I'm feeling defeated. I'm supposed to protect my family, and I failed. My emotions and heavy burden must show. Logan puts his hand on my shoulder and squeezes, "None of this is your fault, brother."

Quinn, Bella, Austin, Blake, and Jake come walking through the automatic doors, and the first thing out of Bella is, "Where's my sister, Gabriel? God, please tell me she's okay." Fresh tears fall down her face, and Logan pulls her close. The rest of the men I know will start showing up soon. The ones in front of me are waiting for answers.

I look down at Bella, "She was taken to labor and delivery. Nothing physically wrong with her other than she's in labor." I'm about to tell Logan to fill the guys in on Reid and Leyna when screeching tires cause all our heads to turn toward the emergency room entrance, and Agent Taylor comes bursting through the doors into the waiting room. "Where the hell is Leyna!?" he roars.

I don't know who the fuck he thinks he is. Badge or no badge, this prick has no business coming up here asking for my sister. I step in front of him, stopping him mid-stride. My brothers form a barrier behind me, anticipating trouble. Logan pushes Bella off to the side behind him.

"What the fuck you doin' here asking about my sister, Taylor? This is a family emergency, and you are not family. Get the fuck out of here," I growl as I square off with him. I don't need this shit right now. That thread is about to snap, and it's all going to be projected right onto the asshole standing in front of me.

"I was on the phone with your sister, motherfucker, while that crazy son of a bitch was terrorizing them. I heard the whole goddamn thing play out. Where the fuck were you? Now, either get out of my way or give me answers before we have a problem on our hands." He stands his ground, clenching his fists at his side.

I think everyone heard that one nerve I had left snap. Before I can lunge, I'm grabbed by three of my brothers. Two security guards rush up, inserting themselves between Agent Taylor and me.

"Gabriel," Dr. Evans' voice carries over the commotion, and whatever fight I had is pushed to the side when she says the next few words, "Gabriel, Alba's in a room. Come on. I'll take you there myself. The rest of you men sit down. I'll be back to give you an update on Reid and Leyna."

I follow her to the elevators, "Your sister is out of surgery. She is going to be fine. A few days in the hospital and she should be able to go home. The doctors are finishing on Reid." The elevator stops on the third floor, and we make our way down a few halls before coming up on another set of double doors. She pushes the button on the wall, and we walk through and pass the nurses station to my right, "I'll let the others know what I've found out. Alba is waiting for you," she says, stopping at room number 312.

"Thank you, Dr. Evans." Walking in, I find Alba in the bed and hooked to several monitors—one of them filling the room with our son's heartbeat. This is happening. She's about to bring a life into this crazy, fucked-up world and make my life more beautiful than the day she walked into it. Calmness washes over me, taking the place of all the worry and anger I was feeling before walking into this room.

My woman gives me that—comfort, peace, a sanctuary from my inner struggles. She smiles at me, trying to hide her own fears and worries. I set her mind at ease when I walk to her bedside and take hold of her small hand in mine. "Leyna is going to be okay, babe, and I have a feeling that Reid will be too." My emotions start to try and get the best of me, so I clear my throat, "Has the doctor been in yet? Are we close?"

Alba takes a deep cleansing breath, "Yeah, she was in here earlier, I'm at five centimeters. The anesthesiologist will be in soon to give me an epidural," she says, as we hear a knock on the door.

"Miss Jameson? I'm here to start the epidural," the older man says as he enters the room along with Mila.

"Mila," Alba says brightly, "I'm so glad you're here. I was hoping I would see you."

"I was surprised to see you on my floor this evening. You aren't due for another three weeks," she mentions.

"It's been a long day, and it's a long story, Mila. Listen could you check and see if my sister has made it—"

I interrupt her, "She's here, Cariño *Sweetheart*. Downstairs in the ER with the rest of the family."

"She's probably a mess with worry," Alba's shoulders slump.

"Let's get this epidural done before another contraction hits, and I'll see if I can find her for you okay," Mila offers.

They get everything prepped and have Alba sit on the edge of the bed with her legs hanging off the side and tell her to arch her back out as much as she can. Mila takes a solution and rubs it over a large area of Alba's lower back. I watch as the anesthesiologist places a big-ass needle into the spine of my woman then carefully removes the needle, leaving a tiny catheter in its place. After placing tape over it to keep it from moving, they clean her, and Mila helps her lay back on the bed.

"You should start feeling numb soon. I'll be back in with the doctor later," he informs us before leaving. Mila hugs Alba then leaves herself. We sit here in the quiet sounds of the room listening to the baby's heartbeat, and as the medicine takes effect, I noticed how relaxed Alba gets. She's tired and worn out from everything.

"Take a nap, mi amor, *my love.* I'll stay right here by your side," I whisper in her ear as I brush her hair from her face.

"Okay," she responds in a sleepy voice, closing her eyes.

She sleeps for almost an hour—the quiet doing me some good as well. Mila poked her head in a couple of times to make sure we were both okay and to let me know that most of the guys, along with Bella, were down the hall in the waiting room. I asked her to give them an update for me because I wasn't leaving Alba's side.

Dr. Evans also came by to inform me Leyna was awake, and Bella was in with her, which puts me at ease, knowing she isn't alone. She also said that Reid is heavily sedated and will probably remain that way for several hours. She was going to give the guys an update. My brother has a long road to recovery ahead of him, but he's strong, and we'll all be there to help him along the way.

Alba starts to rouse with a small moan. She shifts her body in discomfort, and I help her to sit up. "Umm, Gabriel, something feels different. I feel a lot of pressure down there. I think you need to get the doctor," she says through another long moan.

Pushing the button on the side of her bed, I page the nurses' station, "We need the doctor."

A couple of minutes later, the doctor walks in. "So, what are you feeling, Alba?" she asks as she slips on some gloves and starts to examine her.

"Pressure, a lot of pressure," Alba tells her.

"While you were sleeping, this baby decided he was ready to make his appearance. You're crowning. Get ready to push. It's time to have this baby," her doctor says cheerfully.

Holy shit!

I have no time to prepare or to even tell my brothers. The doctor positions her legs into the stirrups, and Mila, along with a couple of nurses come walking in with their gear in tow. It looks like we're having a baby. So many things are happening at once as they prep. I start feeling a bit lost until I feel Alba's hand grab for mine. Her face seems to mirror my own. Fear, excitement, worry, determination, pride—but mostly love.

"Let's do this," my brave woman says.

It's all over almost as soon as it began. After about five hard pushes, my son is born, and I'm cutting the cord. He has a head full of thick, black hair, and he is a big boy. I feel my chest swell with pride. They quickly clean out his mouth and nose, wipe him off, then place him on Alba's chest, skin to skin.

I stand there and look upon the most beautiful sight I have ever experienced in my life. My son and his mother—soon to be my wife. My old lady.

No words can describe what I'm feeling. I'm so sucked into the moment I think I forget to breathe—all the fear I had in becoming a father vanishes.

If it's possible, she becomes even more beautiful as she cradles our son in her arms. Alba lifts her blue eyes to meet mine, wearing a smile that outshines the fuckin' sun, "Come meet your son."

Settling beside her, I dip my head and place a soft, gentle kiss to my son's forehead before placing my lips on Alba's.

"You did good, mi amor *my love*," I whisper to her. The three of us share a few moments together before the nurse walks up to retrieve my son. Wearing a smile, she extends her arms, "I'll bring him right back. We need to check his weight, length, and few other things before we get his footprints along with his ID bracelet," she finishes saying as she gently scoops him from his mother's arms.

I watch intently as the nurses quickly and thoroughly do their job before turning my attention back to my woman, "I'm going to step over to the window and call Jake and let him know a new member of the family has arrived." I kiss her one more time.

Smiling, she gives me an approving nod.

Turning my back for a moment, I stare out the window, collecting myself as I dig my phone from my pocket. I pull up

Jake's number and hit call. He answers before the first ring even finishes, "What's the word, son?"

Swallowing my emotions, I speak, "We have a healthy baby boy, Prez, and Alba is good too," I beam.

"He's here! Both Momma and baby are doing fine," he calls out, and a room full of cheers erupts through the speaker of my phone. "Let us know when you guys are ready for visitors. Congratulations," he tells me, his voice full of pride.

"You got it," I answer before shoving the phone back in my pocket. Turning, I walk back toward Alba. I'm not one to show much emotion, but as the nurse starts to walk back with our bundle wrapped tight and warm in her arms, she rounds the end of the hospital bed and heads straight toward me.

"He's a big boy—nine pounds, seven ounces, and twenty-one inches long. Would you like to hold your son?" she asks me. The nurse helps by gently placing him in my waiting arms. The moment I feel the warmth of his little body against mine, my heart swells.

Besides the first time I laid eyes on his momma, this moment trumps all others in my life. Lifting my head, my eyes connect with Alba's. "Cariño *Sweetheart*, thank you for such a beautiful gift."

Not long after, we get settled, and the nurses finish with all the well beings of my boy and his momma, the guys come piling into the small room, but not before Bella comes bounding in and immediately starts fawning all over the baby and her sister. Watching them and their special bond makes me determined not to wait long on giving my boy a brother or sister of his own.

"Congratulations, brother," Logan walks up and pulls me in for a hug.

"Gracias *thanks*," I tell him.

"It was all worth it, ya know. Everything we've ever been through in life. This right here; our family, it was all worth it, brother," Logan remarks.

"Sí, mi hermano *Yes, my brother*. Worth dying for."

Our family left thirty minutes ago, and Logan literally had to throw his woman over his shoulder to get her to leave Alba's side.

With the room finally quiet, my exhausted woman takes a much-needed nap as I hold my son, Gabriel.

Gabriel Martinez, Jr.

Alba insisted he be given a good, strong name and wanted that name to be his father's, and I will make damn sure I make him proud to carry it.

EPILOGUE

Alba

When we brought home baby Gabe twelve weeks ago, Gabriel announced we were getting married. There was no asking, just a demand. That's pretty much what I would have expected from him. Gabriel may not be a bended knee type, but he's my type, and he's perfect.

I originally wanted to wait until the fall to have our wedding because Montana is beautiful at that time of the year, but Gabriel wasn't having it. The two of us argued about the subject for all of ten minutes before I gave in and said yes. As long as he gave me enough time to plan something small and he had to wear a tuxedo. He agreed to a dress shirt and jeans and gave me no longer than three months.

Now here we are. Standing in front of the altar on the edge of the lake out at Bella and Logan's house. I'm wearing a long, flowing white wedding dress with a halter style bodice. Beautiful white jasmine flowers have been delicately intertwined into a loose braid that is swept over my right shoulder. Simple and elegant.

Gabriel is making good on his promise. I'm about to become Alba Martinez.

Logan is standing at Gabriel's side and my sister by mine while she holds a sleeping Gabriel, or as most of us like to call him, baby Gabe. He is a complete replica of his father, aside from his blue eyes, which are a mirror image of my own. That little boy has filled us with more love than I could ever imagine.

After Gabe was born, Gabriel declared he would be giving his son a sibling right away. I told him he was out of his mind. No way was I having another baby for at least another couple of years. I should have known by the wicked gleam in his eyes that he was going to prove otherwise.

So, when I woke up three mornings ago sick to my stomach and throwing up, I knew Gabriel had gotten what he wanted, and the positive pregnancy test I took later that day proved him right. I plan to tell him tonight.

We decided to forgo a honeymoon and instead opted to let Bella and Logan keep Gabe for the night. Gabriel and I have never been away from him, so I'm predicting we won't make it through the night before coming back over to my sister's house to pick him up.

As I prepare to walk down the aisle, I watch our friends and family begin to take their seats. My heart sinks when I see Reid struggle with his wheelchair. Mila goes to help him, but she quickly withdraws when he snaps his head up at her and says something I can't make out. I can't help but feel guilty.

"I know what you're thinkin', sweetheart. It's not your fault, and nobody blames you, not even him," Jake says from beside me. Giving him a slight nod, I try not to think about the what-ifs. Instead, I focus on the man waiting at the end of the aisle for me.

"You ready?" Jake asks while offering me his arm. Jake is the closest thing I have to a father. Asking him to give me away was a no brainer. When I hear the music start, I look to Jake and take his offered arm, replying, "yes."

Looking into Gabriel's eyes, I recite the vows I have written. He doesn't know this, but after I wrote them, I asked Leyna to teach me Spanish so I could surprise him.

After being released from the hospital, Leyna went back to Seattle with Lex. We have been using FaceTime every day for her to teach me. To say things between Gabriel and his sister are a little strained is an understatement. Still, I told Leyna I was proud of her for following her heart, and I had no problem calling Gabriel out on being an asshole.

Some people may call us crazy for letting Quinn officiate our wedding, but when we made the announcement, he was so excited I couldn't tell him no. At first, we were all a little skeptical when he announced he had his license, but Gabriel had Reid check into it, and sure enough, he was legit.

With all the people I consider family watching on in support, I deliver the last line of my vows to Gabriel. "Tú eres mi hogar. *You are my home.*"

"I don't know what you just said, but it sounded sexy as hell," Quinn says as I complete my vows to Gabriel.

"What the hell are you waitin' for, brother? Kiss your woman," Quinn urges with a goofy grin.

Not paying any attention to his usual antics, Gabriel wraps his arms around me, lifting me off the ground and sealing his mouth over mine, making us husband and wife.

Pulling back, he nuzzles my neck and whispers into my ear, "Llegas a mi vida como un sol. Tú eres la luz de mi oscuridad. *You arrive into my life like the sun. You are the light to my dark.*"

CPSIA information can be obtained
at www.ICGtesting.com
Printed in the USA
LVHW081210210123
737580LV00008B/109

9 781734 754636